THE PRION PARADIGM

Garrett Davis

Published by GJD Publishing

ISBN: 979-8-9855302-0-9 (paperback)
ISBN: 979-8-9855302-1-6 (eBook)

Library of Congress Control Number: 2022900606

Cover Photo: by Tim Strater, licensed through Creative Commons and adapted
Cover Design: Andrew Neighbour
Editing and Interior Page Design: Mary Neighbour

Printed in the Unites States of America

This is a work of fiction. All characters, organizations, and events portrayed in this novel are either products of the author's imagination or are used fictitiously.

*Dedicated to my wife, Ruth,
who has always accompanied me
on any life adventure worth having.*

Chapter 1

I HELD THE BEATING HEART IN my hands—a surreal experience, no matter how many times I've done it. How to describe that palpable instrument of life, rhythmically moving between my fingers? Impossible. Even though it's not a human heart, all my senses honed in on knowing each and every beat is necessary to maintain life, and any error could abruptly end that life.

Timing really is everything. The puppy had been diagnosed with a persistent *ductus arteriosus*, a congenital defect of a large, delicate blood vessel, dangerously close to the heart, which connects the pulmonary artery to the aorta. The telltale sign of the problem is a continuous heart murmur that any first-year veterinary student could detect with a ten-dollar stethoscope. What the pet owner often misses are subtle signs, such as a puppy who is slightly smaller than her litter mates, who wants to sleep a lot, or even has an occasional low-grade cough.

When all things necessary for life come from the mother, blood flow through the open ductus arteriosus is required to protect the young, developing lungs. At birth, when air hits the lungs for the first time, things change in a heartbeat, literally. The body needs to force the ductus to instantly close, allowing blood to carry oxygen throughout the body. If it doesn't close, life will not be sustainable for very long. Like I said, timing is everything.

Several seconds of intense silence passed. My surgical resident, Samantha, looked up and asked, "Is everything okay, John?"

I guess I had been holding the heart pensively, a bit too long for her liking. The most dangerous aspect of the surgery was coming up, and Samantha had been anticipating this moment for years. The hardest part about teaching student surgeons is letting less-experienced doctors take over, even when death is a possible outcome. Though essential for training, any mistake she made could be fatal for the puppy and would reflect poorly on me and the hospital.

"Do you want to take over for a bit?" Even behind the surgical mask, I saw the grin.

"Sure, I would be happy to—if you think I'm ready," she answered in a timid voice.

To be honest, I wasn't absolutely sure, but she had been assisting and observing for months now, and it was time. Her hands trembled as she started to dissect around the delicate vessel. I knew the shaking wouldn't go away for years, if ever, caused by the adrenalin that comes with anything new and potentially dangerous. We both knew the perils tied to this paper-thin blood vessel, which should have closed off months ago. If it ruptured, the dog would die within seconds. No wonder this is where most residents start to fumble a bit.

"Try to relax your entire body by taking deep breaths," I suggested.

It seemed to settle her marginally as she found the right tissue plane. In some ways, my situation was harder than hers. I experienced the slow torture of standing aside and watching someone do something dangerous, knowing a more experienced hand could accomplish the same task more efficiently. I needed to control my own breathing and relax. My hands were steady, but it felt like my insides were slowly starting to boil. I tend to get quiet in stressful circumstances. Most people misread this and assume I'm fully in control and calm. I never bother to correct anyone.

After what felt like an eternity, the right-angle dissecting forceps appeared on the far side of the vessel. "Was that okay?" she asked in a shy voice.

She knew it was, and now I smiled behind my mask. "It was perfectly adequate," I replied. This is an old joke with my residents. Nothing is perfect, because *perfect* implies no future improvement is possible—rarely the case in surgery. But they all know what *adequate* means. She had done well, and her eyes beamed with pride. The dangerous part was over, and the rest was relatively straightforward. All that needed to be done now was to pass two sutures around the abnormal vessel and tie them, forcing the blood through the correct channels.

The physiology of the body fascinates me to this day. There is always cause and effect, action and reaction. As soon as the sutures were tied, the heart rate decreased, and the blood pressure increased. Both reactions signaled the heart was becoming a more effective pump, similar to how shutting off a leaky valve in a water pump balances the pressure in the system.

"What just happened?" I slyly asked.

"The Branham reflex," she responded, suddenly much more confident.

Well, I guess she *was* ready, after all. She had been doing her homework. The earlier tension in the room dissipated. My anesthesiologist, Andy, let out a deep breath she had been holding—obviously I wasn't the only one aware of the potential for problems with the delicate surgery.

"How about a little Frank Sinatra on Pandora?" she suggested. Andy, a bona fide introvert who is naturally quiet, is one of the smartest doctors I know.

Since I was the one scrubbed into surgery, Andy knew I had no choice but to let her play what she wanted, and Ol' Blue Eyes was always her reward when surgery went well.

"Why not?" I agreed.

The door opened and the prep nurse poked her head in.

"Dr. Osler, someone needs to talk to you."

"I'm in the middle of surgery," I responded without looking up. "You'll have to take a message."

"I already tried that, and they are rather insistent about talking right now."

She usually wasn't so demanding while I was in the OR. Something must be off. I sighed, so tired of privileged, rich people expecting instant access to their veterinarian. But the customer is always right, and we are a client-service industry.

"I got this," Samantha bragged, feeling very sure of herself.

"Well, okay, I'll take the call," I said, slightly annoyed. "What line are they on?"

"Sorry," the nurse continued. "They aren't on the phone. They're in the parking lot. It's pretty strange. There are six of them, and they're in suits. They won't come inside."

Working in a wealthy section of New Jersey has pros and cons. The level of veterinary care my hospital provides is one of the highest in the nation. Many clients come to our surgical practice because no one else has been able to help their pets. Of course, that level of care always comes at a cost, though apparently, it's easy for some to forget that part when the bill comes due.

We also attract eccentric millionaires. Just last week, a woman brought in her Pomeranian that had been paralyzed as a puppy. The dog had lived with fecal and urinary incontinence for the last five years. She told me in the examination she had hired a personal assistant to bathe the dog several times a day. The expression on her face told me she wasn't kidding. Moreover, she had actually installed an elevator in her house so the dog could go upstairs and sleep in her bedroom. This pet had a much better life than most people. I wanted to ask how much a personal dog bather made a year, but I managed to restrain myself.

So it's not unusual to have clients ask strange things. Six personal assistants seemed a bit much, but what do I know? I walked through the busy waiting room with purpose, praying no one would corner me and ask me questions about their pets. Some clients I recognized, but most I didn't. I always take this as a good sign, since long-term clients typically mean the problem has not been resolved.

The parking lot was unusually empty, but many of the doctors in the practice didn't see appointments over lunch, and my stomach told me it was about that time. In the back corner of the lot was a sizeable, black Suburban next to a black town car. Both had tinted windows. Someone did not want to be seen in the waiting room.

Over the years, we've had our fair share of celebrity clients, and most would rather not be famous when they are at the vet's. As I approached, the four doors of the Suburban opened in unison, and four nicely dressed gentlemen in matching gray suits stepped out. All had short haircuts and were conspicuously well built. I put on my best smile and walked up to the group. Without saying a word, two of the men politely but firmly directed me to the town car.

"Would you mind talking in the car?" they suggested—though it felt like more than a suggestion.

One of my escorts opened the back door of the town car, and as I peered in, it took my eyes a few seconds to adjust to the dim light inside. I expected to find a dog or a cat, and when I saw neither, I felt a bit nervous. Clearly, however, the man holding the door expected me to climb into the car, so I reluctantly clambered in and took a seat next to the only other occupant. The door firmly slammed shut, and my escort stood like a bouncer outside the door with his arms folded across his substantial chest, a deterrent to anyone who would try to see in, though his presence merely brought more attention to the car. People are crazy, I thought to myself.

An older, gray-haired gentleman sat alone, reading documents in a manila folder. He didn't raise his eyes for a full thirty seconds. I didn't say a word, preferring to study his appearance. I judged him to be about sixty years old. The lines on his face indicated a lifetime of scowling. Deep furrows, like small, recurring waves in a pond, creased his forehead. Tightly pressed lips created substantial indentations on either side of his mouth, and his gray ponytail extended to the middle of his back and matched the color of his bushy eyebrows. He was dressed in a suit similar to what the other men wore, but his skinny physique did not comparably fill out the uniform. I couldn't see what was written on the papers he was studying, and I got the impression from the way he held them that he didn't want me to. Whatever it was, his body language told me he was not happy about it. I shifted uncomfortably in my seat, and he finally looked up, feigning surprise.

"Dr. Osler?" he questioned.

"Please, call me John," I responded with a smile designed to diffuse the tension. The smile was not returned, nor did he introduce himself. I extended my hand to shake his, but when he made no effort to mirror the gesture, I awkwardly pulled my hand back and folded my hands in front of me. "What can I do for you?" I asked.

"Can we take a short ride?" he asked.

A house call! This guy probably owned one of the multi-million dollar mansions scattered along on the waters of the Jersey shore. With this many personal assistants, someone could have simply brought in his pet. Annoyed and cautious, I asked, "Where would we go on this short drive?"

"New York City."

"I don't think so," I responded. Although I was free the rest of the afternoon on an unusually short surgery day, New York City was about a forty-five-minute drive, if there was no traffic. "You are welcome to make an appointment, and I would be happy to see your pet any time, but I don't do--"

"I work for the United States government," he interrupted. "And I have no interest in pets." Incongruously, he matter-of-factly added, "I understand your daughter is a second-class cadet at West Point."

"Yes, she is." I could hear the paternal pride in my voice. "But what does that have to do with anything? And how do you know that?"

"It is our agency's responsibility to know a lot of things," he responded. "For example, right now she is in Dr. Ball's government class. It would be a shame if we needed to pull her out and ask her a few background questions."

"Now wait a minute," I said, growing alarmed at the thinly veiled threat of embarrassing my daughter.

"Just kidding," he said, although his expressionless face told me this was anything but a joke. "I think it would be easiest if you would agree to take a meeting in the city. I promise you will be back here in several hours, and when you hear the purpose of the meeting, you will consider it worth your time."

"Can I see some identification?" I asked.

"No," was his curt response.

I rapidly weighed my options: agree to go, try to get more information from Ponytail, who was as stone-faced as they come, and assess the threat to my daughter, or get out and walk away. I had noticed both cars had government plates, so I didn't think he was lying. If he wanted to kidnap me, he could already have driven away with me. The government wouldn't intentionally embarrass a nineteen-year-old girl just to get back at me for not cooperating, would they? Paternal protection kicked in, and I decided to play nice. "Let me notify the hospital and grab my bag."

"Fine," responded Ponytail. "But make it quick, we have a schedule," he said, checking his watch with irritation.

I also have a schedule, and you were not on it, I thought, opening the door with annoyance, forcefully hitting the back of the man guarding it. I had forgotten about him. He backed up as I exited the vehicle. I took a step forward, but he blocked me, standing so close I could smell the stale coffee on his breath. He stared at me without blinking or saying a word. For a second, I didn't think he was going to let me walk away. His eyes darted to the back of the car, and I assume Ponytail gave a nod of approval, because he finally stepped aside.

Back in the hospital, I checked on things. Surgery had finished, and the puppy was in recovery. There were no pending disasters in the emergency room. I made the decision that my residents could finish the day without me, and the paperwork I was planning on catching up with could wait another day.

Chapter 2

Several minutes later, back in the town car, heading north on the Garden State Parkway, I asked, "Where in the city are we going?"

Ponytail didn't answer right away, instead gazed out the window as we drove over the Raritan River. I was about to ask again when he silenced me with a deliberate, expressionless stare.

"I think you misinterpreted the purpose of this drive. I am not a tour guide or a babysitter, and I certainly am not here to provide you any information. My mission is to deliver you to a certain place at a certain time, and since I graciously let you walk back into your hospital, we are now running about ten minutes behind schedule."

I have always had a problem with being too optimistic and way too trusting. "Am I being kidnapped?" I asked nervously.

His eyebrows arched in exaggerated surprise before actually managing a faint smile, which instantly faded away. "Technically, you got into this car willingly and agreed to take a ride, so this is in no way a kidnapping," he responded.

"A short ride," I mumbled under my breath. "Well, can you at least tell me anything about the topic of the meeting I am heading to?"

"We need help with crocodiles," he responded slyly.

"I'm not an exotics veterinarian. I think you've made a mistake."

"We know exactly who you are and where your skill set lies, and we don't make mistakes."

"Well, then, can you tell me who you are and what branch of government you work for?" I persisted.

With an exasperated sign, Ponytail answered, "I work for the NSA."

We rode in silence for the next thirty minutes. Living so close to New York City, I had been through the Holland Tunnel hundreds of times over the past twenty years. My kids always liked to remind me that the bottom of the Hudson River is less than one hundred feet away, and if the tunnel starts to leak, we would be crushed by millions of gallons of water almost immediately. They often said things like this when they were younger to try and get a rise out of me, and it usually worked. The game we often played while driving through the tunnel was to spot the painted line that designated the transition from New Jersey into New York. Whoever saw the line first tried to extend a foot or an arm forward, so they would be the first one into the next state. It was silly, but the kids loved it. I couldn't help myself, grinning and silently chuckling as I casually stretched my arms and legs forward at the moment we crossed into New York. Take that, Ponytail. I got into New York before you did.

Surprisingly, traffic was light in the city, and we made good time. We headed south toward Tribeca and soon arrived at our destination. I had seen this building before and had taken note, since it was so unusual. The skyscraper rose over five hundred feet into the lower Manhattan sky, yet it had no windows. The design was so strange, and I always thought how bizarre it would be to work in a building where you couldn't see out. Considering the day's surreal events, I now suspected the design's intent was to prevent people seeing *in*.

The car pulled into a side street and down a ramp into a dark garage. As I looked back, a solid door, seemingly made of stone, came down quickly to block out all of the natural light. "You guys really don't like the sun, do you?"

Without a smile, Ponytail asked me to follow him. The elevator we approached had a guard and required both a swipe card and a keypad code for the doors to open. This was certainly someplace they didn't want anyone to wander into by mistake. Inside the elevator, I noticed there was no control panel or buttons of any kind, anywhere.

Ponytail said to no one in particular, "Prism Conference Room."

It was unnerving to be in a moving elevator without lights or displays to determine how high you were going. I estimated the elevator ride lasted twenty-two uncomfortable seconds. Ponytail wasn't fazed. The doors opened to a pale-tan hallway with ten unmarked doors on each side. At the end of the hall were two doors of frosted glass.

"Your meeting is at the end of the hall," he said as I stepped into the corridor.

"You're not coming?" I asked. The doors snapped closed behind me. "I guess not," I muttered.

I couldn't help but try one of the doors on the left to see if it would open. The door was locked, and a voice came from overhead.

"He said at the end of the hall, Dr. Osler."

Someone was watching, but the walls had no signs of cameras or speakers.

"Sorry," I responded to no one in particular and briskly walked to the frosted doors, which opened automatically with a loud hiss when I was two feet away. Inside was a rectangular table with skinny, metal legs and a black, metallic top, around which four people sat in silence. I took the one empty chair; it was unusually hard and cold.

"Now we can start," said the gentleman in the chair directly opposite me. I had the impression everyone had been waiting for me and were none too happy about it.

"I know you all must be slightly confused about what brings you here, but I thank you all for coming. The truth is that the NSA needs your help, and you each have something unique to offer. My name is Mr. Smith, and I am the head of the Prism Division of the NSA. The mission of this department is to pre-emptively identify threats to American citizenry and rectify these threats before people even know they exist. To my left is Dr. Nelly Fleury. Dr. Fleury is with the Johns Hopkins Department of Pathology; her expertise is in rare infectious diseases. Next to her is Dr. Alex King, a neurologist at Mount Sinai, right here in New York, and he is an authority in movement disorders. Next is Spencer Rose, who is a special forces medical sergeant with the seventy-fifth Ranger Regiment. Finally, our latecomer is Dr. John Osler, a veterinary specialist in surgery."

Dr. Fleury had long, brown hair with subtle red highlights that was wound up in a tight bun. Not a single strand was out of place, and her posture seemed rigid. She could have passed for thirty, but I guessed she was closer to forty. Her eyes were a beautiful, light shade of blue that appeared slate gray in the artificial light. Dressed in a dark-blue business suit with a white shirt and a tasteful neck scarf, she could almost pass for a stewardess on an upscale airline. She gazed straight ahead and exchanged glances with no one. The expression on her face was unmistakably one of annoyance.

Dr. King wore a dark-charcoal suit with a vest and silk gray tie. I got the impression his tie alone cost more than any article of clothing I had ever bought. An air of superiority hung about him, suspended between a naturally arched eyebrow on his left and a mouth with turned-down corners, surrounded by a neatly trimmed, slightly graying goatee. He gave me the smallest of nods when we made eye contact.

Spencer Rose sat next to me, wearing green military fatigues. Even under the uniform, I could tell he was a solid brick of a man. The sides of his head were shaved almost to the skull and the hair on the top of his head was not much longer. His nod was a bit more exaggerated, and he sat at strict attention. I guessed him to be the youngest of us, about thirty years old. His eyes were focused, and he gave his attention solely to Mr. Smith.

I still had my light-blue scrubs on, with recycled running shoes. The same outfit I had worn on every surgery day for the last twenty years.

"The issue at hand is crocodiles," started Mr. Smith. Ponytail had told me this much, but I still had no idea what Mr. Smith was talking about.

"A group of crocodiles swimming in the waters of the Great Barrier Reef are behaving in an abnormally aggressive manner and have attacked tourists who were snorkeling and diving. Three divers have already died in the last thirty-six hours, and several others who were bitten are hospitalized."

Dr. King pushed back his chair, which made a cringe-worthy, high-pitched scraping noise on the floor. "Are you kidding me with this shit? With all the cloak-and-dagger act, I thought you had something serious to discuss. You put me in a room with a doggy doctor and talk to me about reptiles halfway around the world. Do you know what I charge clients for an hour of my time? I certainly have more important things to do than this."

Mr. Smith was neither impressed nor flummoxed by this outburst. "Give me a second to explain," he continued with a level voice.

"I don't have a spare second to give to you or anyone else right now," he exploded. "I am leaving and there is not a thing you or your oversized, brainless associates can do about it."

"Okay, Dr. King, you are free to go," said Mr. Smith with an icy stare that actually made me shudder. The conference room doors opened, and Ponytail was ominously standing by to escort Dr. King out. "Just one more thing, Dr. King. Before you go, I would like you to see this," said Mr. Smith, sotto voce. He handed Dr. King a manila envelope from his briefcase.

"Do you even know who I am?" sneered Dr. King, raising his eyebrow even higher. "I think I'm going to bill you for my time.

You will likely be hearing from my lawyer." He pulled open the envelope and, after a quick scan of the contents, slumped back into his cold, hard chair, with worry abrading his smugness. "Okay, I will listen for ten minutes, and then I will be leaving."

As if the outburst had not even occurred, Mr. Smith continued. "Like I said, a number of saltwater crocodiles are attacking divers along a very specific portion of the Great Barrier Reef."

"Is that so unusual?" asked Dr. Fleury. "Aren't saltwater crocodiles supposed to be in the ocean?"

"Yes, they are in the ocean, but to see one at the reef is a once-in-a-lifetime occurrence, I am told, so a large group of them being there is highly unusual," answered Mr. Smith.

"I still don't see what this has to do with me," sputtered Dr. King, struggling to keep the attention focused on him.

Unfazed, Smith continued. "The divers who died did not only die from the bites. They were showing a wide range of abnormal neurological behaviors. The crocodiles are also behaving in a very bizarre way. Besides being about forty kilometers farther out in the ocean than they should be, they are also expressing neurological dysfunction. We did manage to capture two crocodiles and do a postmortem examination. Their brain tissue showed changes identical to the changes seen in cases of Mad Cow Disease. Shockingly, similar lesions were seen in the three people who died, and those who have been bitten are starting to show rapidly progressing symptoms."

With a jolt, I realized why I was here. As a veterinary student at Cornell University, I had written several papers on Mad Cow Disease. To be fair, the research had primarily been done by a PhD student named David Fowler, who worked in the same lab I did. I applied for the position because I thought it would bolster my resume. My job really consisted of assisting David as he collected and analyzed brain samples from affected cows, and I entered data and looked for patterns in the positive cases. This lab work lasted over two summers, and on and off throughout the school year. David and I became friends and spent a lot of late-night hours in downtown Ithaca, drinking beers and discussing science, girls, and football. After the second summer, David became involved in an unsavory incident with an under-age undergraduate and was unceremoniously kicked out of the university.

I felt partially responsible, because I had introduce David to Adrienne. She was a seventeen-year-old freshman I had met at the gym one day. They dated for a month before she turned eighteen. I never understood the penalty, since the relationship was consensual, and David eventually went on to marry Adrienne. I guess the whole mess at school was compounded by rumors that Adrienne became pregnant. I doubted the rumors, because she and David never had any kids.

On the day he was expelled, he handed me three years of his raw data. "This stuff is too important to be archived—or worse, *classified* by some government asshole. The world needs to know how supremely unbalanced nature has become. You publish whatever you can, buddy."

Timing is everything. That data led to three papers on Mad Cow Disease, which did add sparkle to my resume. In fact, it led to a spot in a coveted veterinary surgical residency. His data also mapped out the disease throughout Europe and, in retrospect, probably saved hundreds of thousands of animals and possibly even some human lives.

"I am asking the four of you to go to Australia to investigate this outbreak," continued Mr. Smith. "I fully realize you do not specialize in the outbreak of novel diseases, and there is an entire team in place already, evaluating things from an epidemiological perspective. Each of you has unique knowledge which will be valuable to this department as we put together our investigation."

"That is a big ask," said Dr. Fleury and I, at the same time.

"Strange you two used the same phrase," uttered Mr. Smith. I looked at Dr. Fleury, but she did not return the glance, instead staring rather coldly at Mr. Smith.

"You said the purpose of this agency is to identify threats to citizens," said Dr. King sarcastically. "I suppose it was some rich politician who got bitten by a stupid alligator, and that is why our lives are being disrupted."

Mr. Smith could no longer contain his growing annoyance. Placing both hands flat on the table, he towered over Dr. King as his ears turned a bright shade of reddish purple. I suspected he was a man who was not often questioned or challenged in his authority.

"First off," he said, "I referred to *American* citizens. Second, they are *crocodiles*, and third, I don't think you have a choice, given the contents of that envelope. If any of you need more motivation, there is currently an outbreak in Memphis, Tennessee. Early indications are that this is the same disease that is occurring in Australia. So far it hasn't made the news, since only four people have died and no one has made a connection. But the brain histopathology from the four who died is identical to the three in Australia. Another twelve people are showing similar symptoms at various Memphis hospitals."

"How could you have possibly put all this together so quickly?" asked Dr. King, somewhat subdued. "When I ask for a lab report, it takes me a week to get an answer."

"Unlike you, who thinks he is important, I actually am," said Mr. Smith, with a hint of superiority. "I am giving you each twenty-four hours to decide. Mr. Rose, you are military, and as such you don't have the luxury of deciding for yourself. I have talked to your commanding officer, and you will be leaving for Queensland."

Spencer got up without a word or a change in expression and walked out. How strange it must be to have major decisions in your life entirely decided by a faceless military system.

"We will be in touch," Mr. Smith said to the rest of the group, and he also walked out.

The three of us exchanged identical blank expressions.

"What just happened?" Dr. Fleury asked.

"I don't know about you two, but I'm getting the hell out of this place right now," replied Dr. King.

He stood up and walked out the door. We followed closely behind, down the hall. Mr. Smith had disappeared, and I wondered if he occupied one of the offices behind the unmarked identical doors that lined the hall. I didn't try any of the handles this time.

When we were two steps from the elevator, the doors opened. We all got in and Dr. King shouted to air, "I would like to leave this building."

The elevator started moving and opened to what I assumed was the ground floor. Similar to the last floor we were on, a long hall stretched out, with the same tan paint, but without doors or anything on the walls. At the end of the corridor, an unmarked, brown door automatically opened with a hiss when we approached. The bright outdoor light was a contrast from the artificial light we had been bathed in. I squinted, and it took my eyes several seconds to adjust as we walked into an ally. Behind us, the door hissed shut and clicked. Apparently, a security guard is unnecessary when nothing opens or moves unless the unseen wizard wills it to.

Chapter 3

D R. FLEURY WALKED NORTH ON Thomas Street without a word, and Dr. King headed in the opposite direction. It appeared Ponytail's mission didn't extend to getting me back home. Miffed, I looked around to get my bearings, trying to figure out the direction of Penn Station. I started walking the way Dr. King had gone, thinking that it felt like *north*. As I turned the corner, I was almost hit by a blue Honda Civic, which must have been at least ten years old.

Spencer rolled down the window. "Do you need a ride back to New Jersey?" he asked. Seeing no better option, I jumped into the passenger seat. The inside of the car was immaculate. Not a speck of dirt on the floormats.

"Thanks," I said to Spencer with a smile. "I was not eager to take public transportation."

Spencer looked me up and down and immediately confessed, "I didn't just happen to come around the corner. I was hoping to get some intel. I don't like being in a situation I don't understand."

Tell me about it, I thought. "What intel can I provide?" The phrase sounded strange coming out of my mouth. I have never been in the military, and this is not how normal people talk.

"First off, you can tell me what Mad Cow Disease is and why you were recruited."

"Mad Cow Disease is a neurological disease caused by a prion."

"What's a prion?"

This surprised me, and I asked in the nicest way I possibly could, "Where did you go to medical school, Dr. Rose?"

"I never said I was a doctor," he responded, a bit insulted.

"I thought you were introduced as a *medical* sergeant," I asked.

"I am a special forces medical sergeant. It means that besides all the special forces training, I have been trained in basic medical procedures. As you can imagine, most of my training is focused on stopping bleeding from bullet wounds so my fellow rangers don't die in the field. Essentially, I'm like a frontline triage nurse, though also trained to kill."

"Sorry for the misunderstanding. I never meant to offend."

"It takes a bit more than that to offend me," he replied. "Back to the issue at hand. Tell me about this disease and why you three were chosen by Mr. Smith to go to Australia and investigate."

"I have no intention of leaving New Jersey."

"We'll see," muttered Spencer. "Mr. Smith can be rather persuasive."

"Well, since we have a bit of a ride, let me tell you what I know about Bovine Spongiform Encephalopathy—BSE. And before you ask, that is the same thing as Mad Cow Disease."

"And prions?"

"Prion diseases were first discovered a few hundred years ago. They probably have been around for thousands of years, but like most diseases, the medical technology to properly identify and diagnose these things is relatively recent. Prions cause some of the scariest diseases on the planet, because the particles that cause these problems are so small, and the diseases they cause are nearly impossible to treat. Prion diseases were identified in sheep and goats in the mid seventeen hundreds. The medical community at the time didn't even know bacteria existed, so they had no idea the etiology of the disease. It was called *Scrapie*. In humans, it is called *Creutzfeldt-Jakob Disease.*"

"Let me guess," Spencer grinned. "That's KJD?"

I smiled back. "CJD—but close."

"So the same prion can infect across species?"

"Actually, no. The protein is slightly different within each species, as with variations of bacteria—different bacteria may still cause similar infections and responses in a host. The reaction may be remarkably similar, but different organisms are at work. These prions, which are proteins—neither virus nor bacteria—attack the central nervous system. They are unrelenting and almost universally fatal.

"The history of the disease is interesting, which really formed the basis of my publications back in veterinary school. This disease in sheep has been around for hundreds of years, but it never caused a serious problem. Small outbreaks occurred here and there, but huge populations of animals weren't dying, and it wasn't spreading to any other species, so most people didn't pay attention. A significant outbreak in the beef cattle of Great Britain changed everything. That's when people started taking notice. We think the rendering processes of cattle feed were at the root of the problem. Shortly before the outbreak, the feed manufacturers had begun focusing on increasing protein levels in the feed. The more protein they could pack into what the cows ate, the quicker they would grow, and the more money everyone would make. One less month of feeding a cow before they reach a marketable size translates to huge profits for the cattle industry.

"In the interest of making money, feed companies started experimenting with ways to get more protein into their products. The companies needed a cheap source of protein, so they turned to products no one else wanted. Naturally, they looked within the cattle industry itself. When a cow is slaughtered, the meat that can be sold in the market is harvested, and what is left is a carcass that can't be used for much. The carcass is destroyed or buried or whatever. The feed companies decided the carcasses could be used, and they started buying them from the slaughterhouses for pennies. They took these previously wasted bits, boiled them, and essentially ground them up into gross bits of unidentifiable sludge."

"Let me guess," said Spencer, grinning again, "that's where scrapple and bologna come from."

"I'm not so sure, but I wouldn't rule it out," I chuckled. "As far as I've heard, the components of scrapple are an industrial secret that has been closely guarded for hundreds of years. I bet Mr. Smith has the recipe. You could get it from him and make millions in a competitive scrapple market."

"The stuff isn't bad, as long as it's deep fried."

"I think you could deep fry a ten-day-old dead skunk that would be halfway decent, but I think we're getting a bit off topic," I continued.

"Please, by all means, tell me more about sludge."

I was enjoying our banter and, for the first time that day, pleased to be involved in this strange adventure. "The meat industry used this sludge to make protein-rich powders, which farmers bought and added to the feed to grow cattle as quickly as possible. This went on for a while, and everyone was happy. The cows were getting bigger, quicker, and the farmers and the feed companies were making more money.

"Then, in the early eighties, no one knew how or why, some cows started getting sick. Strange stuff. The cows would wander around in circles until they dropped dead; some would walk up to a wall and press their head against it for twelve hours at a time; some would walk like they were really drunk; and others had seizures. It was a sight to behold. Cattle farms began to resemble insane asylums. But most ranchers didn't care. As long as the sick cows were large enough to be sold, they were sent to market anyway. The feed companies followed suit and used some of the diseased cow carcasses to make feed, and even more cows got sick.

"By the early nineties, things were so bad the world started to take notice. At which point, however, no one yet knew it was the feed causing the acceleration in the disease. Hundreds of thousands of cattle died, and millions more were slaughtered to try and stop the spread of whatever was going on. Too late, as it turns out, because some humans started getting sick with the same symptoms.

"The world closed down importation of beef from the United Kingdom, the epicenter of the disease outbreak, and beef prices went through the roof. People became paranoid about eating beef *anywhere*. In fact, I think this whole crisis led to the popularity of vegetarians in the world.

"Anyway, governments around the globe eventually got involved and changed the regulations for the way meat and protein products were produced, and the sick cattle started to decrease over time. There were some smaller outbreaks in other parts of the world, but once people figured out how to slow down the disease, by culling entire herds of cattle, the outbreaks were shut down pretty fast. In fact, a small outbreak occurred in Montana that would have devastated the meat market in the United States, but it was *dealt with*."

"What do you mean dealt with?" asked Spencer.

"This is where things get a little hazy, and I'm sure I was not supposed to know about it, but no one ever asked me to keep it a secret," I responded, looking around as if someone could overhear. "When I was back in vet school, my friend David was getting samples from hundreds of cows a week to determine which ones were infected. The vast majority were from Great Britain, but one Friday afternoon, about fifty samples showed up, marked for urgent-priority testing. David and I had planned to meet some undergrads for a few drinks when the samples came in. Being the good students that we were, we canceled our dates and worked on the samples. Of course, we played rock, paper, scissors to see who would go down to the local gas station and get forties of malt liquor to help make the night pass more smoothly."

"Classy," replied Spencer.

"Hey, working in a lab didn't pay enough to afford more than that, so we did what we could. Well, halfway through the samples, we found a return address tucked between the samples from a ranch in Montana. I thought it was strange, since the previous samples were all from overseas, but there it was, Sarowitz Ranch, with a return address in the middle of Montana. And all fifty samples were positive. That in itself was terribly unusual. We were seeing positives at a rate of about three percent from most ranches. Also, with the Sarowitz cows, histological changes in the brain tissue were much more severe than anything we had seen in the past. The strange thing was that the next week, I read a news story about an immense forest fire in the middle of Montana, where a ranch was completely destroyed. Four people and all of the livestock perished. Guess what the name of the ranch was?"

"Sarowitz."

"Correct. And the next day, all our lab samples disappeared, along with all our results from that night. Come to think of it now, it was the next week when David was accused of a scandal and kicked out of the University. Damn, I never really put those two events together. You don't think . . ."

"I'm not sure I would run that theory by anyone else, if you know what I mean," advised Spencer.

"Well, everything worked out. I became a surgeon, and David landed a cushy job in a research lab. He and his wife seem to have locked down the 'happily-ever-after' scenario. The positive samples never made the papers, and I didn't follow up on anything since I was only twenty-four at the time. But if the news had become public, it would have destroyed billions of dollars in the US cattle industry. I did stop eating beef for two days after we tested those samples."

"Two whole days?" asked Spencer with obvious sarcasm.

"I don't think I was built to be a vegetarian," I said. "Let's get back to your intel gathering, shall we? This is where the prion comes in. The scientific community of the world, and especially in Great Britain, grew increasingly concerned that if the disease remained in the meat, it was only a matter of time before significant numbers of people would get sick. Neurologists internationally started to connect with the prion. Not many people were affected, but a few sick people were enough to cause widespread panic. I came to the conclusion that in the world of public opinion, one sick person is worth one hundred thousand sick cows. Globally, fewer than fifty people may have gotten sick from eating beef, but it was enough to set up worldwide safeguards to try and protect populations from Mad Cow Disease. To this day, there are countries where the importation of beef is not possible, and most regulations can be traced back to the outbreaks in the eighties and nineties.

"Anyway, things have been relatively under control over the last twenty years, so eating beef in this country is safe. Every once in a while, a case pops up, but it doesn't usually make news and certainly doesn't cause a panic."

"Did they develop an antibiotic to treat this thing?" asked Spencer.

"Being a protein, antibiotics and antivirals do nothing. It's simply a naturally occurring protein; it's not even alive."

"So, how does something that is dead kill you?"

"I didn't say it was dead, just that it's not alive. Here's where biology gets a bit tricky with definitions, and things can get a bit blurred. A prion is a small particle. Smaller than a virus and much smaller than a bacterium. It can replicate even though it has no DNA. Since it can't replicate on its own without another organism, it is not classified as a living thing. I don't make the rules here, talk to biology professors."

"Sounds like science fiction," replied Spencer.

"No, it's very much real and a super-scary particle. For animals or people who get sick, it's usually fatal, since no treatment exists. The truly interesting—or terrifying—thing is how it causes disease. Are you ready for this? It dissolves your brain."

"You're exaggerating," said Spencer, doubtfully.

"No, really. The reason it is called Bovine Spongiform Encephalopathy is because a brain from something with this disease looks like a sponge, with holes throughout."

"For something so gruesome, how come I've never heard of a prion?" asked Spencer.

"Well, the diseases they cause are pretty rare, and people only tend to know about things that affect them or someone they know. Lots of ghastly diseases are around, but if they don't affect a lot of people, the general public remains blissfully unaware. Rabies, for example, is one of the most frightening diseases on the planet. That virus kills almost anything it infects. Once it takes hold, there is virtually no cure. Actually, hundreds of cases a year are reported in animals in the small county I live in, but the reason people don't lock themselves in the basement with baseball bats is because, statistically, few people become infected. Besides, most people know early on when they are bitten by an infected animal, so countermeasures can start immediately after any exposure."

"You're a cheerful car companion," muttered Spencer.

"Hey, I just wanted a free ride to New Jersey. This is your intel session."

"So, how do you find out if someone has Mad Cow Disease?"

"Well, the easy way is to view their brain under a microscope."

"That's the easy way?"

"Well, not easy for the patient. But easy for the pathologist. Before we get to the point of looking at people's brains, a neurological examination will produce abnormal findings. I am guessing some other tests can be done, but my experience is with cows, and once cows start developing neurological problems, they are typically euthanized, and samples are collected. You can have an intel session with Dr. King if you want to talk about diagnosing neurological diseases in people."

"Dr. King doesn't seem like the kind of fellow who likes to chat," responded Spencer.

"As an expert in movement disorders, I'm guessing a disease like this is precisely in his wheelhouse," I said.

"The dynamics of this team are starting to come together, but there is one thing bothering me," said Spencer.

"What is that?"

"Well, I was not brought in for my knowledge of rare neurological problems. So why does an army ranger with basic medical training get assigned to this team?"

"To babysit us?" I offered.

"My skill set doesn't include babysitting. In fact, most of my skills are what people would consider not very nice. The situations I get sent into are usually volatile and violent, and my job is to subdue and eliminate threats. I think it's likely Mr. Smith is not giving us all the facts."

"Is that part of why you offered me a ride?" I asked.

"Let's put it this way: the more intel I have about a mission, the more comfortable I feel about achieving the desired outcome—and right now I'm not very comfortable. The missions I've been involved with in the past inevitably entailed subduing people or organizations who are planning acts designed to cause harm to the United States. I can't help but wonder again: why am I here? I can't overrun or rout a disease process."

I gazed out the window and noticed the clouds rolling in. I wondered what kind of information Mr. Smith would be withholding and why. It didn't much matter, since I had no intention of going anywhere near Australia. I turned to ask Spencer, but he seemed like his thoughts were miles away. We sat in silence for the rest of the drive back.

It was near dinner time when we pulled up to the hospital. My phone rang with an unknown number. I thanked Spencer for the ride and exited the car to pick up my call.

Mr. Smith asked, "Did you have a pleasant ride back to New Jersey with Spencer?"

"How do you know where I am?" I asked, scanning the parking lot.

"It is my job to know things," replied Mr. Smith confidently, as I silently waved goodbye to Spencer. "Have you made a decision about traveling to Australia?"

"In fact, I have made a decision, and I wish you all the best, but I can't go," I answered, hoping that was the end of the discussion. "I have a lot going on professionally and am not the type of person who goes to Australia at the drop of a hat, even if it is for a worthy cause."

"I am sorry to hear that," said Mr. Smith. "I really was hoping to appeal to your tendency to make selfless decisions, but you leave me no choice but to try and persuade you by other means."

He abruptly hung up as I headed inside. I didn't give his words much thought, naively assuming the whole ordeal was behind me.

Chapter 4

THINGS WERE STILL UNDER CONTROL in the hospital. A dog needed surgery after eating a corn cob, but the residents could handle that without my help. The puppy from the morning surgery was up and wagging her tail. She already had eaten a small dinner and was asking for more. I scratched her under the chin as I listened with my stethoscope. It was hard to hear, through the constant squirming and the puppy's persistent attempts to lick my face, but the murmur was gone, and the heart sounded normal. She would do well and should make a full recovery. After rounding with the next shift of emergency doctors, I walked to the basement garage to my car and started the fifteen-minute drive home.

The phone rang again, and I couldn't help but smile when I saw it was Sarah, my nineteen-year-old daughter, calling from West Point. The cadets were not allowed to use their phones very often, so each call was cherished. "Hey, Sarah. How are things going?"

I knew right away things were not going well. She was a strong-willed girl, and even though that challenged her throughout high school, I knew it would serve her well in her life. It was not like her at all to sound over-the-top.

"What's wrong, honey?" I asked.

"They accused me of a regulation violation," she answered, with an uncharacteristic tremble in her voice.

"What's that?" I asked.

"They said I failed a drug test last week!"

"Is that possible?" I asked, immediately regretting my choice of wording.

"Are you kidding me?" she exploded. "Do you think there is any chance I would take drugs at West Point? Do you even know me?"

"I'm sorry, Sarah, that was the scientist in me," I said, with a bit of embarrassment. "It must be an aberrant test that will get cleared up."

"Well, I'm not allowed to leave my barrack for the next twenty-four hours, and they just took blood, urine, and hair samples," she said, her voice cracking a bit. "They said if any are positive, I will be sent home and likely expelled."

My blood was boiling, because I knew what was going on. "Tests are never perfect. You have nothing to worry about because you did nothing wrong," I said, hoping to console her.

"Dad. You know that's not the way the world works," she replied.

I was always surprised about how mature she sounded for a nineteen-year-old.

"I need to go," said Sarah. "I'm not supposed to be on the phone, and I think someone is coming down the hall."

"Please text me the second you hear anything."

"I will," she responded. She was always good about keeping me in the loop.

Throughout high school, Sarah swam competitively and played softball. The higher the challenge, the more she would rise to it. When she was twelve, a much bigger boy thought it would be fun to bully her. He came up behind her, knocked her books out of her hand, and then slammed her head-first, hard, into the lockers, in front of all of her friends. She turned around, and without a second thought, swung her fist and knocked out the kid's two front teeth, dropping him to the ground. The bully started crying as he covered his face with his hands. Sarah felt terrible and even helped the boy to the nurse's station before walking to the office to call home. I had taught her to punch when she was five years old, and occasionally we would spar for fun. She had developed her skills to the point that she packed a mean punch, despite her young age. There was, of course, a meeting with the principal, the boy's parents, and me. I found it hard not to laugh when both kids gave their side of the story. To this day, she maintains she was aiming for his chest and didn't even swing especially hard. But it was the last time anyone tried to bully her at school.

West Point was the perfect environment to challenge her, and I remember the day she was accepted. It was like all of the Christmas mornings in my life wrapped together. Her hard work had finally paid off in a single moment. The feeling of sheer joy is not easily described to someone who doesn't have children. Your child's pain is always your pain, but their successes bring an elation no other emotion comes close to.

Her mother, my beloved wife Julia, had died in a car accident when she was nine. Julia was coming home from coaching and was hit head-on by a drunk driver. The tragedy shook the family for years, but it hit Sarah particularly hard. Her salvation was driving herself in everything she ever did, and she excelled in nearly everything.

Now, I worried Mr. Smith was carrying through with his threats. I next called my son to check on him, though he usually let calls go to voice mail. He picked up after three rings. "Dylan, how are things going?" I asked, as casually as I could.

"Things are great, Dad, but I have an exam tomorrow in parasitology, and I'm having trouble memorizing all the names and life cycles of the organisms."

I always had trouble with that as well. He was a third-year veterinary student at UC Davis in California. Like his sister, he was hit hard by his mother's death. His solution was to bury himself in his studies. He rarely got less than a ninety-five on any test, and the prospect of getting a poor grade in parasitology would drive him crazy. I offered the typical fatherly advice.

"I'm sure you'll do fine, and one test doesn't matter that much."

"Do you have something in particular on your mind, Dad?" he asked.

"Nope, just checking in."

"Okay, I'll talk to you later," he said and abruptly hung up.

Relieved that things were fine with Dylan, my attention returned to Mr. Smith. I was going to rip this guy apart. It's one thing to inconvenience me, but to attack my daughter? No way. I pulled into my driveway and grabbed my phone, ready for a fight, but instantly realized I had no way to reach him. The incoming call from Mr. Smith had been ID-blocked, and I never got contact information from anyone at the NSA. I remained behind the wheel, briefly contemplating a drive back into the city to confront him inside the strange building. No, that wouldn't work, even if I could get inside; it was too impenetrable. The frustration of not having anyone to yell at made me angrier.

I walked into the house through the garage, and Tallie met me at the door with kisses and unwavering excitement. It's hard to stay in a state of rage with a seventy-pound pit bull who only wants to spend time with you.

"Okay, I missed you too," I said, as she licked my face with dire urgency. I let her out to run off some of her energy in the backyard while I sat on the deck and contemplated my options. A quick search of the internet let me know there was no contact information for the Prism Division of the NSA. In fact, I couldn't even confirm the division existed. A quick search of Mr. Smith and Prism yielded nothing. Stupid to even try. I had serious doubts whether that was even his real name. Was any of this real?

Pushing my laptop away, I closed my eyes and tried to relax. When things got tense professionally, I had the ability to relax my body, allowing my mind to quickly follow. This time it didn't work as well as it usually did, but I felt my heart rate slowing down, nonetheless. I've always loved my backyard this time of night. While Tallie chased leaves and imaginary monsters around the yard, I enjoyed the fiery horizon as the sun sank below the treetops. The sunsets from the deck were always peaceful, and numerous. Around the time of Julia's death, they protected my sanity when I was convinced my world had ended.

I slumped deeper into my chair as reality sank in. I could try and fight with this guy, but I had the distinct feeling Mr. Smith was not the type of person who tolerated losing. Faced with defiance, he would retaliate, and the resources he had at his disposal were essentially limitless. While I had no weapon or tool but an old laptop—and a limited understanding of the internet. Sarah would be vulnerable at West Point, a military institution under the control of the US government. A guy like Mr. Smith must have far-reaching influences in that world. The academy had a storied reputation for not tolerating any nonsense from students. They made that clear from day one. Cadets were there to follow orders and develop the skills to learn and lead, in that order. Sarah's first week, four newbies were kicked out for sneaking a six pack into their room on a Saturday night. No questions asked; just leave. According to Sarah, they were given ten minutes to pack their bags, then they were escorted to the entrance and told not to return. No parents were called, no meetings, discussion, or appeal. You are no longer welcome at this institution.

My heart rate ticked up again at the thought of that happening to Sarah; she wouldn't easily recover from such a blow. Even if it came to that, to what other lengths was Mr. Smith prepared to go? Deep down, I knew I would do anything to protect my children, and even though I hated the thought of giving in to a bully, what else could I do?

I remembered the faint resignation in Spencer's eyes when he was told he was going to Australia—no argument, no question. He needed to follow orders, and clearly, Mr. Smith had the ability to give them or at least control those who could. Once I accepted this problem was not going away and that my family's best interests relied on me going along with this plan, my path became clear. I picked up my phone and called my next door neighbor. We weren't exactly friends, but we got along, shared an occasional beer, waved, and chatted small talk every time we passed each other walking on the street, he with his chihuahuas and me with Tallie. Our dogs got along well, and I didn't complain about the shrill barking of his dogs, at all hours.

"Hey, Hank, would you be willing to watch Tallie for a few days?" I asked with artificial cheer.

"Sure, the girls love having a playdate," he responded. "When do you need me to do it?"

"Can I drop her off tomorrow?" I responded.

"That's short notice. Is everything okay?"

"Yes, everything is fine. Something's just come up, and I need to head out of town for business."

"Business? You're a veterinarian."

"Can you do it or not?" I snapped, much too abruptly.

"Easy, John, of course, I can do it. I'm just slightly concerned about you," Hank replied.

"Sorry, I am under a bit of stress right now. I really do appreciate your help, and I'll drop her off at seven tomorrow morning."

I hung up before he had a chance to respond. Hank regularly walked "the girls" at six in the morning, so I knew it wouldn't be a problem. Next, I texted the kids. "Have to go on a quick trip out of town, so if you need anything, use the cell and not the home phone." No need to get into specifics right now. They were both busy with school and tended not to ask too many questions. My son immediately texted back with a horse head emoji. This was an inside joke that had been going on for years. Essentially, it meant everything was fine and always made me smile.

My daughter's response was a bit more concerned.

"Is everything okay?" she texted.

"Everything's fine. A last-minute trip has come up, and I didn't want you to worry if I didn't answer the home phone," I texted back.

"Okay."

This superficial explanation satisfied her. Now, on to taking care of work. I knew my residents would still be at the hospital, so I called in to the surgery office. Appointments had been slowing down, but I still had several that needed to be changed. Samantha got on the phone, cheerful as ever. I wondered if I had an upbeat attitude all the time when I was twenty-five. I could vaguely remember when going into work every day was an adventure, and life responsibilities revolved around social arrangements and getting out of work on time to have drinks or dinner with friends. Life was very hectic as a resident, but in many ways simpler. She agreed to make the necessary calls to reschedule appointments, and I knew the other veterinarians would cover for me as needed. We were a tight-knit group, which was one reason I had worked there my entire career.

My stomach rumbled, but I was not much in the mood to cook. My reliable fallback when I was tired or stressed was to go down to the local pizza parlor and have them heat a few slices of whatever was behind the counter. I went to Sal's enough that the owner called hello whenever I walked in.

"You look tired, Dr. Osler," Sal observed as I ordered two slices to go. The stress of the day was surely catching up with me. Sal seemed to work twenty-four/seven, and he'd been serving pizza to the locals for years. Decades ago, he moved from Brooklyn with his wife and two children, but he had never lost the accent. Slightly overweight, dressed in an apron and baseball cap, Sal always appeared chipper.

"I had a long day," I responded as he put my slices in the oven. "Let me ask you a question, Sal," I said, since we were the only two people in the place. "What would you be willing to do to protect your kids?"

He gave me a concerned gaze. "There is nothing I wouldn't do to protect those two. If someone hurt them, I would be making pizzas in the prison system. Is Dylan or Sarah in trouble? Do you need me to take someone out?" he offered with a smile, patting the broad wooden pizza peel he was holding. "I would risk getting into big trouble to protect my two favorite customers." My kids ate a lot of pizza, and whenever friends came over, Sal was the unofficial caterer.

"No, I don't need you to take someone out," I chuckled. "The kids are fine. Someone was just picking on Sarah."

"Are you kidding me?" said Sal with a smile. "I still remember the time she knocked that kid's teeth out when she was only twelve. If someone has the balls to take on Sarah, with her military training, I think it is the other kid who will need protection, not Sarah."

"I guess that's true enough," I conceded. Sal placed my two slices in a box and put them up on the counter. I got out my wallet to pay and Sal waved me off.

"These two are on the house, Dr. Osler."

I thanked him and slid a ten into his tip jar as he turned around.

"I saw that," said Sal, as I walked out of the place. Like most parents, I guess Sal has eyes in the back of his head.

I collapsed into the couch and turned on the television. Tallie rested her head on my lap. There is nothing like the security blanket of a canine companion. The pizza tasted delicious, and I immediately wished I had gotten more than two slices. I laid my head back and closed my eyes, trying to remember how long it actually takes to get to Australia. Twenty years ago, my wife and I took a trip to the Great Barrier Reef. We were young and didn't have a ton of money, but I remember two things. First, it took an excruciatingly long time to get to Queensland in Northern Australia, where the Great Barrier Reef could be best accessed; and second, it was one of the most magical places I ever visited. For a moment, I started to look forward to seeing that part of the world again.

The phone rang, and the caller ID told me the number was blocked. But I knew exactly who was calling.

"I trust you have reconsidered your position," said Mr. Smith, without emotion.

"You intentionally hurt my daughter, and that's unacceptable!" I yelled into the phone, gripping the device so hard I was worried it would crack.

"I know, but I don't have the luxury of time, and my priority is much higher than keeping people happy. I do what I need to do to get the outcome I want, and I don't apologize for it. That being said, if you agree to go tomorrow, I will have a car pick you up at eight a.m., and your daughter's tests will all be negative. In addition, the positive test from last week will be determined to be from a faulty batch of samples, and the superintendent will issue a formal apology to Sarah."

"That's not good enough!" I screamed into the phone. "If I do this, I need assurances my children will never be used for leverage again."

"Fine," agreed Mr. Smith, with no elaboration.

I wasn't entirely sure I believed him and silently cursed myself for losing my temper. If he needed proof that he had pushed the right buttons, he had it. From what I was learning about Mr. Smith, he had no compunction manipulating people to do what he wanted, and he seemed to know the right buttons to push. He certainly did with me, and from Dr. King's reaction in the meeting, he did with him as well.

"So you agree to go?" he asked with the same unexpressive voice.

"Yes, I agree to go, but--" The line went dead. Mr. Smith had engineered the outcome he wanted, and he was no longer interested in the rest of the conversation. I felt my blood boil as I slammed the phone down. What just happened must be illegal in some way, but my mind had been made up. I would go for the sake of my family. I thought of what Sal said about making pizza in the prison system. Most parents I knew would do anything to protect their children. Was this hardwired into us or something learned over time?

Turning to the task at hand, I went to my office, a converted spare bedroom with a desk, pulled out my old papers on Bovine Spongiform Encephalopathy, and started reading. I needed to do something to keep my mind off of how angry I felt. I read until I heard a clock downstairs strike midnight. My eyes were blurry, and it was becoming hard to concentrate; time to call it a night.

I was experienced at packing light and managed to get everything I needed into a medium-sized duffle bag, which would fit into a plane's overhead compartment. It was after one in the morning when I drifted into a restless sleep. I could never sleep well when I was agitated, and there was no question I was still on fire due to the circumstances of the last twelve hours. I woke several hours later and quickly showered, and then made an egg and cheese sandwich with a pot of coffee. Since I never had a meal at an airport that didn't make me sick to my stomach, I like to have a full stomach whenever I travel.

I made time to give Tallie a short walk before dropping her off at Hank's and again apologizing for the lack of notice. He was polite, but very short with me, still a bit miffed by our interaction last night. He'll get over it. I'll bring him back a didgeridoo.

At exactly 8:00 a.m., a black town car with tinted windows and government plates pulled up. The driver was dressed in a gray suit and didn't say a word as I threw my bag into the trunk and slid into the back seat. These guys really don't switch it up very much, I thought. A red manila folder on the seat contained about thirty pages detailing what had been going on in Australia over the last several days. I started reading.

The pages covered the attacks at the reef, those who died already, and four others still alive in the hospital. Those four, despite minor injuries, had started to develop a variety of neurological signs, including incoordination, seizures, and blurred vision. The three who died already had full pathology results, including gross and histological pictures of their central nervous systems. The amount of information available, and gathered so quickly, was impressive. Reports like these typically take days, if not weeks, to prepare after a patient's death. A team of pathologists must've been standing by, waiting to study these poor victims.

The degree of brain damage sustained in such a short amount of time astounded me. One diver's crocodile bites were so severe, she died before the boat was able to reach shore. The histopathology samples of her brain were normal, and the cause of death had been determined to be exsanguination. The two others who died—a husband and a wife—deteriorated over seventy-two hours after being bitten. Their bite wounds, miraculously, were not life threatening.

Dredging up what I could remember about crocodiles, I knew this couple should have been crushed. The bite strength of a saltwater crocodile is the strongest of any animal ever recorded. And once they bite, they don't let go, rolling violently and pulling their prey underwater. Whatever animal is unlucky enough to get snatched will typically drown in the murky water of a river or swamp. If normal crocodiles had been hunting out in the ocean, these people would have been devoured, their bodies never to be found. Minor wounds from an attack made no sense. I jotted a quick note on the page, coming to the conclusion the crocodiles responsible were obviously not exhibiting normal behavior.

Examining the human brain imaging delivered another shock. The spongiform changes in the deceased were profound. Each had lost over thirty percent of brain tissue, with diffuse changes that almost entirely demolished the structure of the cerebellum. If this happened in only seventy-two hours, as the report suggested, this prion, by far, was the most aggressive I had ever heard of.

MRI reports on the four survivors showed minor changes within their brains, suggesting a similar mechanism was in play. Serial MRIs showed the size of the lesions were roughly doubling every day. I put down the folder in disbelief. A prion causing this degree of progression, even at the twenty-four hour-mark, was unprecedented. I read the interpretation of the MRI images again, to be sure I hadn't misread it, shaking my head as the words sank in.

Several pages focused on the captured crocodiles. I found these reports more interesting. Training in veterinary school has taught me that despite the huge amount of variability between species, one biology unites all life. People tend to get caught up in how different animals look from one another. I always focus on how similar species are to one another.

Crocodile brains are smaller than a human's, with less development in most areas. Nevertheless, the underlying structure is strikingly similar. Spongiform changes showed less advancement in the crocodiles than in the humans who died, but the parallels were there. In the samples of both species, the majority of the changes had occurred in the cerebellum, with microscopic changes throughout the entire brain.

No data determined how long ago these reptiles had been exposed to whatever made them sick. Nor was it known why they congregated at the reef or why they behaved so erratically. The report concluded these creatures were perfectly healthy except for changes in the central nervous system.

The end of the report detailed the work currently underway. Whatever team Dr. Smith had in place was being directed by the Australian army, with doctors and scientists from the United States and Australia working together. Why the hell are we going here? These people do this for a living—I don't. What a waste of time.

The last sheet of paper, tucked in behind the others, was handwritten. It appeared to have been left in the folder by mistake, but based on everything that happened over the last day, I doubted these people make many mistakes. The note said, "Determine the source of the prion, be it natural or engineered." That gave me pause.

I had assumed we were dealing with a natural outbreak, like that in the cattle industry in the '80s and '90s. Back then, various theories tried to explain why the outbreak was regional and so severe, but most scientists thought the rise was due to evolution of the prion, making cattle more susceptible to its effects. I had assumed this was a similar circumstance. Spencer's suggestion that we did not have all the facts came back to haunt me. Is it possible we were dealing with a malicious actor? Was this particular prion so aggressive because that is what it was designed to do?

Determine the source of the prion. Did I just "volunteer" for something that was inherently dangerous, and is that why the team includes an army ranger? I suddenly didn't feel so good about the egg and cheese sandwich, which was churning in my stomach.

I looked out the window and realized we weren't heading north. In fact, we were on the New Jersey Turnpike, heading toward Philadelphia.

"I thought we were going to Newark," I questioned the driver.

"Then you were mistaken," he curtly replied.

"Well, then, can you tell me where we *are* going?" I said with annoyance.

"To a marine base, north of Philadelphia," he replied. "We'll be there soon."

Arguing would be pointless, so I sat back and closed my eyes to think. Find the source of the prion. I assumed the crocodiles were the source of the infection. So how did *they* become affected? Back in the '80s, when people had become infected with the prion, it was from eating beef from an affected cow. The cows became infected from eating a protein source derived from sheep and goats, specifically their nervous systems. How did those goats and sheep initially develop the disease in the 1750s? No one, surely, engineered biological weapons then, so it must have been a naturally developing disease. Moreover, a similar disease has been seen in elk and other wild game in various countries.

Yet, the possibility of this prion being produced in a lab couldn't be ruled out. This disease strain was significantly different from past outbreaks. It caused a huge amount of destruction in a brief time span. True, science has seen natural precedents for diseases becoming more aggressive in a short amount of time, especially when jumping between species, but it remains rare. Most disease processes stick to one species or at least similar genera. I pondered the facts, trying to come up with a helpful theory, but none materialized.

Several minutes later, the car came to an abrupt stop. "Time to go," said the driver.

The sun was brilliant and the day was warming. It took a minute for my eyes to adjust after viewing the world from behind tinted windows. There were several airplane hangars and a very long runway. We were parked next to a hanger with the most unusual plane I had ever seen. The entire aircraft was jet black. The nose of the plane was extremely pointed, with two small wings near the front, which must have only been eight feet long each. About halfway down the tube, the body expanded into a wide V-shape, creating a pair of larger wings, which must have been one hundred feet across at the back. Six engines were built into the center of the body, with seven individual flaps hanging from the back of each massive, wing-like tail feather. The only windows were those of the cockpit, and they seemed quite small.

In the hangar I saw Spencer and Nelly talking, so I headed that way. Spencer was dressed in military fatigues and Nelly was dressed in jeans and a white shirt with blue stripes.

"That is quite an unusual plane," I remarked as I walked up.

"This the newest model of the Valkyrie," said Spencer, staring at the plane with admiration. "I didn't know such a plane existed. The Valkyrie was initially built to be a high-speed bomber in the nineteen fifties, but the entire project was supposedly scrapped due to costs and the development of cheaper technology. I guess the military has a way of developing aircraft the general public never knows about."

"It looks fast," I said.

"The initial Valkyrie certainty was," replied Spencer.

I couldn't help but notice that Nelly, standing nearby, was absolutely striking in the morning light. In our initial meeting, she dressed more like a business executive; in the morning light, she more resembled a high-fashion model.

"Good morning, Dr. Fleury," I said with a smile.

"Maybe it's a good morning for you, but I am most certainly not having a good morning," she snapped. "I suppose you volunteered to make this impromptu trip across the world?"

"Well, I did agree to go, but it was more like coercion."

"Same here," she said. "I have the distinct impression Mr. Smith is a master of manipulation. What he is doing is criminal. I contacted a lawyer last night for advice, and she cannot believe what's going on. Do know what he did to me?"

Nelly was nearly screaming now, at no one in particular. Spencer and I, not knowing how to respond, maintained blank expressions.

"The head of pathology at Johns Hopkins told me if I don't volunteer for this trip, funding for my research will be cut off. I have worked with this department with an impeccable record for the last fifteen years, and just like that, they want to take away my research lab." She paced back and forth between Spencer and me, her agitation rapidly mounting. "I threatened to transfer to another hospital and take my funding with me. I applied directly to the NIH four years ago, so the money is linked to me personally, and not Johns Hopkins. The hospital director was getting upset with our confrontation, and he stepped away to take a call. When he got back, his response was creepy. He made it clear the funding wouldn't only be cut off here, but the money would be suspended wherever I went. He has no authority over the NIH. In fact, I don't even think it is possible to take away someone's research money once it has been appropriated. But he made it crystal clear the decisions were not being made by him but by someone who can manipulate the NIH. Who *is* this Mr. Smith, and what right does he have to disrupt our lives in this way?" Somewhat exhausted after her rant, she looked at the ground and kicked a small stone that went flying into the side of the bunker, making a clanging sound that reverberated around us.

"Mr. Smith is the head of one of the most powerful organizations in the world," offered Spencer, deliberately. "He doesn't play by the same rules as the rest of us, and it's his job to fuck with people and get his way. Let me offer some unsolicited advice to both of you. He knows more about each of you than you could possibly imagine. He really doesn't care about either of you—or me—and once he sets his mind to something, it's best to go along. He can be rather spiteful; crossing him is the last thing you want to do."

"You've been on missions before with him?" I asked.

"Yeah, and there was a so-called volunteer who didn't play his game. That poor guy's life was uprooted and his career was destroyed. He hired a lawyer to plead his case, but after one day on the case, the attorney abruptly dropped out, even refusing to speak with his client again."

"From what I've seen in the last twenty-four hours, I'm not surprised," I said. "I'm still not sure why we were chosen, but this entire thing is crazy. I don't like it, but each of us is in no position to challenge Mr. Smith. Speaking of which, our little party is about complete." I nodded to another black town car, just pulling up.

Alex got out. If looks could kill, his expression would have sent us all to an early grave. As he walked up, the door to the plane opened, and Ponytail appeared.

"The gang's all here," he said with a mock cheer that was not well received. He was not smiling, mirroring the looks on all of our faces. "Grab your stuff and get on board. It is time to go."

My phone pinged with a message. Sarah texted me that all of her drug tests had come back negative; the initial positive test was due to a lab error. I could hear the brag in her words when she said the school superintendent had called her with an apology—which never happens. I felt a weight had been lifted. Well, at least Mr. Smith had held up his side of the bargain. I texted back a short message, punctuated by hearts and smiley faces. Now that my daughter was back in a safe place, I felt much better about leaving the country.

Chapter 5

THE PLANE'S INTERIOR WAS NOT designed for comfort. In the main cabin, eight gray chairs with shoulder straps faced each other, four on the left and four on the right. The windowless cabin was dimly lit.

"You are going to want to strap in," Ponytail advised. Alex and I sat on the left of the cabin facing Nelly, Spencer, and Ponytail. Thirty seconds later, the engines turned on with a deafening roar. The plane jolted, and I could tell we were being towed out of the hangar toward the runway.

"You will all want to put these on if you want to hear anything for the next three days," Ponytail said, handing each of us black noise-canceling headphones. The silence was almost deafening as the headphones covered my ears. The plane stopped moving, and my seat reverberated as the big engines received more power from the cockpit, but I heard nothing. Without warning, all of the seats rotated ninety degrees toward the front of the cabin, and we were no longer facing each other. I practically jumped out of my seat as the voice of Mr. Smith came across the headphones. I glanced around the cabin. The sound was so crystal clear, I was sure Mr. Smith was sitting right next to me.

"Thank you all for volunteering," he said, as the plane jolted violently forward.

"Like we had a choice," I muttered.

"You did all have a choice," he responded curtly.

"Sorry, I didn't know you could hear us," I responded, a bit unnerved, feeling my face turning slightly red, even though Mr. Smith was not in our physical presence.

"I can hear and see everything," responded Mr. Smith with an ominous voice, as I was pushed back into the seat by the awesome power of the six engines. "I trust you all read the briefing packages I provided," stated Mr. Smith. After ten awkward seconds he added, "I will take your silence as a yes. The trip will take four hours. That gives you all time to become acquainted."

"I thought we were going to Australia," I said, confused.

"Yes, you are going to Port Douglas, to be precise," answered Mr. Smith. "This plane has the ability to go very fast, and I need you all there as soon as possible. The situation has grown a bit worse over the last twelve hours, and time is of the essence. Please use these four hours wisely to plan. I need to know what is going on, and your mission is to provide me with answers."

The plane must have reached the end of the runway since we were at a dead stop. All of a sudden, the pressure compressing us into the back of our seats increased, and I imagined if it abruptly ceased, I'd be shot out of my seat like a human missile out of a cannon. Several seconds later the front of the plane rose up dramatically, to nearly a ninety-degree angle. The relentless G-force made my stomach churn. The lack of windows and the way my body was being torqued reminded me of the tilt-a-whirl that I used to love as a kid. I wasn't loving it now, but I had little choice but to close my eyes and concentrate on not vomiting. I endured this for several minutes, and I unsuccessfully tried several times to lift my head forward and look around to see how the others were doing. It was no use; I was an unwilling prisoner in a torture device. All I accomplished was to make my head throb.

After several minutes of this wretchedness, the pressure finally eased, and the plane leveled out. Without warning, the seats turned, and we once again faced each other. The complete lack of sound coupled with the sudden absence of any forces on my body created a strange sensation. I knew from high school physics it meant we were no longer accelerating. I wondered how high we were and how fast we were going. Doing some quick math in my head, I determined we were heading to the other side of the planet at speeds I didn't even know planes could achieve.

I could tell from the gray faces of Nelly and Alex that they had suffered through the experience as much as I had. Spencer and Ponytail seemed unfazed by what had just happened. A two-foot-wide, eight-foot-long table rose from the floor of the plane and Ponytail got up and walked silently into the cockpit and closed the door.

"What the hell was that?" asked Alex. "I thought we were going to die. I think a little heads-up that we were about to be launched in a damn rocket ship would have been appropriate. And I hate the fact I was essentially bribed to be here."

"We all were," I said, "but since we're in this situation, I suggest we come up with a game plan."

"What game plan?" sneered Alex. "We're not coaches, we're not sleuths. Do any of you know anything about dealing with an outbreak? Because I sure as hell don't. My plan is to pay my debt to this psychopath Mr. Smith and try and get back home as soon as I can."

"The quicker we come up with something useful for him, the quicker we can get this whole ordeal over with," I reasoned. "We were all obviously chosen for a reason. Why don't we start with what we are good at? Back in veterinary school, I wrote several papers on Bovine Spongiform Encephalopathy—commonly called Mad Cow disease—and examined thousands of histopathology samples of cow brains."

Nelly met my eyes for the first time when I mentioned *histopathology*.

"And what did you determine in all of this vast research?" asked Alex sarcastically.

"First off, prion diseases are relentless," I responded, not acknowledging Alex's sarcasm. "The outbreaks in Britain were fueled by the prion being present in the feed, and our work produced no successful way to treat the disease within a population. Reluctantly, we made the recommendation to cull large herds of animals. Any cows showing symptoms were slaughtered, as well as others that may have been exposed. Ranchers cumulatively lost billions of dollars.

"Even after destroying the affected herds, the disease persisted, so the government got involved to regulate the way feed companies operated. That regulation took years to put in place, and lobbyists from the cattle and feed companies fought the changes every step of the way—which is partly why the outbreaks took nearly twenty years to get under control.

"We also saw multiple cases of cow-to-cow transmission in animals that hadn't ingested tainted feed products. These were free-range cows with no access to factory-prepared products. At those farms, it was thought that one contaminated cow was introduced into the herd, and the others got sick through ingestion of saliva or nasal secretions."

"There is little value in an animal's life, in my opinion," said Alex, who apparently couldn't remain silent very long. "So simply eliminating the sick is a reasonable solution in your world. But culling populations is not a solution when you're talking about humans." As if his haughty tone might not be insulting enough, he added, "If you were a real doctor, you would know that. I have written hundreds of articles throughout my career, and we focus on treating patients, not simply eliminating the sick ones."

I rolled my eyes. Why was everything a pissing contest with this guy?

"I wrote an article on Creutzfeldt-Jakob's Disease in Britain in the early nineties," he continued, scanning our faces as though he was giving a lecture at a podium. "We had hundreds of cases in a short amount of time, and people assumed it was from eating contaminated beef. We were only allowed to report on twenty-three cases in the end. The journal editor said we were unable to prove cause and effect on the others, but I know better. These people were getting sick, and they didn't want widespread panic. We even tried to write a second paper on the ranchers who were getting sick."

"What ranchers?" asked Nelly.

"A disproportionate number of ranchers were getting sick, as compared to the general population."

"But don't ranchers eat a lot of beef?" suggested Spencer.

"I have no idea, but I suppose it's likely," responded Alex. "But the ranchers saw what was going on earlier than anyone else. In my research, I found twenty cases where ranchers gave up beef altogether, yet they got sick. My theory was that their close contact to the cows' salivary secretions made them sick. Despite my impeccable methodology, with a lot of supporting evidence, when I tried to have it published, it never made it past the first review—suppressed for political reasons."

"Did you pursue another journal?" asked Nelly.

"No, at the time I was busy with my career, and I had lots of projects. One lost publication was not going to affect my career." Alex turned to Nelly. "So what brings you along on this adventure?"

"Neuropathology is a big part of my work. Fifteen years of looking at brains in a dark room by myself brings a lot of experience with the diagnosis of a disease like this one."

"Fifteen years locked in a dark room sounds wonderful," I joked.

"I love the work, and the science is really fascinating." Nelly flashed a partial smile and immediately returned her face to neutral. "Most of my research has been focused on CTE."

"As the resident non-scientist, what is CTE?" asked Spencer.

"Being in the military, I'm sure you have heard of it—you just don't know the scientific terminology," responded Nelly. "CTE stands for chronic traumatic encephalopathy. Basically, it's the reason that some professional football players and boxers can't finish a sentence when they are in their forties. Repetitive brain trauma causes functional damage. In these patients' brains, everything appears normal until you apply special stains to the tissue, and then profound damage is exposed. I actually developed one of the stains myself, to allow pathologists to diagnose this disease more quickly," she said modestly. "It used to take neurologists and pathologists a long time to figure out what was going on. I can tell you Creutzfeldt-Jakob Disease is much easier to diagnose. The brain resembles swiss cheese. No special stains are necessary."

"So, apparently, we all have knowledge about prion diseases," I said. "That must be the reason why Mr. Smith selected us."

Alex countered, "Either that or he knew he could force us all to do something we obviously don't want to do. I don't trust the man, and I think this whole situation stinks. What about the people who devote their entire careers to diagnosing outbreaks of diseases? None of them are on this plane. If I haven't been clear thus far, I don't want to be here; I'm being blackmailed."

"Since you bring it up, what does he have on you?" asked Spencer.

"I'm not discussing that."

"You don't have to tell me anything you don't want to, but my job is to keep everyone here safe, and believe it or not, I can do that a lot better if I know more about the people I'm trying to protect," said Spencer in response. He leaned in toward Alex and continued, "In fact, it seems like the better I like a person on my team the more likely they are to survive."

I doubted what he said was true. More likely, Spencer had had enough of Alex's superior attitude.

Regardless, it did the trick, and Alex sat back, taken down a peg. "I'd rather not give specifics, but if we are going to be working together, I'll tell you this," said Alex. "I'm involved in a malpractice lawsuit, which was not going well until the woman suing me lost a piece of critical evidence. There was no malice, and I didn't really do anything wrong, but with the way the biased justice system in the United States is set up, I could have lost millions in a civil suit. She's in a wheelchair and will most likely never walk again, and juries eat that shit up."

"So what did Smith do?" I asked.

"You remember the manila folder he handed me at our first meeting? In it was the missing piece of evidence, in an envelope addressed to the woman who is trying to sue me."

"That would do it," replied Spencer with a wry smile.

"Where do we go from here?" asked Nelly. "I mean what are we going to do once we land?"

"I assume you guys got the background information from Mr. Smith. Did you all get the handwritten note at the end of the file?" I asked.

"Yes, that was a bit strange," replied Spencer. "Determine the source of the prion, be it natural or engineered."

"It kind of creeped me out," I said. "The implication is that some deep conspiracy may be going on."

"Well, if this is not a natural disease outbreak, it does explain Mr. Smith putting me on the team," reasoned Spencer. "If this disease is some kind of biological weapon, then someone made it. In my experience, people who make biological weapons are not very nice. My job is to eliminate threats to the United States when ordered to. Those who develop or try to obtain biological weapons tend to be the worst of the worst. I have some experience in this area and believe me when I say these are people you never want to tangle with."

"Do you think Mr. Smith knows more than he's telling us?" I asked.

"I would bet my meager life savings on it," replied Spencer.

"Well, if this is a biological weapon made from a prion, that would be a terrifying weapon," I said. "Prions are extremely difficult to detect and even tougher to kill. One of the reasons why the prions getting into the livestock feed was such a big problem is that it's not inactivated by anything other than intense heat.

Prions survive quite happily in environments that kill most bacteria and viruses. It also can live in mammals for quite a long time without causing any problems, and then, all of a sudden, you are hallucinating, having seizures, and unable to walk. In fact, people who lived in Britain in the eighties and nineties are still not allowed to donate blood, since they may have the Mad Cow Prion circulating inside them, just waiting to cause a problem."

"Horrifying," said Spencer. "So the basic elements of this prion disease are: one, there's no treatment; two, we can't deactivate it; three, it's typically fatal; and four, when you get it, if you survive, you never get rid of it?"

"Not exactly," interjected Alex. "Not all prions are created equally. The prion in Creutzfeldt-Jakob Disease, for example, causes a slowly progressive deterioration over months to years. It takes a very long time to kill someone. With the cases we are going to investigate, people are dying in a matter of days. My guess is some sort of toxin combines with victims who happen to have a pre-existing neurological problem."

"That would be quite a coincidence," chimed in Nelly.

"What the hell do we know about these people?" continued Alex. "All we have in these cases is a similar pathology to Creutzfeldt-Jakob Disease seen in a postmortem of the brain. I don't trust the level of medicine in that part of the world, so who knows what the neurological examinations showed? It's possible these people were all sick before going to the reef—one last hurrah before they died of a problem they already knew about."

"Do you think the crocodiles were invited to this last hurrah?" I questioned. "A reptile support group for sick tourists, perhaps?"

Alex gave me a quick death stare, and I smiled back, which made him even more hostile.

"It will be weeks before we can test things properly in this part of the world," he grumbled. "This is a total waste of my time. In fact, we have no reliable way of detecting the prion in any live patient, so there is no way to tell who is infected. Why not simply send the samples of the neurological tissue from the people who died to the United States, so it can be properly analyzed?"

"That's not exactly true," said Nelly. "A blood test is being developed for the detection of prions. The basic problem with identifying these diseases is that prions aren't visible under a traditional microscope, and they appear in blood in low numbers. You need an electron microscope to view the protein structures, which can be variable, so even with that technology, imaging is not very helpful. But, like anything else, proteins can be detected if the test is sensitive enough. What we have done in experimental cases, with patients suspected of having disease, is take their blood and replicate the protein to easily detectable levels through a process called protein misfolding cyclic amplification. Essentially, if the prion is in the blood, the process adds proteins to the blood that have the potential to become prions. The diseased blood converts these harmless proteins into prions, whereas normal blood does not. Once there is enough protein, you can detect it with a standard Western blot.

"Spencer this is for you: a Western blot takes a sample and places drops of an unknown substance on a rectangle of jelly-like goo, and then runs an electrical current through the goo. The proteins in the substance travel different lengths depending on their properties. Then you can add another protein to the goo to get the protein you want to light up, voila: you can see if the blood has a prion in it or not."

Spencer smiled at Nelly, enjoying the simplified explanation. "Wait, are you saying prions can convert normal, non-harmful protein into deadly protein?"

"That's exactly what I'm saying, and this happens very slowly over time in people with the disease," replied Nelly.

"So what would cause the process to speed up and make people get sick very quickly?" asked Spencer.

"Proteins are not that complicated," answered Nelly. "They're merely strands of amino acids linked together. Different proteins are formed by the different ways the strands are shaped and folded. In the case of the prion we're talking about, the strands are only about two hundred amino acids long. Change just one of the amino acids, and the entire structure can fold in a dramatically new structure, which changes everything. The real destruction of these molecules is caused by how the body reacts to them and forms more noxious proteins or inflammation."

"Yes, well those protein things kill people in terrible ways," said Alex curtly. "Enough of the science lesson. Can we get back to focusing on what we are supposed to do about this problem?"

"The question we were asked was to determine the source of the prion," I offered as a starting point.

"More specifically, is this prion engineered," added Nelly.

"When we began determining the cause of Mad Cow Disease, we started by looking for common threads," I stated. "According to our most recent intel," I couldn't help but grin at Spencer when I used the phrase, "all the people who have gotten sick were bitten by the crocodiles. So the common thread is obviously the crocodiles. But we don't know how the reptiles got sick. I think we need to start there. When we land, I suggest going out to the Great Barrier Reef and evaluating the marine life to see if there are any common characteristics or any other sick animals. At least that way, we'll form an impression as to how widespread this thing is in the environment."

"I know nothing about crocodiles, and since I don't care to know anything about crocodiles, that's a terrible idea," said Alex.

"Well, I wasn't actually inviting you, and I need to start somewhere," I said.

"Perhaps we can find a local who knows something about crocodiles," suggested Nelly.

"That's a good idea," I conceded. "The second question is how we can determine if this prion is natural or engineered. Is there a difference between natural proteins and proteins made in a lab?" Glancing around the table, no one had an answer. "I think I know someone who may be able to answer this question," I said. "My friend, David, who researched BSE with me, went on to get his PhD in molecular biology. His thesis was on the folding of proteins. I can call him when we land to get some insight."

"You can call him now," said Mr. Smith.

His voice made me jump. I had no idea he was on the line. Had we said anything derogatory about him? I realized I didn't really care. "Have you been listening this entire time?" I asked.

"Of course I have," he answered immediately. "This is my mission, and I am here to help in any way I can." His voice lacked sincerity, even through the headphones. "Okay, the call is going through now."

"I didn't even tell you his last name--" I started to say, but a ringing phone sounded through the headphones. David answered after three rings.

"Hello unlisted number," he answered with a cheerful tone. David was always a bit smart-alecky.

"Hey, David. This is John."

"John Osler?" he asked.

"In the flesh," I replied.

"Hey there, old buddy. I haven't heard from you in months. What's new? Are you in town? Do you want to get a beer tonight? Dinner perhaps? Catch up?" David had a habit of asking several questions without waiting for an answer.

"Sorry, David, I'm not in town. I just called to talk about proteins."

"Proteins are what I do, all day, every day. What do you want to know?"

"Well, I was hoping you could tell me how to differentiate between a natural protein and a synthetic, manmade one."

"Sure. A natural protein has a pleasant brown appearance with one-piece tan lines, and a synthetic one is more orange, with skimpy tan lines or very small bikini lines or, in some cases, no tan lines at all. In addition, when you talk to them, the natural ones talk about wholesome things, like growing corn or the church social, and the synthetic ones talk like the girls who hang out at the Jersey shore. You know the type; the ones with names like Candy who moonlight at the Coco Loco Lounge at night and know their way around a stage with a pole, if you catch my drift. In fact, you should be an expert at such things, spending as much time in Jersey as you have."

"David," I interrupted, "Can you please be serious?"

"Wow, you need to relax a bit, buddy. I think you should come out to Illinois for a vacation. Get away from the hustle and bustle and chill."

"I like this guy," said Nelly.

"Who is that?" asked David, surprised.

"I'm with some people, and we're trying to figure something out," I said. "I should have also told you that you're on speaker."

"Speaker phone, discussing proteins," said David, his voice abruptly changing to a more professional tone. "Okay, here goes. As you know, all proteins are made up from twenty amino acids. And though there are only twenty ingredients, trillions of different configurations are possible. Even the same combination of amino acids can interact in different ways, causing the proteins to fold in multiple ways, depending on the order in which the amino acids were linked and environmental factors. Scientists have been creating artificial proteins for years. When they first started, they were rather clunky at it. You know, simple stuff, short-strand proteins that don't occur in nature. Back then, it was pretty easy to tell synthetic from natural. Nowadays, scientists have been able to recreate naturally occurring proteins, like antibodies in small mammals such as mice, with the intent of using them to treat natural diseases. Advanced stuff. The proteins being created today can't be differentiated from the ones mother nature has created."

"So, in most cases, you can't tell the difference between something made in the lab and ones made in nature?" I asked.

"Well, that's really the point," continued David. "If I can tell the difference in my lab, then the human body can also tell the difference, and the body wouldn't mount the same immune response."

"Could someone make a synthetic prion which mimics the prion that causes Mad Cow Disease?" I asked. An uncomfortable silence ensued, for at least twenty seconds. I thought the phone had gone dead. "David, you still there?"

"Sure," answered David, reluctantly. "A protein is a protein, but labs don't dedicate resources to *making* diseases. There's no money in it. Most of the work is focused on proteins to cure diseases. If you could make a synthetic protein that causes a person's immune system to attack a disease like cancer or the virus that causes the common cold, a big pharmaceutical could cash in on a cure. Hundreds of labs across the country are trying to perfect the creation of antibodies for any number of diseases. I predict that in twenty years, chemotherapy will be a thing of the past, and more natural cures for cancer will be available—with none of the horrendous side effects. Immunotherapies are all the rage in oncology right now."

"Could someone design a prion to be more aggressive than a naturally occurring one?" I asked.

After another long pause, David responded, "That's a dangerous and dark question. What exactly are you trying to do?"

"We are trying to solve a bit of a mystery," I responded.

With a deep sigh, David continued. "Prions cause disease by recruiting other proteins to cause local damage to the central nervous system. The difference between one that doesn't cause much of a problem and one that causes destruction in the brain is based on the shape. Think of it this way, a harmless prion is like a circle that other proteins don't care about. The ones that cause damage are more jagged and other proteins take an interest, attach to the prion, and form massive accumulations of these structures in the brain. To make a prion more aggressive, one only needs to figure out how to make it more jagged."

"Could it be done?" I asked.

"Be warned, my friend. It can probably be done if you want to spend the rest of your life locked in a jail cell," he responded. "Moreover, the science behind something like that would be trial and error. And I'm not saying you would be successful. You'd be facing a painstaking process where you change one little thing and then look for a response; then change another thing and then another and on and on. You could spend a lifetime manipulating proteins and never come up with one that does what you want it to do. Science is torturous patience combined with a little skill and a whole lot of luck mixed in."

"I'll write down the recipe," I chuckled. "Thanks, David."

"John, whatever it is you're doing, I advise you to be careful. "People have gotten into trouble just by asking these questions. I would be very selective about the company you're keeping."

"That's why I called you, buddy."

"John, I'm not joking. You're talking about engineering a biological weapon," David said. "Rogue nations have tinkered with this stuff, but their science is about twenty years behind the major labs in the United States. However, science, like most things, does advance. It's only a matter of time before some Dr. Frankenstein creates something the rest of the world will suffer for. Once the genie is out of the bottle, it's really hard to stuff him back in."

"Okay, I'll build a bunker in the middle of some forest," I joked.

"If someone creates an aggressive prion and a way to get it into people, it won't matter if you are hunkered down in a bunker," David said in a very grave tone. "There will be no place to hide."

His voice had now become ominous and even unfamiliar. Hairs stood up on my neck. "I hear you, man. Thanks for your help. I promise I will make it out to Illinois soon, and we can have that beer and catch up."

"John, no joking—why is a veterinarian asking such questions? What are you up to?"

"I am looking into--" The line abruptly went dead.

Mr. Smith's voice came out in a threatening tone. "You can use any resources you want to try and figure this situation out, but the specifics of what you are doing and where you are doing it are classified. Try and remember this for your own good and for the good of the people you care about. Focus on the task at hand."

All of us stared at each other for a solid minute. Did someone create an aggressive disease—which we were seeing in its early stages—and which we were going to confront?

Chapter 6

Alex broke the silence, nervously clearing his throat. "In all reported cases of prion-related diseases to date, the assumption has been that the prion was ingested or directly injected into the bloodstream through a transfusion or transmitted by bodily fluids. In most, the source of the disease was determined to originate with eating contaminated meat containing bits of nervous tissue. There have even been reported cases of people getting the disease from cannibalism."

"You can't be serious," I responded.

"Yes, that's accurate," said Nelly. "There used to be a sacred ritual in New Guinea. When someone died, the people ate the brains of the deceased. If you review history closely enough, you can find plenty of cases of ingesting bits of the living or the dead."

"That can't be true," said Spencer.

"It *is* true," continued Alex. "Hundreds of cases were documented in the fifties and sixties of people who believed eating the brains of the dead helped guide the spirits into the next world and allowed their spirits to live on in those people who participated in the ceremony."

"I thought cannibalism was a myth," said Spencer. "I find it hard to believe any modern culture eats their grandparents when they die. That's the stuff of science fiction."

"Is it so hard to believe?" persisted Alex. "Millions of people in different religions go to church every weekend. Many symbolically drink the blood and eat the flesh of Jesus as a sign of respect for his sacrifice. Religions from only a few hundred years ago practiced ritualistic sacrifice, where the high priest drank the actual blood of those who died. The Aztecs practiced cannibalism on a large scale. Even the Australian Aborigines ate the dead as a sign of respect."

"I thought I had seen it all, but I am shocked by the world we live in," said Spencer. "People never cease to amaze me."

"Let's get back on topic," said Alex. "If we believe what's going on in Australia is due to a mutated prion—keep in mind I said *if*—then the prion likely got into the humans through bite wounds. That's unlike anything reported in the past. Admittedly, it's not much different than the transmission through saliva or nasal secretions, but in those cases, the theory is that contamination took place over months to years. For transmission of this disease to occur with a single bite, the amount of protein which would need to be present in the saliva would be astronomically high."

"Bear in mind, every disease host in the past has been an herbivore," I offered. "And most herbivores don't bite other animals. The very nature of the host makes it unlikely salivary levels would have ever been analyzed critically—so we can't dismiss that mode of transmission."

"Let's get back to basics. How do we even know that what's going on in Australia is due to a prion?" asked Nelly.

"Good question," I said.

"Just because a disease looks similar to something we've seen in the past, it doesn't mean that it *is* the same disease," reasoned Alex. "This is what I've been saying all along. I think the first question we need to answer is whether or not this is a prion disease."

Nelly, hearing her own words co-opted, rolled her eyes.

"Personally," continued Alex, "I need to start by doing a neurological examination on the people in the hospital. I need to review the records and the tests that have been performed. If the disease process is as rapidly progressive as the reports indicate, then following these patients along and making sure they are being treated appropriately would be my first step. Not sightseeing on the reef."

"And I need to examine the samples we have from the patients who have died," offered Nelly. "I can also look under a microscope at the nervous tissue of the crocodiles, for similar patterns. I wish I had access to my lab. Several stains could be useful for detecting the prion. I also would love to be able to amplify the protein and run a Western blot, which could help determine the cause of the lesions and prove that a prion is responsible."

"Your requests have been passed along and you should have what you need by the time we land," Mr. Smith's voice came over the headphones.

I kept forgetting this creepy guy was listening to everything we said, though I no longer jumped when he spoke. And at least he seemed capable of getting things done in a hurry.

"So, do we have a plan?" asked Spencer.

"The start of one, at least," I responded. "I'll head out to the reef to examine the observable wildlife and try to determine if the crocodiles are the only animals affected. I'll also observe the reptiles for ongoing neurological deficits. Nelly and Alex can go to the hospital to examine the patients and the samples that have been taken. Ultimately, we need to see if we can prove whether this is a prion disease and, if we get lucky, try and trace things back to an origin point.

"I think I need to talk to the local authorities and see what they have come up with," said Spencer. "In my experience, there is no greater resource than locals on the ground."

"No," came the voice of Mr. Smith. "If Dr. Osler is going out to the reef, I need you, Spencer, to accompany him."

"Why?" I asked.

"Because we are not yet sure what is safe and what is not," responded Mr. Smith. "I have people in the hospital standing by to watch over Dr. Fleury and Dr. King, but I don't have anyone who can protect Dr. Osler on the reef."

"Why do we need protection?" I asked, but was met with silence. "Mr. Smith, are you still there?"

"I am still here," he responded after an uncomfortably long pause. "I will name three reasons why you all need protection. First, Queensland, Australia, has more things that can kill you than just about anywhere else in the world. The area may be beautiful, but it can be deadly in many surprising ways. Spencer has been all over the world, and he knows how to avoid dangerous situations. Second, I need someone to monitor what you say and who you say it to. You have yet to prove to me you know how to keep information to yourself. And third, I don't know for sure what is going on. Believe me when I say that there are very few circumstances when this is the case. When I have found myself in that rare situation, disaster often follows."

Those words hung over all of us. I blinked rapidly and tried to organize my thoughts. Were we in danger—other than from this disease? Or could Smith possibly be manipulating us again, trying to get us to trust, or rely upon, him?

"In the side pocket of each of your chairs," Mr. Smith continued, "you will find updated information on the Australian outbreak more specific to your area of expertise. As additional information comes in, I will keep you apprised."

No click indicated that Mr. Smith had disconnected from the conversation, but clearly he had no more to say. I suspected he was always listening, or at least he wanted us to think he was.

My folder contained information mostly on the crocodiles. Their neurological behavior was bizarre. The two captured crocodiles were not brought back to the mainland alive. Each had drowned. Since these creatures can hold their breath for up to two hours at a time, I suspected they had aspirated water due to their condition. Those left in the water demonstrated abnormal behaviors, such as swimming in circles for hours, rolling over continuously, or showing unprovoked aggression toward nothing other than open water. It sounded like Captain Cook's worst nightmare. According to the reports, besides these reptiles, no other part of the ecosystem *seemed* out of the ordinary, but the Australian authorities had shut down all travel to this area of the reef as a precaution.

Koch's Postulates came to mind. In veterinary school, I had first learned about these basic rules, which state that for a pathogen to cause a disease, three criteria must be met. First, the organism must be present in each sick patient. Second, it must be isolated from the host and be able to be reproduced in a lab. Finally, it must cause the disease when another patient is injected with the same organism. So in order to prove one disease is causing everything, we have to find it, grow it, and then infect something else, and wait to see what happens. The postulates were simple, but they'd be difficult to prove.

The headphones were starting to give me a headache, so I slid them off. I immediately regretted the decision, as the deafening sound of the engines made me cover my ears with my hands. I quickly slid them back on.

"I should have warned you," said Nelly, chuckling. "I tried taking them off a few minutes ago, and I still can't hear right."

"They didn't design this thing with the passenger in mind, did they?" I said as I smiled at her. For the first time since I met her, she genuinely returned the smile.

"Can you isolate a specific protein to prove it's present in all of these cases?" I asked.

"I'm not sure, but I think it's possible," she responded. "It's the first thing I'll tackle. According to the files, the doctors found characteristic changes in all the samples, but they haven't been able to isolate the offending pathogen yet. I can see why they wanted me there. This stuff is exactly what I do in my Baltimore lab."

"What about trying to grow a prion in a lab?" I asked, suspecting I already knew the answer.

"Well beyond my skill set," she responded.

Koch's Postulates, as I predicted, were not going to be satisfied easily. I closed my eyes and reviewed all that had happened in the last twenty-four hours. Quite the day, I thought. I must have drifted off, because I was jarred awake as my seat turned toward the back of the plane. The plane angled forty-five degrees down, and I could tell by the way my body was being pulled and my stomach twisted that we were decelerating and descending at a rapid rate. The descent was rather quick, but equally violent to the takeoff. We were all sitting facing the back of the plane being pulled in ungodly ways for several minutes before the aircraft leveled out. The absence of windows made for an eerie sensation. I suspected we were approaching the ground, but without any visual cues, I couldn't be sure. We let out simultaneous gasps as the tires hit the runway. As the plane gradually decelerated, I cautiously slipped off the headphones. It was still loud, but it felt good to have them off my head.

The cockpit door opened, and Ponytail walked out. "We're here. Grab your stuff—your transport is waiting," he said. The plane's door opened, and Ponytail returned to the cockpit.

I was surprised to see it was pitch black outside. "What time is it here?"

"That would be three-fifteen a.m., local time," responded Spencer.

Talk about a time warp. We left in the morning from the East Coast and arrived even earlier in the morning after the elapse of four hours. "Is it the same day we left?" I asked.

"Does it matter?" responded Spencer.

"I guess not," I muttered.

Two open-air jeeps awaited us. "Dr. King and Dr. Fleury, you're in the first jeep. Dr. Osler, you're with me in the second jeep," said Spencer, leaving little room for argument. The drivers were dressed in military fatigues, identical to American camouflage. I suppose there are only so many ways you can do green.

We spoke little as we drove away from the airport. Several miles down the road, the first jeep took a left and we took a right.

"Where are we going?" I asked.

"I thought you wanted to see the Great Barrier Reef," responded Spencer. "You know, catch some sun and go for a snorkel."

"So, you do have a sense of humor," I laughed.

"When I need to," replied Spencer. "The other two are going to the hospital in Cairns. We are heading about thirty miles north to Port Douglas, where a lot of the reef tourist companies are stationed. That's the closest point to where the crocodiles are."

"Do you have a map of the area?" I asked.

"Um, that's what phones are for; nobody uses maps anymore," remarked Spencer.

"They do if they're in the middle of nowhere, without a cell tower nearby."

"Point taken," he conceded. After a short conversation with the driver, we found a map, and I started finding what I wanted.

"How far to get to the Daintree River?" I asked the driver.

"About a half an hour north of where we are going," he answered. "The roads up there are not the best. Why do you ask?"

"I'll need to go there after I visit the reef," I answered.

"That's dangerous country up that way," he answered, glancing back at me as the jeep drifted into the other lane. He faced forward again and jerked the wheel to bring the jeep back onto his side of the road. "You'll need a local guide."

"Can you make the arrangements?" I asked Spencer.

"I'll see what I can do."

At about four in the morning we arrived in Port Douglas. "No sense in going out to the reef now," said Spencer. "We won't be able to see a thing. I'll drop you off at your hotel and pick you up in three hours."

Chapter 7

THE TOWN WE RODE THROUGH was small and quaint, and you could tell most of the businesses catered to sightseeing. Our small hotel complex consisted of independent, one-room suites scattered around twelve-acres, with a pool central to everything. Spencer dropped me off at house in the front of the property, and I guessed a single family lived here and ran the business. I met no one inside and rang a bell on the desk. Based on his disheveled appearance, the teenage boy who checked me in had been sleeping. He showed me to room 204, at the rear of the property, and sluggishly trotted back to his office to return to his nap. My room was small, but the two full beds and the bathroom were clean and tidy. There wasn't much else. All the pictures on the walls were of wildlife from the reef. I laid down on the bed and closed my eyes, but sleep would not come. Every time I started to drift off, a feeling of deep dread jolted me awake. Finally, at five thirty in the morning, I decided it was useless and opted to stretch my legs. I walked out toward the front of the property and nearly knocked over Nelly as she rounded the corner.

"Hey there. What are you up to?" I asked her.

"I just got back from the hospital. There's nothing for me to do at this hour, without any additional support staff. Reviewing the histopathology samples they have, the people who died certainly looked like they had Creutzfeldt-Jakob Disease. I have never heard of a prion causing destruction so rapidly. They even had excellent histopathological samples from the cerebellums of the reptiles that were recovered. The brain tissue appeared microscopically identical and could have been in a textbook for spongiform encephalopathy from any species."

"Sounds like a pretty good hospital."

"Yeah. Everyone dealing with the sick patients is in full hazmat gear, though, and it's obvious the entire staff is pretty freaked out."

"Until we figure out what's going on, it's the smartest strategy," I responded. "I can't imagine this protein would be spread through the air, but better safe than sorry. Did Alex come back with you?"

"No," responded Nelly, with a knowing grin on her face. "He said he wanted to personally reexamine everything that has been done, since neurologists in this part of the world are mostly incompetent."

"That sounds like the Alex I've come to know and love," I responded. "I hope he can turn up something that will help treat these poor victims."

"I talked to the staff at the hospital and confirmed the supplies I requested via Mr. Smith would be there later on this morning," continued Nelly. "I figured I might get a few hours of sleep before I head back in and start on some tests. Are you heading to the reef?"

"Not for another hour and a half," I responded. "I'm going to walk around and explore the area a bit. I tried to sleep, but too much is rattling around in my brain. Besides, my legs are really tight from traveling."

"Want some company?" she asked.

"Sure, if you're not too tired," I responded cheerfully.

"I'm fine," she said, seeming a bit insulted. "I wouldn't have asked if I was too tired to go."

"Sorry, I didn't mean to offend you," I said.

"No, it's not you," she said. "I just can't stand it when other people try to determine what I want and what is best for me. I can do that all by myself," said Nelly, as she started walking briskly toward the direction of the town.

It took several steps before I was able to catch up with her. She was a fast walker, and I think was trying to make a point that she was in the lead here. "I have a twenty-two-year-old son and nineteen-year-old daughter who react the same way every time I do that to them," I said, as a partial apology.

"Then why do you do it?

"It's the parenting genes. I think this stuff is hardwired into me."

"Is this pace too fast for you?" Nelly asked. "I know I walk fast, and most people can't keep up."

"I'll manage," I replied, and resisted uttering, *I hate it when other people try to determine what's best for me.* We walked for about ten minutes without saying a word. I enjoyed the quiet of the early morning, broken only by the occasional, distant bird call. I've never found silence awkward. In New Jersey, most people feel the need to fill every waking minute with mindless chatter, so I tend to prize silence. I think it's really the only way to truly appreciate your surroundings. I wondered if Nelly felt the same way.

As we strode the empty streets of Port Douglas, I struggled to keep up with her. But I didn't want her to know it. I stole a few glances in her direction. She truly was stunning.

Nelly was the first to break the spell. "So, what's your take on all of this? Do you think we're faced with a natural disease outbreak or something more sinister?"

"Well, Nelly, I typically keep an idealistic view of the world, so I have to believe this is a natural outbreak that we can easily contain, and we'll be home in a day or two." I hoped I didn't sound out of breath.

"Nell," she replied.

"Pardon?"

"No one calls me Nelly," she explained. "Not since the first grade. My friends all call me Nell."

"Okay, then Nell it is," I answered. I was relieved when she started to slow down a bit as we passed by the shops.

"I'd like to believe that, but I think if this were a natural outbreak, we wouldn't be here with an army ranger to babysit us," she reasoned methodically.

We both glanced around simultaneously, and not a person was to be seen. Was danger actually nearby? The shadows from the streetlights began to play tricks on me, and I imagined figures in the alleyways. I started to feel eyes watching me. A mild state of unease crept up my spine. Had Mr. Smith withheld information? According to Spencer, most likely he had. He had worked with this guy in the past. In what capacity, I couldn't guess.

"I have been accused of being too optimistic at times," I said, trying to downplay my unease.

"I've never been accused of that," Nell responded with a weak smile. "My life has not been exactly easy at times."

"Why is that?" I asked, immediately regretting it, as the expression that flashed across her face could only be interpreted as anger, but then it softened slightly.

We continued to walk silently through the town for several minutes. Enough time passed that I was sure she was just going to ignore my question. I was about to awkwardly change the topic entirely when Nell inhaled sharply.

"Well, my parents died when I was fifteen. I didn't appreciate it at the time, but parents are important in the teenage years. I thought at fifteen I had all the answers to life's important questions, but of course I didn't have a clue. Then I lived with my grandparents, who were more interested in watching *Jeopardy* than what I was doing. For a while, I enjoyed my newfound freedom, doing what most rebellious teenagers do. I got myself into trouble with boys, drinking, and drugs. You wouldn't believe the interest college boys have in a teenage girl."

"Well, you are beautiful," I made the mistake of saying.

Nell let out a groan of deep frustration and stopped abruptly. She turned to me with a deathly serious look. "You don't understand that being beautiful in some sort of conventional sense has been a curse for me," she screamed. "It is for a lot of women, and men never get it. I don't think any guy could possibly understand it."

"I can try," I said softly. "I've been through some stuff myself."

"Let me guess," said Nell. "You are a surgeon with a beautiful daughter, a successful son, and a wife who drinks martinis at a beach club on the weekends. Your idea of *going through stuff* is a bad PTA meeting or your kids being rejected from their first-choice of college and having to settle for Brown over Harvard."

"Wow! That's a lot of emotion. I don't exactly know what I did, but I didn't mean to antagonize you."

"Well, I've known a few surgeons in my life, and all have been what I would accurately refer to as scumbags," Nell said with venom. "In fact, most are the types of guys who would go for a quiet walk with an unknown woman in a strange town and call her beautiful, hoping that in the stress and emotion of the moment she decides to go to bed with them, even though they only left home twelve hours ago. Don't think just because you're more subtle than most that I haven't noticed your glances. Men are always staring at me like I am some sort of object. Some sort of toy."

"That's not me, and that's not what is happening here," I responded, glad it was still dark and Nell couldn't see my face turning red with a mixture of anger and embarrassment. "I don't know where all this is coming from, and I wasn't implying anything. Not to make you feel badly, but so you don't misjudge me, my wife died about ten years ago in a tragic accident, and I'm still coping with that. I don't have anyone in my life I'm betraying by taking a walk with a woman, and I'm not trying to get you to do anything."

We both started walking slowly forward again. The next few minutes of silence I did find awkward. Even in the dark, I could see a tear streaking down Nell's cheek. I knew enough to let things be until she spoke again.

"It's a curse," she finally said, quietly.

"What is?" I gently asked.

"Being beautiful. Oh, sure, when I was a teenager and my parents were gone, there was no lack of attention from the boys. With a void in my life, I loved the attention. I needed the attention. But inevitably, they only wanted to be with me physically, and as soon as that happened, they didn't stick around. At first, being the popular girl with the boys felt great. But the more the boys paid attention, the cattier the girls got. I never had a close girlfriend in my life. By the time I got to college, I would have ten messages a night from boys asking to spend time with me. My roommate hated me for it. I started to despise the messages and the constant attention. I actually smashed my answering machine with a hammer. None of them liked me for me. All they saw was the beauty. Like, if I was beautiful, then I had nothing else to offer. I was a trophy to be shown off. It didn't matter if I was smart or had an opinion on things. No one cared about the deeper stuff."

The tears were streaming now and dripping down her cheeks and onto the sidewalk. She made absolutely no attempt to hide them.

"It was like that in medical school too. I drew attention from the older faculty. Mostly the married surgeons. I even made the mistake of being with one for a short time. Of course, his wife found out and confronted me. The things she called me burned into my soul. She never once blamed him. Just the beautiful girl who seduced her poor, innocent husband. She made him the victim and me the devil. I haven't dated since. That's why I went into pathology. I can be by myself in front of a microscope in a dark room, and no one cares what I look like. I can pursue my research and perhaps people will start respecting me for *me* and not for my bone structure."

"I really didn't mean to irritate you," I said, quietly.

"You didn't," Nell responded. "Well, yes, you did. But I guess it's not entirely your fault. I went all psycho and unleashed five years of frustration on a relative stranger."

"To be fair, I think it was actually closer to twenty years," I said with a smile.

She stopped and met my gaze, ready for round two, and then her entire body relaxed slightly. "Okay, I'll give you a pass on that one," she said and smiled back. She truly was beautiful, but I was never again going to make the mistake of telling her so.

We came to a beach. "Do you want to walk a bit more?" I asked.

"Perhaps ten more minutes; between my emotions and the stress of everything, I am getting ready to crash."

We headed up the beach. Twenty-five years ago, on vacation, the thing about Australia I loved most were the beaches. I once walked along a beautiful, pure-white shoreline for two hours without seeing another person. It was like heaven. In New Jersey, you can't get to the water without stepping over dozens people and their paraphernalia. The world is indeed getting crowded.

At times I regretted where I had raised my children. The fifty miles surrounding New York City is one of the most congested areas of the US. On the other hand, while the land mass of Australia is about the same as the US, the population is less than a tenth of the US. Walking with Nell, the pristine sand was free of pollution, people—and the only faint sound was the breaking of tiny waves. In the heavens, the stars were brilliant. A hint of morning hung in the ghostly, still air, and the ocean was dead calm.

Nell was keeping the same casual pace beside me, and I risked a quick glance in her direction. She appeared deep in thought, and her eyes were fixed on the sand about ten feet ahead. Suddenly, a loud crash boomed from the trees.

"What was that?" asked Nell, grabbing my forearm tightly.

"I have no idea." Immediately, I had the same uneasy feeling I had in town. I turned around and could only see the dim lights of civilization about a half mile down the beach. I wondered how long it would take us to run that distance. "Let's go back," I said, wishing Spencer was walking with us.

"Good idea."

Our pace quickened as we retraced our steps. There it came again, a loud crash, this time closer. A lone figure approached, walking away from town as we headed back. The dim lights of the distant town along with the growing morning light gave the figure a phantasmal quality.

"I don't like this," said Nell, no longer trying to hide her panic. "Should we go into the woods?"

I estimated the figure approaching was about one hundred feet away. "No," I answered, trying to sound confident, though my voice cracked. "It's probably nothing." I tried to quicken our pace, but the thick sand made it difficult. "Let's head for higher ground. We can duck into the woods if we need to."

We turned away from the water to keep some distance between us and the approaching person. Strangely, they seemed intent on the ground—skipping occasionally!

A third boom from the trees caused us both to jump and look over our shoulders to the darkness of the trees behind us. When we turned around, the figure was only a few feet away, and we both relaxed. It was a girl, about ten years old.

"Hello," I said with relief. I felt a bit silly we both had become so spooked by a little girl.

"Hey there, you two," she replied in a playful voice. "Don't you love walking in the early morning light?"

"Yes, it is very peaceful," said Nell. I was surprised by the maternal softness in her tone.

"You just need to be careful not to step on a bluey," the young girl said.

"What is that?" asked Nell.

"You know, the blue jellyfish that wash up on the shore," she responded. "They can kill you if you don't pour vinegar on your feet right away. My mom says that if I go into the water, the blueys will get me. So I stay on the sand."

"Do you live around here?" asked Nell.

"No, I live in Montana, but I've been here about ten times."

"Really?" I asked. "We're a long way from Montana."

"I know, but I come here with the tours," she answered. "My mom runs them, you know."

"What tours?" Nell asked.

"Mostly for rich people who want to come and see the reef. We travel around the world all the time with rich people. I help run the tours," she bragged. "They couldn't do them without me."

It came again, a loud crash from the trees. Nell and I looked back nervously. I imagined figures darting between the trees, peering at us in the darkness. I was sure my eyes were playing tricks on me.

The little girl picked up a rock and threw it into the ocean. "Don't worry about the noises," she said.

"Why not?" Nell asked.

"It's only the coconuts falling off the trees," she responded, throwing another rock and watching it cause gentle ripples in the water offshore. "The palm trees at the resorts don't have coconuts, so most people have never heard a coconut fall. But I know what it sounds like. It can be really loud. I'm not allowed to walk in the trees either."

Nell and I exchanged grins—we were clearly out of our familiar environments.

"My name is Ella," said the little girl bouncing on one foot. "I am ten years old. Actually, I'm almost eleven, but for another month I still have to tell people I'm ten."

"Hello, Ella, my name is Nell, and this is my friend John." Nell added, "I like your hat."

Ella wore a bright-orange hat, shorts, and a sweatshirt that said *Off the Grid Tours*. She had light-blond hair cut in a cute bob, which almost came down to her shoulders. She picked up another rock and threw it into the surf.

"Thanks," said Ella. "It's my favorite hat, but I have two others. One is green and the other is blue, but I almost always wear the orange one since orange is my favorite color most of the time. "

"My favorite color is purple," said Nell.

"That's a funny favorite color," said Ella. "I like bright colors better."

"Well, it was very nice to meet you, Ella," I said in my best fatherly voice. "Have a great day."

"I will, but we're leaving today, and I need to go pack in thirty minutes, so I'm going to walk for twelve more minutes before I turn around," said Ella.

"Just watch out for a bluey," I said.

"I will," said Ella, and she skipped away down the beach.

"You have to love the innocence of youth," I remarked to Nell. We walked the rest of the way back to the hotel in silence. I couldn't help but glance over my shoulder several times on the way back to be sure we weren't being followed. Nell pretended not to notice.

"Have a good time on the reef," said Nell when we parted. "And please be careful," she added, almost as an afterthought.

Chapter 8

SPENCER MET ME IN MY room promptly at seven, with a coffee in each hand. I grabbed one with a nod. "Thanks, I'm going to need this."

"The boat is at the dock. Are you ready to go?"

The walk from the hotel to the dock was brief. Only a few people were out in the predawn, preparing for the day, hosing off decks, and setting out life preservers on the larger tour boats. We walked to the end of the pier to a forty-foot McKinna dive boat named *Deep Calling*. Two others were on board, and Spencer called them both by name.

"Good morning, Sebastian; good morning, Bill." Both seemed tired and merely nodded. "Bill is the pilot, and Sebastian is a local naturalist who agreed to take us out," he explained.

"Did Mr. Smith need to convince them to help us?" I murmured.

"In a way," remarked Spencer. "He gave me a hefty chunk of discretionary spending money. They weren't happy when I woke them up in the middle of the night, but they were less upset when I forked over a pile of cash. The ride out to the reef will take us about an hour."

"Okay, I need to talk to Sebastian about some things anyway," I replied. With that, Sebastian gave me a curious glance. I took a seat next to him in the cabin where we could talk.

Sebastian was slight in build and couldn't have weighed more than one hundred thirty pounds. He was dressed in sandals, jeans, and a blue windbreaker. Bill was gruff-looking, with a bushy, unkempt beard. He must have been at least six feet, five inches, with a great beer belly protruding to the limits of a tight, red T-shirt.

Bill cast off with the help of Spencer, and the boat churned out of the marina at low speed. Once we cleared the end of the dock, Bill pulled back the throttle, and the boat lurched forward. The marina grew smaller behind us. Gazing at the shoreline, I observed how the trees of the rainforest connected the hills north and south of the marina. The sun broke over the horizon, causing the green vegetation to glow with life. A sight to behold.

"I'm being well paid for this trip, so what do you want to know?" Sebastian asked, breaking the silence.

"Tell me about the relationship between the reef and the rainforest," I asked.

His eyes widened. "Most people just want to know about sharks or, in this case, crocodiles. This entire situation has freaked people out, and the crazy crocs are all anyone talks about lately. Everyone has theories, but I'm mostly worried about the tourists. The bleaching of the reef dramatically decreased the tourist business, but once word gets out that there are killer reptiles on the reef, business is going to stop altogether. Humankind can't help but screw the planet up, can they?"

"I understand the bleaching is due to global warming, but you think humans have something to do with the crocodiles?" I asked Sebastian curiously.

"There is no question in my mind."

"What makes you so sure?" I questioned.

"Nature is balanced, with gradual, subtle changes that occur over a long stretch of time," Sebastian answered, while admiring the receding coastline. He had a distant look in his eye, and it took him a minute to continue. "Nature is beautiful. It isn't always kind, and it's rarely merciful, but it is balanced. I have lived in this part of the world my entire life. When balance is disrupted, it is invariably due to people messing things up. The current situation is unnatural, and unnatural always means manmade."

"I take your point," I said, "but I still want to hear more about the overall ecosystem before we talk about the crocodiles."

"I much prefer to talk about the global ecosystem anyway," continued Sebastian, "though I'm not sure how it'll help you."

"Humor me," I responded. "We have an hour to kill, and then we can talk about the crocodiles."

"No problem. Let's start at the beginning. The beginning of this particular ecosystem, anyway. Thousands of years ago, the Great Barrier Reef was right at the edge of the continent, and in some ways it still is, but most people don't want to know about that part of the reef. They want to see the dramatic structure with the bright coral and the big fish. I don't think of the reef like that. Without the entire system, the reef would die out in a matter of years. Like most of nature, all things are connected, and the health of one part supports the health of another. The way to think of the reef is not only as a specific place but as an enormous living organism. Did you know the reef is the only living creature that you can see from space?"

"No, I didn't."

"Well, it is," he continued. "This one structure is over twenty-three hundred kilometers long and has the most biodiverse ecosystem on the planet. In my humble opinion, the reef off of the coast of Port Douglass is the most vibrant and diverse aspect of the entire system, and this is in great part due to the Daintree Rainforest. For me, the reef is broken into three distinct but closely related systems. The inshore reef and mid-shelf reef are below us right now. No one wants to see those because the animals are not very big, and the coral is not very pretty. The water is also not all that clear because of the run-off from the forest. Yet without these portions of the reef, the outer reef, where we are heading, would not exist in its present form. You see, the shallow waters near the shore with the mangroves, as well as the mid reef, don't have the populations of predators the outer reef does. This area is a natural nursery, safe for the babies and smaller animals to mature. Well, as safe as any ecosystem in Queensland, which is to say not safe at all, but safer than the outer reef. Did you know they say nine out of ten things that live in Queensland can kill you, and the other one just hasn't yet figured how to?" Sebastian chuckled.

I was less amused. "How comforting," I said, sipping the strong black coffee.

"The water runs down from the rainforests, filled with nutrients and minerals that allow the nursery to thrive," continued Sebastian. "Essentially, the rainforest is a giant filter purifying the water and filling the thriving, offshore ecosystem with food. The animals in the water benefit from these nutrients and grow bigger and stronger until they are able to join the big boys at the outer reefs. Without this system, the biodiversity would not exist.

"What do the rainforests get out of this system?"

"Protection. The reef is essentially a giant storm break that extends along the entire coast of Australia. Did you know that without the reef, the weather systems of the entire continent would be dramatically different? There is a distinct symbiotic relationship between the great forests and the reef, and neither one would survive in its present form without the other. Humans are doing their best to destroy both of them, however, and lately we are seeing the damage firsthand. The forests are being cut down, which leads to a massive runoff of silt and non-nutrient-rich sludge into the shallow reefs near the shore, effectively choking off the nurseries. In the reefs, a measurable decrease in the biodiversity can be seen, thirty kilometers offshore in the areas where the forests are being decimated. We are lucky in Port Douglas, because the Daintree is protected, but it won't take long for people to mess that up, I suspect.

As industrial machinery churns more poison into the sky, the planet is getting warmer. Slowly, but measurably. And what most people don't realize is that the balance is delicate. If you tip things just a little bit, the entire system can come crashing down. The water warms, and the coral responds by turning white. If the coral dies, the marine life will quickly follow. It's a true tragedy. People are gradually destroying the world, and no one seems to care. We are on the frontline of a relentless, evolving ecological disaster, and humankind is knowingly making this happen. Anyone who cares about the environment should be infuriated by what is happening."

Sebastian was really worked up. His passion for the ecosystem matched his anger at the environmental injustices he felt powerless to stop. It was time to change the subject. "Tell me about crocodiles," I said. "How often will you see them at the outer reef?"

"Try never," responded Sebastian. "This is not really their playground. We call them *salties* because they can quite happily survive in the ocean, but they much prefer the rivers and shallow inlets. These magnificent beauties can get up to five meters long, weighing up to five hundred kilograms. It's rumored they can live for one hundred years or longer. This is their world. They were around long before us, and I suspect they will long outlast us."

"I've seen documentaries about them. It's terrifying to see these predators in action."

"You better believe it," continued Sebastian. "I have seen these marvelous creatures in the wild. Once they grab hold—game over. No more efficient killer exists on this planet than a saltwater croc. They attack smaller swimming animals as well as land prey that drink on the banks. But they typically are not deep-ocean hunters. There is nothing for them way out here. Over the last thirty years, I've yet to see a saltwater croc on the outer reef."

"So you've never been up close and personal with them?"

"I've seen these impressive creatures my entire life, even relatively close, from the safety of a boat, but they demand respect. I keep my distance. Every year, people are killed by crocs, but the stories are all much the same. The people were either swimming in the wrong spot or wading in shallow pools in the wet season. In some cases, plain bad luck—say, a boat capsizing in the wrong part of the river—puts humans in jeopardy. In every case, it's hard to get mad at the croc. You don't get mad at the lion for eating the zebra. That's simply a lion being a lion. Don't trespass on their territory, or they might eat you, is what I say."

"So where do they come from?" I asked.

"Around here," responded Sebastian, "they all come from the Daintree River."

"Are you sure?" I asked, happy that Sebastian had reaffirmed my suspicions.

"Either the main river or a tributary. And yes, I am sure."

"Are you familiar with that territory?" I asked.

"As familiar as anyone else you will find. It's my home."

"Can you take me there when we get back from the reef?" I asked.

"Does your buddy have any more cash?" he said, pointing at Spencer, who had been quietly listening in the corner.

"Yes, I do, and I suspect you will take us there," he responded dryly.

"I think this is the start of a beautiful relationship," smiled Sebastian, almost bellowing the word *beautiful*.

"I have another question for you," I said to Sebastian.

"Sure," he answered. "What do you want to know?"

"Why do you think an entire group of crocodiles ended up in the same spot?"

"Obviously, I don't know for sure."

"But you have a theory?" I pressed.

"Sure, theories abound. It's all people have been talking about for the last week, and everyone always has a strong opinion about everything in this town," he answered. "I don't know if this happens in the United States, but every several years, a group of whales will end up stranded on a beach in Australia."

I nodded to Sebastian. "I've heard about this and seen several reports."

"Well," he continued, "theories abound as to why this happens. I have heard everything from space aliens to secret military projects that throw the animals' internal compasses off. But what I think actually happens is a subtle change in the whales' brains. Let me ask you, how can a monarch butterfly, one of the most delicate creatures on the planet, fly thousands of miles through all kinds of conditions and end up exactly where they want to be in southern Mexico? This happens every year without fail, like clockwork. A butterfly's brain is the size of a pinhead, and yet they make this trip that most humans could not make in a lifetime. Call it instinct, an internal compass, whatever you want, but the butterflies just know. Whales similarly migrate. And when something gets messed up, they end up dying on a beach.

"The way I see it, crocodiles on a reef are not much different than whales on a beach. The top rumor is that the salties are suffering from something in their brains. Rumor also is that what they have is contagious, resulting in a bunch of sick people in the hospital. Port Douglass is a small town, and there are no secrets. And now, two Americans show up, drag me out of bed, hand me a stack of cash, and want to see the crocodiles on the reef. You two are not tourists. That much is clear. So *you* tell *me*. What's going on here? Are you two scientists? Military? Whoever you are, I think you know more about this than I do."

One look from Spencer told me to keep my mouth shut. "I do appreciate your expertise on all of this, Sebastian," I replied with a warm smile. "My friend and I are trying to piece some facts together, and the more information we have, the better we can do that."

"The other group didn't seem to fix anything," said Sebastian casually.

This comment caught Spencer's attention. "What other group?" asked Spencer.

"Like I said, Port Douglas is a small town, so people take notice of things. Three days ago, another group went out to see the crocodiles. The area is off-limits to tourists and is patrolled by the Australian Navy, so this particular trip naturally caught people's attention."

"Who were they?" asked Spencer.

"I don't know for sure," answered Sebastian, "but the rumor was that they were American scientists sent to study the crocs. Strange thing is, they never made it back to shore, according to the rumor mill."

This piqued Spencer's curiosity. "What do you mean they never made it back to shore?"

"Out here, everyone knows everyone, right?" answered Sebastian. "Well, no one recognized the boat that went out. And none of the local pilots were missing. However, this conspicuous boat never came back in."

"For a small town, this is a busy place," said Spencer. "Any chance the boat was just missed when it came back, or it went back to a different port?"

"Whenever anyone asks me a question starting with 'any chance,' the answer must be yes. A *chance* is always feasible," answered Sebastian. "But I don't think it's the case here. Not many boats have been going out, since the reef is off limits, and there is nothing much to see above the water. So people have been watching all the activity at the marina closely. No other port is close, and why would they start from one port and then go to another? Most popular conjecture: the boat sank. Though admittedly, people like rumors better than facts."

Spencer and I exchanged glances, both thinking the same thing: something was amiss, and we didn't have all the facts.

Sebastian saw the concern on our faces. "Come on, mates," he said with a smile, "Chins up. Nothing is going to happen to us out here. Bill is the best pilot in Port Douglas, and I don't even think he's hung over today." With that comment, Bill grunted deeply. "Don't worry about him," continued Sebastian, "I know these waters like the back of my hand."

Sebastian's comments gave me little comfort. Choosing my words carefully, I said, "I'm a veterinarian from the United States, and this is my partner. We are trying to find out as much as we can about these animals at the reef so we can fix this before the situation escalates." My explanation about our involvement wasn't technically a lie, but it wasn't exactly the truth either. It didn't matter, because the desired effect was achieved. Sebastian sat back in his chair and relaxed.

"Why didn't you tell me you guys were veterinarians?" Sebastian said warmly. "I was assuming you two were American CIA spies or something. I was worried that if I saw something I wasn't supposed to, I would end up disappearing myself." He stood. "We should be at the reef soon. Why don't we go up on deck, and I can point out where the crocodiles have been congregating?"

The reef was as beautiful and as scary as I remembered—far enough offshore that you couldn't see land in any direction. If the boat sank out here, good luck getting home. We passed by several smaller reefs, some of which appeared as only a change in the color of the water. Others were shallow enough that the waves broke over the reef, and occasionally bits of coral were visible above the surface. Bill started to slow down in front of a huge reef that must have extended a mile in all directions.

"Welcome to Opal Reef, one of my favorites," said Sebastian. "It's about six kilometers long and currently is off-limits. You're about to see why."

Looking into the distance, I could see waves breaking over a shallow part of the reef, and directly in front of that, continuous thrashing within the water. As we grew closer, I could make out the bodies of at least ten huge reptiles. They were slithering through the water like snakes and blindly bumping into each other. When that happened, there was more wild thrashing and clamping of tremendous jaws into nothing but air and water. Even over the breaking waves, I could hear hissing and growling that sounded like prehistoric fury. The violence of the animals was unnerving. Several of the large crocs were no longer moving on their own and merely floated back and forth with the waves.

"We need to try and get them out of the water," I said.

"You must be joking," said Sebastian. "These animals are a minimum of three hundred kilograms, crazy mad, and biting anything that moves. No way." Of course, he was right, but if some of our theories were correct, these things could hypothetically pass on the prion to anything they came into contact with. Talk about an upset in balance!

"There has to be a way," I pleaded with Spencer. "If they're loaded with the prion and the ocean predators start to tear them apart, it will only be a matter of time before things spiral out of control."

"I hadn't thought about that," confessed Spencer. "Let me see what I can do," and he picked up his satellite phone.

"Have any of the other animals at the reef been acting in an abnormal way?" I asked Sebastian.

"The last time I went into the water was five days ago, and everything was normal," he answered. "I'm not going into the water to check now, but if you want to, be my guest. I can tell you no one has reported any abnormal behavior anywhere along the reef but right here. I have friends up and down the coast who run tours. In places other than Port Douglas, it's business as usual."

"So are you sure all the crocodiles are isolated to this one area?" I asked Spencer.

"As far as we can tell, yes," answered Spencer, covering the mouthpiece of his phone. "The Australian Coast Guard and the Royal Australian Navy have been patrolling the reef in the immediate area nonstop, and tours have been suspended in a forty kilometer area, just to be safe. No other reports of abnormal activity have come in, although no one has been in the water since the crocodiles were first sighted." Spencer held up a finger and went back to his phone call.

We now were within about twenty feet of the massive reptiles, and I could see them clearly through the crystal water. As I studied the animals swimming, a pattern developed. Most swam in tight circles to the left and a few to the right. Two rolled continuously, and all displayed signs of extreme aggression whenever they bumped into each other. No attempt was made to avoid hitting another animal, and the crocodiles were so tightly packed into one area that a collision was occurring every few minutes. I got out my notebook. Their actions appeared to involve a combination of prosencephalic and cerebellar signs, with possible targeting of the amygdala and hypothalamus. Some of the animals appeared to be blind. A diffuse neurological impairment was the only diagnosis that made sense. Moreover, the behavior was consistent with the analyses of the pathology samples. The entire brain was being affected, and the clinical results were quite dramatic.

"We need to see what is happening with the animals along the rest of the reef," I told Spencer as he got off the phone.

"We'll talk about that in a second," he said. "For now, the Australian authorities agree with you. We need to get these animals out of the water to prevent possible spread. If there were an outbreak along the reef which prevented people from diving here, the effects on ecotourism would be devastating. The Coast Guard is escorting a small whaling boat here to collect the crocodiles."

"Any chance they could bring one in alive?" I asked.

"You can ask them if you want, but I think we both know the answer to that one," Spencer said, watching the thrashing animals.

"Can we at least take the boat around the reef to see if anything else looks off from the surface?" I pleaded with the group.

"No problem," grunted Bill. "I really don't like being here anyway. I don't think I'll ever go in that water again." Over the next hour we slowly made our way around to the back of the reef. From the surface, everything appeared normal.

"I still need to see if the animals are acting normally underwater," I reasoned with Spencer. "We have no idea if the crocodiles are the entire problem or the tip of an iceberg. In fact, we don't even know if this is transmissible to other marine life. Relatively few diseases cross species so efficiently as this seems to be doing with humans."

Spencer nodded. His silence encouraged me to continue. "Let's say the whaling boats get rid of the crocodiles, and then a week later tourists come back out here, and someone figures out that, under the water, hundreds of species are just waiting to wreak neurological havoc. We have an obligation to check this now, while it remains a potentially manageable problem. The source could be right here, ten feet under the surface."

He turned away from me to peer over the side of the boat.

"This is what we were asked to do," I said.

"Any decision we make here comes with significant risks," Spencer replied carefully. "I have an obligation to uncover facts but not at the expense of our lives. If we go into this water and end up getting sick or attacked, then we are not doing anyone any good. Least of all us."

"So what do you think we should do?"

"I think we can take a quick dive, but we must take precautions. I was hoping we didn't have to use them, but I stowed dry suits onboard. These are highly modified with a fully enclosed helmet to protect our mouths and prevent any direct contact with the water. We'll have to pipe our air in from the boat, which means we won't be able to go that far."

He retrieved the equipment from a compartment on the deck. I guessed he did this last night after negotiating with the pilot.

"We have no idea what is in this water," Spencer continued. "So one thing I want to make perfectly clear: what I say goes. If I say to return to the surface, then that's what we do, without question. Agreed?"

I nodded in agreement.

"Unfortunately, we won't be able to talk to each other, since the suits don't have coms. I will signal a resurface by holding my hand out—stop—and then pointing upwards. Understood?" Spencer gestured the hand motions he would use.

"Understood." I was relieved by the way he thought this through.

Spencer handed me a suit. "These suits are used by the military for wreck salvage. They'll keep the water out, but they're no protection against big predators, so we need to scan the area frequently. Also, the suits are a bit clunky. Are you a strong swimmer?" asked Spencer.

"Seven-time All-American in college," I replied.

"Well, hurray for you. You can't wear your medals under the suit," he kidded.

"What I mean is that I am comfortable in the water and won't panic," I replied. "And my medals remain in a shoe box under my bed," I added with a wink.

It took twenty minutes to get into the dry suits. They were awkward to get on, but they fit well and were actually rather comfortable. According to Bill, the boat was positioned over a reef wall that dropped to over fifty meters straight down. This was a popular place to dive, due to the abundance of marine life along the wall and the tendency of the currents to be mild, he explained. Since the reef was shallow along the top of the wall, hypothetically anything big swimming into the area would have to come from behind the boat, where Sebastian and Bill would be standing guard.

"Are you sure you want to do this?" asked Spencer.

"Find the source, right?" I said, hoping I didn't look as worried as he did.

Chapter 9

S PENCER GAVE SEBASTIAN AND BILL a quick lesson on the device providing the air supply, and they worked out a system where, if there was danger, we would be pulled up quickly by the tubes. We were ready to go. The helmets were fastened tightly over our heads and snapped into a rubber seal on the neck of the suits. The air tubes were connected to the helmets, and we slid into the water. Spencer was right, the suits were a bit clunky, but all we needed to do was go down and make a quick assessment.

What a spectacular place to dive! The top of the underwater cliff lay only a few feet under the surface, but the rock face disappeared into the murky depths of the dark, blue sea, giving the impression that there was no bottom. The marine life was as brilliant as I remembered, although the coral had turned a light shade of tan and white. What a shame; it once was radiant.

We slowly made our way down the face. Schools of fish enveloped us in the shadowy water as we submerged past ten meters. The marine life seemed normal, but would I recognize a neurologically damaged fish if I saw one? Three green sea turtles swam by in formation. Their motions were slow, effortless, and smooth, with no tremors or shaking. About eight meters below us, a whitetip reef shark meandered through the coral. She swam with no signs of incoordination. Along the edge of the wall, a brilliant-turquoise parrotfish fed on the coral. A small school of blue tangs passed in front of us, moving as one unit, turning in a synchronous dance as if performing a ballet. Keep swimming, I thought to myself, smiling under my helmet. Everything was as it should be, and I couldn't help but get caught up in the splendor of this magical environment.

In surgery, I had a bit of a sixth sense when something started to go awry. It was hard to explain and impossible to teach. I knew it wasn't premonition, because there were always clues that a problem was developing. Good surgeons were able to recognize these clues earlier than others. A subtle change in heart rate or a change in the internal pulses, for example, could be overlooked unless one was fully in tune with what they were doing. In medicine, like in life, avoiding a problem is considerably easier than trying to fix one.

This feeling had served me well in my career, and many disasters were avoided due to this developed sense. I started to get a similar feeling right then. Something was amiss, but I couldn't place my finger on it. It was just a general state of unease that made my senses tingle. We passed fifteen meters deep, and Spencer signaled to stop our descent, and he gave me the thumbs up. I didn't return the gesture. Perhaps I was being paranoid, but my unease would not go away.

Strangely, my left leg felt cold. With a shudder, I understood: water had gotten in the suit. I turned to Spencer with an expression that said all was *not* okay. The cold crept to my thigh, and then my right leg turned cold. I continued to descend with the weight of the water filling my lower suit. I saw a steady stream of bubbles from over my left shoulder, where none should be.

Don't panic! Panic leads to bigger problems. I inhaled slow, deep breaths and kicked my fins to maintain my depth. Nevertheless, I continued to sink—and I was expending a lot of energy. The cold reached my abdomen as I passed twenty meters.

Spencer appeared right next to me and grabbed my arm, trying to pull me closer to the surface. With our combined efforts, we managed to maintain the same depth, but there was no way to ascend.

Despite my best efforts, I was losing my battle to remain calm. The continuous stream of bubbles seeping from the shoulder of my suit accelerated as the cold reached my chest. I watched as the bubbles gently meandered to the surface, which seemed so far away.

It had taken twenty minutes to get the suit on, so there was no way to remove it with the time I calculated I had until the water reached my mouth. Think, think!

The tubes! The tubes that were pumping in oxygen were a lifeline to the boat. My hands fumbled several times before I was able to reach behind my head and grab my tube. I started pulling myself, hand over hand, closer to the surface.

Looking over at Spencer, I saw the worry in his face. The cold had reached my neck, and he saw the water through my helmet. With considerable effort on both our parts, we had managed to rise back to ten meters, but the increasing weight in my suit made the ascent increasingly difficult.

At seven meters, the cold water splashed against my chin. Was I going to die here in this suit of death? Nightmarish images of sinking to the ocean bottom sloshed around my brain, my thoughts became muddled with an onslaught of images and memories and sensations: crocs, Smith's voice, snorkeling with my wife. My thoughts split apart, some remaining in a twilight zone and others cleaving to some still-rational part of my brain that registered on what was happening. My arms and legs were on fire from the effort of trying not sink.

Exhausted, feverish, and stuck, I couldn't go any higher. I tasted salt in my mouth, and tried to breathe through my nose before it succumbed to the water. There was no more time.

Spencer reached down to his leg and grabbed a diving knife. He gave me a pleading look as he took the knife and cut into my suit. In my delirious state, I thought he was trying to stab me. The water rushed in, and my vision became blurry as the saltwater rose above my eyes. I could no longer breathe or see.

Then I understood. Spencer was trying to cut off the suit. For a second, I let go of the air tube to try and pull the suit off from where Spencer was slashing with his knife. As soon as I let go, I felt myself plummet deeper before I was able to again grab the hose. I was powerless to help. I needed to hold on to buy as much time as I could. I could feel the arm of my suit become free and risked letting go with one hand to allow the arm to slip off and sink away. I could feel Spencer slashing down the side of the suit. He cut across the waist and my legs were free as the lower half of the suit sank away. The weight pulling me down was considerably less now, but my lungs were on fire.

How long could I hold my breath? When I was younger, I once stayed underwater for ninety seconds to win a bet, but I wasn't so young now. Spencer cut up the torso of the thick suit as things started to go a bit black. I knew my blood oxygen levels were dropping dangerously low. The effort required to sustain this level, combined with panic, were draining me.

Don't inhale, I commanded myself. Once water fills your lungs, it's game over. A rush of cold hit my head, and Spencer ripped the rest of my suit off and removed my helmet. I lost control of my legs and my arms, and I felt myself slipping into unconsciousness, and then all went black.

I opened my eyes to the blazing sun glaring down on me. The wide, blue sky contained not a single cloud. I was gently rocking, and despite the intense sun, I was cold. My arms and legs still were not working. Did I die?

Spencer's voice brought me back to reality. "I said, are you okay?"

"I don't know." I tried to lift my head, then gave up. A jag of coughing blended with images of bubbles, sinking, and drowning returned in a confusion with the strained look behind Spencer's helmet. His face now remained lined with anxiety.

Finally, my voice raspy, I managed, "What happened?"

"You almost died," responded Spencer. "I got you to the surface as fast as I could, but I fear some water may have gotten into your system. We don't know if the water is safe to take in. I'm so sorry. I should have never agreed to this."

"No, I mean what happened with the suit," I said. "I thought they were military grade. How did mine leak? Everything happened so quickly."

"I have no idea, but these things are tested to two hundred meters. It should never have happened."

My arms and legs were tingling, but I was starting to get some function back. I tried to sit up, and Spencer and Bill helped.

"Can you sit up by yourself? Take it slow." Spencer cautiously let me go.

"Chill, man," I smiled. "I'm fine." But when I tried to sit unaided, I rolled over and my face struck the deck with a thud.

"You're not fine, John," said Spencer. All three men helped me into a seat. Spencer said, "We've done all we can out here on the water. Let's get you back and checked out."

Sebastian sat beside me, Bill returned to the wheelhouse and the powerful engines started to churn as we began the journey back toward shore. Spencer disappeared around the corner pulling the phone from his pocket. "I need to make a call," he said.

I wrapped myself in a blanket and tried not to shiver as I curled into a ball. "This sucks," I muttered.

Sebastian fetched hot tea, which helped, as I slowly regained my strength and coordination. "What did you guys see?" he asked.

"A whole lot of nothing," I replied. "Which is to say that everything seemed normal. The marine life we saw was acting as it should."

"That's good, right?" questioned Sebastian.

"Yes, but it doesn't necessarily mean there's no danger."

I had a pounding head, but after finishing the tea, I did actually feel much better and was able to stand. My arms and legs were cooperating again, but my hands and feet still felt like they were submerged in ice. I knew it was my circulation coming back to normal, and it was only a matter of time before I warmed up. The tropical sun helped as I held the deck, rail and watched the waves break over shallow parts of the reef.

Returning to deck, Spencer said, "I need to talk with you in private." His face remained as grave as death. I followed him down the stairs to the lower deck. "Okay, I just got off the phone with my sources," said Spencer. "Those suits were state of the art. They came with us from the States, on our plane, and were delivered to the boat as soon as Bill agreed to take us out. The military uses them all the time for salvage, and they were pressure tested a week ago. A small leak is possible if you hit something really sharp very hard, but your suit didn't have one leak."

"What do you mean?" I asked.

"A leak in the leg or the arm wouldn't cause the suit to fill with water," Spencer explained. "There is constant pressure being applied by the air hoses. Only a leak in the bottom and a leak in the top would allow it to fill with water. The chances of that happening are almost nonexistent. Besides, we didn't bump into anything sharp that could have caused this."

"So what are you saying?" I asked.

"Someone wanted this to happen. This was a deliberate attempt to cause harm, and we need to proceed with extreme caution."

"How, though? No one even knows what we're doing out here."

"We need to proceed under the assumption that's no longer true," said Spencer. "Someone *does* know we are out here, *and* what we're doing. I'm afraid Bill and Sebastian are suspects number one and two. They had access to the suits."

"True enough," I said after some thought, "but I don't think so."

"Why not?"

"If they wanted us dead, all they had to do was drive away. We would have been screwed. Even if we made it back to the surface, land is miles away. They could have caused us harm any number of ways."

Spencer nodded. "And they did bring us to a site that wasn't dangerous. In fact, it was very safe. There were no strong currents. The area was protected, and they could keep watch.

"Also, they had access to our air hoses. One cut and we both would have gone down. They could have made up any story they wanted," I added. We were silent for a couple of minutes, and it occurred to me to ask, "How did you find them?"

"I asked the military guys who drove us her for recommendations. They both vouched for Bill and Sebastian. But I'm a naturally cautious person, so I did my own research on them. Neither has much in the way of records, but they are both well-established professionals who have been taking people to the reef for years. I was satisfied."

"And then you knocked on their doors and woke them up?"

"Yes, I did," responded Spencer. "And Bill seemed pretty hung over.

"How long was that before we actually went out?"

"Two hours. And before you ask me any more leading questions, I get your point. These guys were chosen by me, two hours before they took us out. The chances of them waiting in bed on the off chance they would be asked to assist on a mission they could sabotage is unlikely."

"Just unlikely, Mr. Paranoid?"

"It's my job to be paranoid," said Spencer. "But I agree with you. These two are not responsible for this. Regardless, we need to be very careful about who we trust. The navy wanted the suit back to see what went wrong. They were not happy it's on the bottom of the Pacific, cut into little pieces."

"Yea, I guess that would make it hard to examine," I joked.

"I'm not fooling," said Spencer. "Literally, I am deadly serious."

"Does this mean the prion is a weapon?" I asked, chastened.

"Not necessarily. But if someone is willing to commit murder to try and obstruct us from poking around, they'll be willing to do it again. I don't believe this was an accident. Like I don't believe the other boat these guys told us about went to another port."

"The pieces of this puzzle are more confusing than ever, but I don't like the emerging picture," I mused.

Spencer looked at me with concern. "I'm going to have my suit inspected forensically. When I just checked it, several stitches didn't seem right. I'll have people who know what they're doing check into this. Someone doesn't want us to figure out what is going on here, and they're good at covering their tracks. What I know for certain is that we all need to take steps to keep ourselves out of harm's way."

Keeping to myself on the way back to port, I collected my thoughts. I couldn't stop repeating, *find the source.* One area of the reef being healthy told us little. On the hand, it was *something.* I couldn't imagine the sea water was the source of contamination and that the crocodiles simply happened to swim into a hot spot. They must have been infected where they congregate in large numbers, and then somehow ended up at the reef. I thought back to what Sebastian said about the beached whales, which made sense. I hit my fist a little too hard against the hull in frustration.

I was feeling myself again, but my mind had started going through what-if scenarios—with each conclusion involving the dissolution of my family. I'm the father of motherless children— and I'd taken a stupid risk.

I watched from the deck as the shoreline became visible and steadily grew. The magnificent morning light had brightened, which paradoxically made the forest appear less green. The trip to the reef allowed me to see the effects of the prion up close, in the wild, but we really were no closer to figuring out how the crocs got sick in the first place. The most logical explanation is that the reptiles became infected by eating something containing the prion. After which, they got sick and wandered out to the reef in an altered cognitive state.

The next logical place to investigate, then, was where the reptiles hunted. Scanning the shore, I saw in the distance what seemed the river's likely entrance to the sea—a giant chasm between the hills of the rainforest. Dark clouds hovered over the trees, creating the illusion of smoke. I envisioned fat raindrops falling through the thick, lush vegetation and falling to the mossy ground, making their way into small brooks, larger streams, into the river, and finally out to sea. I thought about the people dying in the hospital, their brains being pillaged until they no longer were the same person and their thoughts were not their own. What if someone I knew and loved were infected with this prion, and doctors were helpless to alter the terrible course of this disease. What If I was contaminated already. I shut this last thought out of my head, not willing to go down that avenue right now. There was nothing I could do. I set my resolve: I needed to move forward and try and help in any way I could. If there was a potential answer somewhere out in the wilderness, then we should try to find it, no matter how difficult.

I entered the cabin. "We still need to go to the Daintree," I said to Spencer and Sebastian.

"Happy to take you, if you're up for it," replied Sebastian. "But if I remember correctly, you were almost dead an hour ago," he joked as he slapped my shoulder playfully. "Haven't you had enough adventure for one day?"

"Let me think about that one," Spencer cautiously replied. "I'm not sure I'm going to let you go."

"I don't need you to manage me, and I don't think I need your permission," I said, instantly regretting taking a hard line with Spencer. Surprise flashed across his face. I quickly added, "We need to move forward, and that's not going to happen until we find out how these reptiles got sick in the first place."

"I know, but since I don't know who sabotaged us, I can't guarantee your safety. I can't protect you *and* investigate what's going on at the same time."

"I can take care of myself," I replied, but even I didn't believe the words, so I doubt anyone else on the boat did either.

"There are lots of dangerous things in the rainforest," offered Sebastian, "but people are rarely one of them. I grew up there, and I can keep him safe," he said to Spencer motioning to the forest.

"Okay, but I don't like it," said Spencer reluctantly.

"Noted," I said, "but I'm sure you will get over it."

"Only if you come back in one piece," he said.

"Spencer, I haven't told you how grateful I am to you for saving my life," I said in a suddenly sober tone. "If not for you, I would be at the bottom of that wall."

After an awkward silence, he said, "I was motivated—every time I lose someone, the paperwork is brutal. Besides," he added, "I find myself liking you. I can't say that about most people."

Chapter 10

THE RETURN TRIP WENT MUCH quicker than the trip out, and soon we were on the dock. "Where can I get something to eat around here?" I asked Sebastian. I couldn't remember the last time I had eaten.

"Inlet by the Sea is what I would recommend. And if you get there in time, you can watch them feed Charly," offered Sebastian. "It's noon. I'll pick you up at your hotel at two p.m. I suggest that you wear long pants, long-sleeved shirt, and hiking boots. The bugs can be brutal."

"Who's Charly?" I asked.

"You'll see."

The restaurant was right down the street from the dock, located on the waterfront, with both indoor and outdoor dining and a nice little bar with string lights. I chose a table close to the water and sat down. The waitress brought a glass of ice water and a menu.

"You can order whenever you would like," she said with a warm smile that instantly made me like her, "but if you go to the dock you can meet Charly. Just come back to this table when you're done."

I did want to meet the mysterious Charly, so I shrugged at the waitress, got up, and walked out to the dock where a small group had gathered. A man with a bucket full of chicken parts ceremoniously dropped sizeable chunks into the water to the delight of the crowd. Charly, a six-foot grouper who lived under the dock, shot to the surface to snatch each offering with a dramatic splash and a glimpse of his immense size. Each time he surfaced, the small gathering cheered and clapped. The children watching were mesmerized.

"Wow! That's a big fish," I said to a man next to me.

"These guys can get much bigger than this," he responded with a slight slur. "I once hooked a grouper three-meters long and the better part of three hundred kilos. It was bigger than my boat, I tell ya. I couldn't bring myself to kill such a magnificent beast, so I let her go."

His friends started in on him. "He tells this story to anyone who will listen, and each time, the fish gets bigger and the boat gets smaller. Wait until he gets a few more beers in him. It will be a rubber raft and a thousand-kilo fish that nearly ate him whole!"

Even halfway around the world, the scenery can change, but fish stories stay the same. I returned to my table, and the waitress came over promptly. I read the menu and felt awkward, but ordered the grouper sandwich anyway. The sandwich was huge and came with a stack of fries and a pickle. It was the best fish I ever had. I ate in a hurry, and the waitress seemed disappointed when I didn't want dessert, but I needed to get back. I felt nearly normal again as I walked to the hotel, enjoying the tropical breeze. Once on the hotel grounds, I saw Nell and Alex sitting by the pool and joined them.

"The neurologists here have no idea what they're doing," complained Alex as soon as I sat down.

"What do you mean?" I asked.

"The MRIs they did are so low-quality, they're barely readable," he began. "In addition, they didn't do all the proper sequences. A ton of subtle changes could be missing. Their neurological examinations were incomplete, and their treatments are way behind the times. This quality of medicine is about fifteen years behind where we are in the US."

"So you found mistakes in the diagnoses?" I asked.

"Actually, no," he admitted. I caught Nell letting out a chuckle as she sat back in her chair and put her arms out with her palms up—the universal sign for *I'm getting some sun.*

Alex pretended not to notice. "The fact is, all the people who are still alive have multifocal neurological abnormalities, which seem to be getting progressively worse, and there's not a damn treatment that is working."

"Are any of them blind?" I asked.

"Two are blind," replied Alex, surprised. "They both have normal retinas, suggesting the problem is deeper within the brain. Why do you ask?"

"The crocodiles exhibited multifocal neurological signs, which could potentially be isolated to the amygdala and hypothalamus. Granted, it's exceptionally difficult to do a neurological examination on a giant swimming crocodile, but I think they may have been blind as well."

"Curious," replied Alex.

"What is?" I asked.

"I didn't even know veterinarians do neurological examinations," he responded.

"We do a lot more than give vaccines," I replied, dryly. I was getting a bit tired of Alex's pompous attitude. "Any updates on your end?" I asked Nell.

"Well, most of the materials I was waiting for have come in, especially the experimental blood tests. I've begun trying to isolate the proteins from the human and crocodile tissues to determine if they are the same."

"Are you using amplification?" I asked.

"There's no need, since the protein should be present in high concentrations, given the states of the neural damage. I've also applied several of my favorite stains to samples from each species. Right now, the samples are running, so I have eight hours of down time to just pull out my hair and wait."

"I have to head back to the hospital soon to check on the patients," said Alex. "The doctors here have already tried most of the basic treatments, but I still have a few tricks up my sleeve. Besides, I need to try and get these doctors up to current standards in practicing neurology."

"I'm sure they'll love that," I murmured, too soft for him to hear. A look from Nell told me she was thinking the same thing.

"Any updates from you, crocodile hunter?" asked Alex, as he got up to leave.

"Someone tried to kill Spencer and me," I responded casually.

"What?" they both gasped in unison, as Alex sat back down, truly concerned.

"Next time lead with that," said Alex.

"What happened? Are you okay?" said Nell in an uneasy voice grabbing my hand.

I went through the story with them as they listened intently to every detail.

"That would explain certain things," said Nell subtly pointing a finger to a man lounging with dark sunglasses on. "The guy across the pool is Australian military. I was getting a bit of a creepy vibe from him, so I approached him to ask who he was and what he was doing here. He showed me his credentials and admitted he was ordered to casually observe and protect us if need be. We also had armed escorts who insisted on following us everywhere we went in the hospital and driving us to the hotel.

"One of them stood guard at the door while I used the restroom," said Alex. "I assumed they were just being courteous, or following orders—not that our lives might be in actual danger."

The word danger brought back thoughts of my own safety. "Nell?" I asked as casually as I could. "Do you have the ability to test for low levels of the prion in the blood of, uh, say . . . me?"

"Oh, my God!" she replied quickly. "You were in the water. You don't think--"

"No, I don't really think I was exposed," I responded. "The ocean is huge, and even if prions were in the water, the chances that I could get this are astronomically low. But if there is a chance, I have to have peace of mind. If there is a way to find out, and you can run the test, then I would appreciate it."

"I can run the test, but not yet," Nell responded with a bit of regret in her voice. "I wish I could, but what I need to amplify the protein is not coming in until tonight. Do you feel okay?" she asked.

I detected a forced calmness in her voice, which only made my anxiety a bit worse. "Yes, I feel absolutely fine," I answered honestly. "In fact, I'm off to the rainforest soon, and I need to change," I said as I got up.

"What rainforest?" asked Alex.

"The crocodiles don't live in the ocean. In fact, it's pretty rare to see more than one out there. In the coastal rivers, on the other hand, they're in high concentrations. The major river system near here is in the middle of the rainforest. If they all got sick at the same time, as I suspect, the source is most likely going to be found somewhere in there."

"Thank you for the nature lesson, but I have more important things to attend to," Alex said. "I'm going back to the hospital." And he left abruptly.

Nell and I exchanged eye rolls as we watched him walk away. I stood up from the lounge chair and started to walk back toward my room. "I'm coming with you," Nell called after me from across the pool.

Remembering that she hated being told what to do, I chose my words carefully. "You're more than welcome, but I don't know how long this will take."

"I have eight hours," she reminded me, "and I surely am not going to sit by the pool being stared at by a creepy bodyguard the entire time."

I wasn't sure if she was coming because she was bored or because she was worried about me, but either way, I found myself smiling. "Okay. Sebastian suggested we wear long pants, long-sleeved shirts, and hiking boots," I said.

"Who's Sebastian?" she asked.

"Our guide," I answered. "He's a good guy and knows a lot about the area and the local wildlife. He grew up around here and is a naturalist."

"Give me ten minutes," she said. "What room are you in?"

"Room two-oh-four," I responded.

"That's easy, I'm in two-oh-five," she said as she walked ahead to her room.

Sebastian got to my room two minutes before Nell.

"Ready to go?" he asked.

"I invited a guest," I responded. "She'll be here any minute."

"She?" he asked curiously. "You're bringing a date?"

"No, she's a neuropathologist, working with the team at the hospital," I answered carefully, trying to reveal as little as I could. I still wasn't sure what was public knowledge and what we were allowed to communicate. As far as I could tell, Sebastian already knew more about what was going on than I did, so I figured a bit of information was fair game. Besides, Mr. Smith had not made an appearance since the plane.

"I have to warn you, I brought a date too. But I think I will probably like your date better than mine," said Sebastian with a devious smile.

"Who?"

"You're—ahem—*partner* has arranged an escort for us," Sebastian replied with a knowing grin.

Nell came around the corner wearing jeans, hiking boots, and a safari shirt. This sensible outfit did nothing to detract from how gorgeous she was. Sebastian's jaw went slack as he watched her approach.

"I definitely like your date better than mine," he said under his breath. "Is she single? I think I am in love."

"No, she isn't," I lied, before she got close enough to hear. "Nell, this is Sebastian; Sebastian, Nell."

"Hello, Nell," managed Sebastian. "I thought Australia had the most beautiful girls in the world, but apparently I'm wrong." Nell managed a fake smile and as Sebastian turned to walk to the jeep, she rolled her eyes at me and just shook her head.

Our "escort" was a six-foot, four-inch soldier from the Australian military with a large gun strapped on his waist and the biggest biceps I had ever seen. He introduced himself as Walter. Leave it to Spencer; I bet he searched for the most intimidating figure he could muster in the two hours he had. We climbed into a tall Jeep Wrangler with a Snorkel and huge tires.

"Where do you want to go?" asked Sebastian as he climbed behind the wheel, his eyes lingering a bit too long on Nell. She pretended not to notice as she stared blankly back at the pool.

"We need to head to the place where we will find the highest concentration of saltwater crocodiles," I responded.

"We'll need a boat to get there," answered Sebastian. "You can't drive along the river for long distances, and to walk along the shore is not a very smart idea. But there's a marina about an hour from here. Stevie's is the name of the place. I know the guy. He'll have what we need."

"Tell us about the rainforest," I prompted Sebastian.

"Beautiful. Eden to look at, but it can be closer to hell if you don't know what you are doing." A mile from the hotel, the road turned to dirt, and I understood why the jeep with the oversized tires was necessary as we bounced along the rough road. "I used to play in the forest as a kid," continued Sebastian. "The thing about the rainforest is that most of the dangerous stuff you never see coming. Everyone worries about the snakes. I've seen my fair share of taipans, brown snakes, and death adders, but they want nothing to do with you. Unless you're incredibly unlucky and happen to step in the wrong place at the wrong time, you'll never *see* one, much less get bitten by one."

"What about other things that bite?" I asked.

"There are plenty of funnel web spiders around, and their bite can be nasty. One bit me when I was a kid. The little guy was taking a nap in my shoe when I put it on. I got plenty sick, but my parents rushed me to a hospital that had antivenom, and it wasn't a big problem. I can tell you I have never put on a shoe without turning it upside down since."

We stopped at a fork in the road, and Sebastian turned around to Nell as he continued. "We even have the only species of bird known to kill a person. If we get lucky, we may see one."

Politely, she asked, "Really, what's it called?"

The jeep started off again down the fork to the left, which led deeper into the forest. The air was getting thick with moisture and smelled of plants—alive, dying, and dead. Sebastian answered, "The cassowary is the size of an ostrich but is a lot prettier. These beauties can stand up to six feet tall. The body is mostly black, but the head and neck are a brilliant blue. And get this, they actually have a mohawk, like the punk rockers in the 1970s. It's best to watch them from a distance, where they'll leave you alone. But get them cornered, and they'll strike out with serious claws. I mean *dagger-like* claws. I'm not kidding when I say this bird has killed humans. I've driven people around this forest for years, and I'll see a cassowary maybe twice a year, but you never know. Ecotourism is huge here. We're very lucky the Australian government set up most of this forest as a preserve. Sadly, surrounding areas were not so lucky. The land was developed and farmed and destroyed. As I was telling John here, the reef depends on the land, and the land on the reef."

Nell was gazing out the jeep's window, not paying attention to Sebastian. The landscape was beautiful but primitive. The underbrush was thick, and I was starting to see what Sebastian meant about needing a boat to get around. We crossed several small rivers running across parts of the road. The deepest parts were only two feet deep, but driving this road in anything other than an all-terrain vehicle would be nearly impossible.

At one of the crossings, Sebastian got out and pointed to a small bush with large, heart-shaped leaves. "You see this plant here?" he said with a smile, "It has tiny spikes on each of its leaves that contain neurotoxins. If you touch the leaf even for a second, the spikes penetrate your skin, break off, and inject the toxin. It can sting you for months and is very difficult to treat." He seemed to be talking specifically to Nell as he jumped back into the jeep. "People love seeing the scary stuff. I can't tell you how many tours I've run where all people want to see are deadly creatures. I'll never understand human nature. Anyway, the forest is filled with ancient trees and rivers. The most dangerous time to go walking is during the rainy season, when the rivers are flooded and the creatures come out. You never want to go wandering into a deep, murky pool. Chances are good you won't come out. Biggest threat there is the salties. Those guys will eat anything."

"What is their natural diet?" I asked.

"Most of the little ones eat small fish and the rodents that get close to the water. They even eat insects when they're really small. The big ones tend to take down full-grown mammals that come to the water to drink."

"So, the little ones consume a different diet?"

"Yeah, I guess that's true," answered Sebastian. "I think if a little croc could take down a wallaby it would, but I don't see that happening."

"Has anyone reported abnormal crocodile behavior in the river?" I asked.

"Nothing I've heard about, but we can ask at Stevie's. All the tours cast off from there, and Stevie knows everyone and loves to chat. If anything is going on, he'll know."

We pulled into the marina about fifteen minutes later. Stevie's was located in a cove with an expansive view up and down the river. Three separate docks jutted into the Daintree. There were several pickup trucks as well as two tour vans in the dirt parking lot. A small store stood at one side of the lot, with souvenirs in the windows and a sign that advertised bait and tackle. Across the parking lot was a long aluminum building with heavy doors. Inside I could see several boats on metal racks. The sounds of a working mechanic shop drifted out. As we pulled up, an immense man came out of the store.

"That's Stevie," said Sebastian. He recognized Sebastian halfway across the lot, and his face lit up with a huge smile. Stevie could have stepped out of an Australian travel booklet. He wore a black cowboy hat with a silver band and one side of the hat snapped up. He had on khaki pants and a blue, button-down shirt with sleeves rolled up above his elbows.

"G'day, mate," he said as he swallowed up Sebastian in a bear hug. "What brings you way out here to mingle with us common people?" he asked.

"Just taking these fine folks for a private trip up the river," replied Sebastian. "I could use a boat. Do you have anything for me?"

"Of course, mate, help yourself," replied Stevie, his eyes now lingering on Nell as she jumped out the back of the truck. "You know where I keep the keys. Today I have three in, and you can take your pick. It's going to cost you drinks the next time we go out, though. If you want, you could invite these fine people along with you. The more the merrier."

"I'm not sure I can afford to buy a night of drinks for you," replied Sebastian with a wink.

Stevie walked in closer and held out his immense hand to Nell and introduced himself. She shook his hand politely before quietly walking down toward the water. After she was halfway down, Stevie finally turned his eyes back to the two of us.

I introduced Walter and myself, as Walter headed toward the workshop, looking bored.

"How long have you worked here?" I asked Stevie.

"Well, I've owned this place for the last twenty years," he replied. "Most days I don't consider what I do work. I have anywhere between five and nine boats, depending on which ones are running. Tours are constantly coming through, and we provide the boats and the pilots to take people up and down the river. Locals use the docks and sometimes the boats to do some fishing. Most of the time, I chat with people and run the bait shop. It's a sweet deal. I inherited the land from my father and built things up from there."

"Do you know the tour directors?" I asked.

"Some," he replied. "But typically they only want to focus on the tourists. Those people are their meal ticket. I have a great group of locals who run my boats, and they know the river like the back of their hands. Most people want to see the salties, and the truth of it is, they aren't hard to find. All of the boats radio one another when they see one basking on the shore, and the boats all go to that spot. The people on the tours love it, and they usually tip pretty well, so the money is good for my crew."

"Have you seen any unusual tours come through in the last two weeks?" I asked as casually as I could.

"That's a strange question," remarked Stevie with a chuckle. "If I'm telling you the truth, I think anyone who pays money to see a crocodile is a bit nuts. As I said, they're everywhere. I don't see what is so exciting about them. They lie around in the sun all day and rarely move. They do most of their hunting at night. And folks will fly halfway around the world to watch these things sleep. I don't see the point. Not complaining, though. I get a cut of every tour that comes through. My boats have been booked out for the last week. Everyone wants to search the river for the killer crocs. It's been great for business. The only reason I have boats today is I just got three repaired and didn't have a chance to rent them out yet. I'm trying to cash in on this rush, before the interest goes away. I know that sounds insensitive, but business is business."

So much for the secret nature of what was going on.

"Has anyone reported any strange behavior with the crocodiles in the river?" I asked.

"Nope, the river crocs are doing normal things," he replied, almost disappointed. "Tours have been going up and down the river for the last week. Any abnormal behavior, and I would have heard about it. Let me ask you something, John?"

"Sure," I responded.

"You guys are not here on a tour, are you?" he said with a sudden, humorless look. "I mean, Sebastian is great and all—we grew up together—but he stays on the reef and in town most of the time. He's not a regular tour guide. So you come in here, with a special guide and a woman who could be a model and an army escort. Something doesn't fit. I'm not prying or anything, but you're also asking questions most people don't ask. So, can I ask you what you're really doing here?"

I thought for a minute and then decided the hell with it. If he can help, then why not tell him the truth? "We're here to investigate what is happening at the reef. I'm a veterinarian from the United States, and Nell is a neuropathologist."

"Brains and beauty," responded Stevie slyly. "You had better be careful, friend; I think she's out of your league."

"She is my partner in this," I started to explain and then opted to just move on. "We figured the crocodiles had to come from the river."

"You're right about that," answered Stevie. "The salties can survive in the ocean, but they live and feed here. The strange thing is, there have been no reports of any croc acting abnormally in these waters. Even though I know they came from here, they must have swum out to sea before they went all crazy. Don't tell people, though. I want them to continue to rent boats from me to hunt for these things. Fact is, I've increased my rates over the last week. Don't tell people that either."

"I won't," I answered, unexpectedly feeling disappointed and now quite sure this trip was going to be a waste of time. I was considering calling off the entire thing and heading back to town when I tried one last question. "Can you think of anything out of the ordinary that's happened over the last several weeks?"

Stevie wrinkled his forehead and gazed at the river. When he closed his eyes, I thought maybe he was nursing a small headache. But he opened his eyes and smiled and snapped his fingers. "A strange incident happened up the river, over a week ago," he finally said with satisfaction, almost relieved he had thought of something.

"What occurred?"

"A marsupial die-off. It was a small third page article in one of the local papers. They found a group of thirty kangaroos, wallabies, and possums all dead by the river. Authorities suspected poisoning, but no one was charged with anything."

"What happened to the bodies?"

"You are a strange man, John. What bodies are you talking about, mate? No one died."

"The animal bodies," I said, trying to hide my excitement.

"Damned if I know. It was close to a picnic area that the ecotours like to stop at, so I'm sure they were dragged away somewhere and disposed of, so the tours wouldn't be affected."

"Does Sebastian know the way to the picnic area?"

"I'm surprised Sebastian was able to find the dock," responded Stevie with a chuckle.

"I heard that," said Sebastian as he walked up the hill.

"These folks want to see picnic area number eight," Stevie said with a slap on the back that sent Sebastian three steps back down the hill. "Do you think you can manage that?"

"I'll try and bring your boat back if I can," responded Sebastian with a smile. "Let's go guys," he shouted loud enough for Nell and Walter to hear.

The boat was a twenty-four-foot, flat-bottomed craft with a small outboard motor. Four chairs on both the left and the right sides of the boat accommodated eight passengers. Sebastian took the helm at the front of the boat. Picnic area number eight was about a mile upriver. The boat was exceptionally fast, and the river was calm. I told Nell about the dead marsupials, and we scanned the banks and the shallow inlets for signs of anything abnormal, but we encountered nothing out of the ordinary.

The river and surrounding forest were astonishingly beautiful. The towering trees of the rainforest sheltered a diverse population of birds, which we both heard and saw. The trees met the edge of the water, and in most spots, I could understand why Sebastian said walking along the river was not possible. The undergrowth along the banks was so thick that we couldn't see more than a few feet into the rainforest. A few small crocodiles basked in the sun in a few clearings, amazingly resembling the stray logs here and there. Stevie was right, they didn't do much but lie perfectly still in the sun.

According to Sebastian, the limited points of access to the water served to funnel animals to a very few spots, providing excellent hunting opportunities for the adult reptiles. We slowed down in these areas but saw no large salties and no prey thirsty enough to want a drink. As we continued up the river, we passed three boats filled with people clicking photographs of the forest or whatever critter appeared interesting to them. Nothing seemed out of place.

"Are there always this many people on the river?" I asked Sebastian.

"Yes," he responded. "Most people come to spend time at the reef, but lots of the tours encourage at least a day to explore the rainforest as well. The type of people who come to Queensland tend to care about the environment and like to see as much diversity as they can. River tours are a great way to see an assortment of wildlife while never having to walk a step. Typically, it's the only place to see the salties, and like I pointed out before, tourists love to see the dangerous stuff."

We arrived at the picnic area, and the boat pulled up to a narrow dock. Sebastian jumped out and tied off the ropes. We were the only boat, although the well-worn grass path suggested this area was heavily traveled. Sebastian offered a hand to Nell as she jumped out of the boat. He followed her along the path, leaving the rest of us to scramble out of the boat ourselves. I could see why it was a popular spot to eat lunch. The panoramic views of the river were spectacular from the two, well-seasoned picnic tables that sat in a slightly elevated clearing.

"This is the place where they found the dead marsupials, according to Stevie," said Sebastian.

"Are there crocs in the river near here?" I asked.

"You could try and swim across, mate, but I wouldn't suggest it," Sebastian answered.

I grinned, taking in the expanse of the river. At this point, it couldn't be more than fifty feet wide. The surface was relatively still, with a few small ripples near the center. I threw a stick into the river, out as far as I could. It immediately took off downstream, verifying that the current was vigorous. I wondered if whoever was tasked with cleaning up the dead animals would have just cast them into the river.

"Would a crocodile eat a dead animal floating in the river?" I asked Sebastian.

"Like most carnivores, they prefer fresh kills, but if something went floating by that looked tasty, I have no doubt they would grab it," he answered.

I wasn't sure what we were going to accomplish here, but we had made the trip. "Let's spread out and see what we can find," I said to the group.

"This is a prime area for leeches," said Sebastian.

"We'll stay out of the water," I responded.

"That's always a sound notion around here, but the leeches live on land and drop from the trees," he said.

"What is this place?" asked Nell. "Things drop from the trees and try to drink your blood?"

"Welcome to Queensland," said Sebastian with a smile. "I could walk with you and show you areas to avoid if you'd like."

Nell again rolled her eyes, saying nothing. While we walked the perimeter of the clearing, Walter kept guard by sitting on a picnic bench and picking at his fingernails. It only took ten minutes to traverse the area. Other than the panoramic view of the water, there wasn't much to see.

The rainforest surrounding the clearing was thick, but the underbrush in areas was not impassable. "Let's enter the forest a bit and see what we can find," I said to Nell. She nodded in agreement.

"Don't go too far," warned Sebastian. "Stay within earshot."

We fanned out to search the area. The massive trees blocked most of the sun, creating an illusion of twilight. The forest floor was soft from years of decaying vegetation. I knelt and picked up a handful of material from the ground. The soil was black and rich and smelled of minerals. Could this place be the point of origin for an evolutionary change that caused the prion to become more threatening? Somehow I didn't think so. I stood and cleaned the residual dirt from my hands on the legs of my pants. We walked in concentric circles for about an hour without finding a thing.

"Are you thinking what I am?" I asked Nell, with a combination of disappointment and sympathy. "I know you were hoping to find a smoking gun here, but I don't think it's going to happen," she offered with a soft voice. "Why don't we head back? On the bright side, the beauty of this place alone was worth the trip." Her warm, blue-gray eyes lingered on mine for a touch longer than necessary, and then she glanced down and started walking quickly back to the clearing.

At that moment we heard Sebastian call out. "John, Nell, I think I may have found something for you."

We found our naturalist wading in a bog on the other side of the picnic area, where the water was a few inches deep. Our boots sank into the mud, creating a soft, sucking sound with each step. About thirty yards into the marsh, near the side of the river, a mangy, brushtail possum bumped into bushes as it walked, and its head was nearly turned ninety degrees to the right. The animal, no bigger than a housecat, was skin and bones and clearly hadn't eaten in days.

This is what we're looking for! "Don't lose sight of him," I said to Sebastian and Nell. I ran back to the boat and managed to find a bit of thin rope and an old tarp. This could work. I threaded the rope through the grommets on the tarp, making a crude sack.

I ran back to Nell and Sebastian. The sick possum hadn't moved more than a few feet; it seemed ready to collapse into the mud. I fashioned a bit of the rope into a crude leash and, without much effort, hooked the possum's neck and pulled him into the tarp. He thrashed and rolled for a minute, and then went deathly still.

"Is he dead?" asked Nell.

"I suspect he's just playing possum," quipped Sebastian.

I felt fully vindicated. This could be a key to the source of the prion. "We need to get him back to the hospital and see if this little guy is infected with the prion." I turned to Nell and asked, "If we can get a blood sample, can you check it for the protein?"

Nell checked her watch and turned back. "In three hours, my supplies should be in."

"They are not going to like you bringing a sick possum to a human hospital," said Sebastian.

"We'll sneak it in," I responded, ignoring the question. "I need to get some blood."

Wrapped in the tarp, the possum lay perfectly still throughout the ride back. I didn't think that he could bite through the tarp in his condition, but we all kept our distance anyway. Now going with the flow of the current, we made it back to Stevie's in about half the time it took us to get up to the picnic area. Stevie met us at the dock and looked on curiously as we loaded the tarp into the back of the jeep.

"What the hell did you catch?" he asked with curiosity.

"A neurologic possum," I answered with a triumphant tone.

"Congratulations," answered Stevie, "but so you know, they taste like shit. You would be better off eating some of the bait I have in the shop." As we pulled away, churning up dust, he called out to Sebastian, "You still owe me a night of beers for the boat."

The sky was turning a magnificent shade of fuchsia as we pulled up to the hospital. Sebastian let us out behind the building at a loading dock with an open door into the basement. We exchanged brief goodbyes and rushed inside, finding our way into a room labeled *pathology*. Two metal tables with drains stood at one end, and a large hose with a spray attachment hung nearby. Not a soul was in sight.

"This is perfect," I said, gently placing the tarp on the tile floor. With a quick search of the drawers, I found what I needed: needles, syringes, blood sample tubes with red, purple, and white tops. In another drawer I found full PPE for Nell and me.

"Can you draw blood from me?" I asked Nell.

"I haven't done it in a while, but I'll give it a try," she answered.

"That's exactly what you want to hear from your phlebotomist," I said feigning worry.

It took Nell three tries to hit a vein as I stayed as still as I could and pretended it didn't hurt. "Sorry, I told you I was a bit rusty," she apologized. Nell squeezed the samples in her hand. "I am sure these will be negative," Nell said with a reassuring smile that did not reach her eyes.

I tried to shut negative thoughts out of my head and turned to the possum. The tarp moved almost imperceptibly up and down as the sick creature breathed.

"Can you run upstairs and see if you can find Alex?" I asked Nell with a playful smile.

"Why would you want Alex to see a sick possum?" she asked.

"Mostly because I don't think he will handle it well," I responded, "but I also wanted his opinion as a neurologist."

After Nell left, I unwrapped the tarp. The mangy animal opened his eyes and didn't move for a while. After a few minutes, he took a couple of steps off of the tarp. I watched as the possum moved around the room. He still had his head turned to the right and occasionally fell over to that side, rocking over to his other side before being able to stand again. He bumped into several of the boxes on the floor and seemed to be minimally aware of his surroundings. Several minutes later, Alex and Nell arrived.

When Alex saw the sick possum, he jumped back and ran to stand behind a chair near the corner of the room. "What the hell is that thing?" he exclaimed in a panicked voice.

"A neurological possum," I responded with a satisfied smile, "and if this animal is infected with our prion, it may reveal the source. I was hoping you could help me do a neurological examination on him."

The possum took two stumbling steps toward Alex and fell over. Alex jumped onto the chair, which tipped backward and almost toppled before he quickly regained his balance.

"That thing probably has rabies, and I want nothing to do with it!" Alex exclaimed in a frantic whine. The possum had bumped into a box and was pushing his head into it, now standing perfectly still. In this state, it was about as threatening as a hummingbird, but Alex was terrified. He refused to even make eye contact with the possum or either of us.

One glance at Nell told me she was enjoying this as much as I was. The possum made a gurgling sound, which was enough to push Alex over the edge. He leapt from the chair toward the door. In his fancy dress shoes, he slipped on the linoleum floor and dropped to one knee. He let out a panicked gasp, ran to the door, threw it open and could not dash through fast enough, letting the door slam behind him as we heard him run down the hall. Nell could not contain it anymore, and we both burst out, laughing hysterically.

"Did you know he was going to react that way?" asked Nell.

"I didn't think he was going to enjoy the encounter, but I am astonished he was so freaked out," I uttered, still regaining my breath.

"Thanks," said Nell. "I really needed that."

"No problem," I responded. "I'm always happy to provide the day's entertainment."

"What do we do now?"

"I do want to get a blood sample of this possum so you can test it for the prion," I responded.

"How do you propose we do that safely?" asked Nell.

"Have you ever hit a vein on an animal?"

"You saw how I butchered your arm," she responded, "but if the choice is between holding this thing down and drawing blood, I will be the blood girl a thousand times over."

We both put on masks, full PPE gowns, and thick gloves. The possum was still pressing his head tightly against the cardboard box. His long snout allowed me to pass a lasso of gauze around his mouth and cinch it down tightly. From there, it was fairly easy to wrap him in a blanket to restrain the sick animal safely. It took several tries, but Nell was able to draw the blood she needed.

"What do we do with this thing now?" she asked.

"I guess we'll see how the tests come back," I responded. "In the meantime," I said, emptying out a box from the floor and scooping the possum into it, "do you know what room number Alex is staying at in the hotel?"

"You wouldn't," she said with a devious grin.

"Just because there are very real health risks, I would not, but I want to keep this thing for a bit, in case we need additional samples."

"I'll need several hours to analyze everything I have. I'll call you as soon as I run the samples on your blood."

"You don't have my number," I said coyly.

She stared at me for a minute and then simply said, "Well?"

I recited my number without making things any more awkward.

She turned toward the door without writing the number down. Before leaving, she looked back. "Catch up with you later?"

I gave a quick nod. "Tell Alex that if he wants a second visit with the possum, he can find me back at the hotel!" I enjoyed hearing her giggle as the door closed.

Chapter 11

THE SUN WAS SINKING BELOW the horizon as I got back to the hotel. For lack of a better option, I placed the possum, still in the box, in the tub. For safekeeping, I settled a picture from the wall over the top of the box, angled so that air could circulate.

I needed to think and had several hours before any additional information would be available. Not wanting to sit in my room alone, I headed to the pool and was surprised to see Spencer sitting by himself in a lounge chair. I took a seat next to him and collapsed, starting to realize I was, in fact, exhausted.

His expression was deadpan. "Several threads on my dry suit were cut in the right-calf and the left-shoulder areas. This did not happen by accident. I'm not sure why mine held together and yours didn't, but this was deliberate."

I shuddered. If his suit had leaked as well, neither of us would have made it back from the reef.

"We have to assume someone knows we are here and what we are doing, and this person or persons doesn't want us to succeed."

Still shocked, I said, "They wanted to kill us."

"The suits were loaded onto the boat several hours before we went out, and there was no security on the dock or the boat. Anyone could have gotten onto the boat and sabotaged the suits. I made a careless mistake—but it won't happen a second time."

"Don't beat yourself up," I said in a comforting tone.

He replied in a numb voice. "I failed, and that is unacceptable. It's only dumb luck we're both alive. Going forward, we need to assume that we'll be targeted again."

I sat back and gazed into the darkening sky. Large birds fluttered from treetop to treetop, but their flight was odd. I panicked, thinking they could be neurologic birds, but then I realized they were giant bats.

Spencer noticed them too and was watching them dart from tree to tree. "What the hell are those things?"

"Megabats," I answered. I recited what I remembered from a National Geographic documentary I had watched years ago with Dylan and Sarah. "They actually call them *flying foxes*. Their wingspan can reach a meter long. But don't worry, they eat fruits and are harmless."

"They look like something from a vampire movie," responded Spencer.

Vampire bats, killer crocodiles, an unseen murderer—I was starting to regret coming on this trip.

"Let's get something to eat," Spencer said tiredly.

We found an Italian trattoria several blocks from the hotel. We both ordered the lasagna special and munched on hot bread while we waited. The service was good, and the food came promptly.

"Where do we go from here?" I asked.

"I requested reinforcements from Mr. Smith," responded Spencer, "but the request was denied."

"Why?"

"Mr. Smith is not in the habit of ever explaining his choices, but the four of us need to get together to discuss safety. The hospital is being protected by the Australian military, and I have people watching the hotel, but the reality of the situation is that if someone does wish to hurt us, and they are patient and skilled, we don't have the resources to prevent that from happening."

"Did you explain this to Mr. Smith?!" My outrage was clear.

"I did, and he didn't seem concerned," responded Spencer. "To him, we're all pieces in a complicated chess game."

"Pawns? Knights?" I asked.

"Based on his denial of additional resources, my guess is that we're closer to pawns at this point," responded Spencer. "But you have my word I will do whatever I can to protect you all. I also asked him about the boat that Sebastian described disappearing. His denial at knowing anything about it was very quick and unconvincing."

"I don't like the feeling I'm getting," I said.

"Let me put it this way," said Spencer while taking a sip of espresso. "If he didn't know anything about it, an appropriate response would have been something like *give me some time to check into it*. By saying he didn't know anything about it, he either didn't care, which would be out of character for someone in the intelligence business, or he already knew the answer and didn't want to tell me. I think this second scenario makes more sense. He knows what happened and wants to keep the information from me, which makes me angry."

"Is there anything you can do?" I asked.

"The guiding principle in the military is the chain of command. Typically you go up the chain, one rung at a time, if you need to accomplish something. For this mission, I was essentially pimped out to Mr. Smith because I have certain skills he finds desirable, and that makes the chain of command irrelevant. My most superior officer reports to Mr. Smith in this current situation. Whether I like it or not, only one rung in the chain separates us—the buck begins and stops with Mr. Smith."

Returning to the hotel, I was a jangle of nerves. Was it just last night that I felt paranoid, walking through the town with Nell? Now, with Spencer, I couldn't help but peer down every alley and search the expression of every face we passed. My mind started to play tricks on me. Were people staring at us, were hidden faces lurking in the shadows? Were we being followed from a distance?

As if reading my mind, Spencer simply said, "It's hard."

"What is?"

"Turning off the noise," he responded. "Trying to distinguish an innocent look from the look of those who mean you harm."

"So how do you do it? My mind is playing tricks on me. I feel *very* paranoid. I doubt I'll sleep tonight."

"It's more a feeling than anything else," Spencer said. "Do you know the ten-thousand-hours theory?"

Without getting into a discussion, I indicated I was familiar with the theory. In fact, I used it with my residents all the time. About fifty years ago, Dr. Simon and Dr. Chase wrote a paper explaining that to become an expert at anything, it takes at least ten thousand hours of practice. Dr. Malcolm Gladwell popularized this in his books. But a correlative is that experts, for whom things appear to come naturally, do not get there without failures and time. Musicians, chess experts, mathematicians, and surgeons who are highly successful all struggle before they become experts. No person is immune to this, and no one is naturally gifted enough to be an expert without excessive practice at a task. At times I believe it, and at times I do not. I have no doubt that practice is important to get good at anything, but some people *are* naturally more gifted. For example, I could practice the violin for ten thousand hours, and while I'll get better at it, I'll never reach the level of the people who play for the New York Symphony.

"Well," said Spencer, "if it makes you feel any better, I've spent the better part of twenty years becoming a *danger expert*, and I know the difference between people with a sinister intent and those without. Call it a sixth sense if you will, but you develop a feeling for when there are actually faces in the shadows or when someone is following you."

"Are you getting that sense now?" I asked, still apprehensive.

He smiled. "We're safe right now."

Somehow, I didn't feel much better. My phone buzzed in my pocket, and I picked it up without recognizing the number.

"You are negative," came Nell's voice over the receiver. Without even realizing how much tension had built up in my body, I felt a flood of relief and relaxed.

"Thanks, Nell. You are the best!"

"I'm going to work on the possum blood now. It shouldn't take long," she said and hung up before I could say anything else. I shared the welcome news with Spencer, and we both returned to the hotel with lighter steps.

Spencer initiated a plan for the four of us to meet as soon as possible to discuss how to proceed safely. Leaving him to call Alex and Nell, I walked to my room, locking the door behind me. Collapsing on the bed, my kids were front and center in my thoughts. What time is it in the United States? What time is it here? Exhaustion overtook me, and I craved a two-day sleep.

I closed my eyes for what felt like a second, but when I checked my phone, over forty-five minutes had elapsed. Tossing the phone on the bed, I headed to the bathroom. I ran the water in the sink for about ten seconds for it to get warmer. It didn't, but I decided the cold water would work better anyway. I splashed my face with a bit of the icy water and blindly grabbed a towel from the rack, burying my face deep into it. The water had helped—my own sixth sense kicked in. Something was out of place. I scanned the bathroom, shocked to see the tub was empty, except for the picture in its frame.

Panicking, I ran out of the bathroom and crashed into the door frame, nearly tumbling to the floor. The chain lock seemed to take forever to release, and I imagined someone attacking me from behind. Not even bothering to close the door, I sprinted to Spencer's room. I pounded on the door, and Spencer answered almost immediately, with a gun in his hand.

"What's wrong?" He said, alarmed.

"Someone has been in my room," I shouted, suddenly realizing how frazzled I was.

"How do you know?" he asked.

"Because the possum is missing," I gasped.

When he responded with confusion, I realized I hadn't told him about my afternoon. It took me several minutes to calm down and another several minutes to fill him in as to why there was a neurologically abnormal possum in my tub.

"Are you sure it didn't simply climb out of the tub and wander away?" asked Spencer.

"And take the cardboard box with him?" I asked.

"Good point," said Spencer, grabbing his bag which was already packed. "That makes my decision even easier. It's time to leave this place."

Nell and Alex had just gotten back from the hospital. We stopped by Nell's room and then Alex's and watched them gather up their belongings before going back to my room. My door was still open, and Spencer took about ten seconds to search the room before allowing me to quickly pack. We were heading out when I looked at my bed and realized my phone was missing. I was sure I had thrown it on the bed, and now it was nowhere to be found.

"Time to go," said Spencer with military authority. "Let's move it."

"My phone's missing. I'm sure I left it on the bed," I explained.

"Do you have it locked with a reasonable passcode?" asked Spencer.

"What do you mean reasonable?" I asked.

"I mean could someone easily crack your secret passcode," responded Spencer sarcastically.

My passcode was my son's birth year. "Yes," I lied.

We headed to a waiting jeep, and Spencer grabbed a computer from the passenger's seat. "We may have caught a break here," said Spencer, his eyes constantly scanning around rather than at the screen as he handed me the computer. "Can you log into your Apple account? I want to try and track your phone."

It only took a second to log into my Apple ID. No signal registered, and Spencer gave a disappointed sigh. "You need to remotely erase the phone," he commanded.

"You can do that?"

"Oh, for God's sake, give me that," said Alex, grabbing the computer from me. It took him a few keystrokes to complete the task. "Can we please head out now? I feel like a sitting duck here."

Spencer jumped into the driver's seat and we drove away from the hotel.

"There are more sophisticated ways we can try and track it, but whoever took it is probably smart enough to know that. We'll try anyway."

"Why would they want my phone?" I asked.

"It's really a matter of reconnaissance," answered Spencer. "You try and find out as much about your enemy as you can so you can anticipate their moves."

Enemy. I'm no one's enemy here; I'm trying to help. A growing unease crept into my stomach as I realized how far over my head I was. I stared into the night as the jeep bounced along the road, trying not to imagine faces peering back at me from the surrounding woods. It took about thirty minutes to get to our destination—an army barracks. Armed guards stood at a gate house, and the entire area was surrounded with chain-link fencing.

"This place is not impenetrable," said Spencer, "but it's a much more controlled environment than the hotel."

We walked to a large metal structure in the middle of the base. Inside was a room to the left, with four cots and makeshift curtains between the beds. We threw our stuff down and proceeded to head to a conference room with a laptop computer on the table. The picture on the screen showed a live feed of a very sour-faced Mr. Smith. We all took seats without a word.

"Where are we?" Mr. Smith asked. "I would like a full report from each of you, starting with Dr. King."

Alex took a deep breath. In a tired and bleak tone, he said, "They are all dead. Everyone who had a wound from the crocodiles has died. We tried every treatment we could think of, and despite our efforts, the neurological signs rapidly progressed. I have never seen anything like this. MRIs showed that the spongiform changes in the brain grew in a matter of hours."

"Unfortunately, that is what we found in Memphis as well," said Mr. Smith. "All sixteen people who developed the disease had severe, rapid progression and died within days. The MRI findings and the findings on the postmortem examination all point to a prion as the cause of death. The people were of varying ages and states of health, but all had eaten at the same barbecue restaurant a day before they got sick. We have shut the place down, of course, and are working on a complete examination of everyone and everything related to the restaurant. No one else is sick, and there are no signs of a residual prion anywhere to be found. Dr. Osler, what have you found?"

"The neurological signs in the crocodiles were consistent with the neurological problems in the people. We asked the Australian authorities to get the remaining animals out of the water so that we can minimize the potential for other animals getting sick. I think we have a connection to an outbreak up the Daintree River. Several marsupials got sick, and if they made it into the river, which is likely, then that's how the big crocodiles got the disease. We even managed to find a sick possum and got blood from it for testing, but the possum was stolen."

Mr. Smith's eyes widened. This must've been the first piece of information he didn't know about prior to this meeting.

"What do you mean?" he asked.

I filled him in on the possum that was taken from my hotel room, along with my phone.

Smith glared at Spencer. "Why was I not told about this?" he asked in an extremely judgmental tone.

"It just happened," replied Spencer, "and my first priority was getting these three to safety."

"I need real-time information. Understood?"

"Understood," said Spencer, unfazed, returning the icy glare. The screen abruptly went blank, and Mr. Smith's face disappeared for about sixty seconds.

"Is the meeting over?" asked Alex.

Mr. Smith's face reappeared, even more irritated.

"We can't track the phone," he grumbled, still glaring at Spencer, who didn't seem to care. "It was disabled in a way I have not ever seen, which may prove helpful over time."

I didn't understand what he was talking about, but he asked me to proceed with my report. "Needless to say, we don't know if the possum had the same disease, so I can't confirm my theory," I continued.

"That's not true," interrupted Nell.

"Explain," said Mr. Smith now turning his black gaze to Nell.

Unperturbed, Nell continued. "I took the blood we collected from the possum through a process called protein misfolding cyclic amplification. We ran it through a Western blot and found a massive spike in a protein at the size of thirty-five kilodaltons, about the same size as the bovine spongiform prion. This protein also lit up like a Christmas tree when I subjected it to a stain with antibodies to the BSE prion. An identical pattern was seen in the proteins from the brain tissue in the people and in the crocodiles. So there is no question this protein particle is causing the disease.

"The only thing that doesn't make sense is that the protein showed up in massive quantities in the blood of the possum, without the amplification. I have never seen this before. That means either something is wrong with the test, or somehow this prion is multiplying in the blood in massive amounts, incredibly fast, which would explain the increase in how contagious this prion has become. Something changed in the protein that allowed it to become more aggressive and much more fatal."

Mr. Smith listened quietly to Nell's presentation, but I had the distinct impression he already knew all of this. "Spencer," he said, "do you have any additional updates?"

Spencer glanced apprehensively at the three of us, "Only that there is undeniable evidence someone knows we are here and what we're doing. I feel we face a significant threat. At least one attempt on our lives has occurred, and I can't protect these three in this country without the allocation of significant additional resources. I don't know who is after us, and therefore I don't know where 'safe' is."

"Then I think it's time for you all to come home," replied Mr. Smith. "I appreciate what you have learned, but there is no more information I can gain from you being there."

The image in the computer instantly flicked off. The relief in the room was palpable. *Home* sounded really appealing.

"What, no 'thank you for your service'?" I asked, with a wink at Spencer.

"Mr. Smith is not a thank-you kind of guy," he responded. "Let's get you three home."

"About time," said Alex under his breath.

Chapter 12

I**T TOOK AN HOUR TO** get back to the plane. At least they were letting us take the supersonic jet to get home. I remembered how long it took to get home from Queensland the last time I flew, and between the flights and the connections, it was exhausting.

Ponytail met us at the door as we climbed up the gangplank. What had this guy been doing the entire time? Sleeping on the plane? We all climbed aboard and strapped into the seats. Somehow, I felt defeated. Did we even help the situation? What was the point of all of this? We were no closer to solving this mystery than we were two days ago, and I had almost gotten myself killed.

It was too much to process, so I closed my eyes as the big engines started to scream. The chairs turned, and I again felt the unrelenting G-force push me into the back of the seat. It wasn't as bad this time. Being through an experience once made it less concerning the second time. I've seen this in surgery. Teaching young doctors the skills of the trade involves no magic—only repetition. Once you perform a task enough times, it becomes second nature. I tried to think: at what point did I reach ten thousand hours? Was there any one thing I had done ten thousand times?

A few minutes later, we reached a constant speed and altitude. The seats again swiveled to face each other, and the middle table rose from the floor. I smiled at my companions. In a little over three hours, we would be home.

"A new outbreak has been reported." Mr. Smith's voice came over the noise-canceling headphones.

My smile vanished and Alex groaned. Disappointment showed on every face. I knew what was coming next, and the prospect of going home and sleeping in my own bed faded rapidly.

"Two Americans in the northern Serengeti were attacked by a hyena. The bites were relatively minor, thanks to the quick action of their safari guide, but both people were airlifted to a nearby hospital in Kenya as a precaution. This happened three days ago. Despite the minor wounds, both were declared dead an hour ago, due to an aggressive and progressive multifocal neurological disease. The bodies of the deceased are being flown back to the United States to be analyzed. Unfortunately, the medical facilities in Kenya do not allow for extensive testing, but it sounds like the same disease we have been tracking. I need you to proceed to Tanzania to investigate the site of the animal attacks to look for parallels to the Australia outbreak."

We started to object, but the lack of response from Mr. Smith told us that he was either off the line or didn't care. In either case, the plane was being diverted to Tanzania.

"This is bullshit," said Alex.

We were all thinking the same thing. We're not military. Although we had volunteered for this, there were limits. Spencer rose and approached the cockpit and pounded on the door. An aggravated Ponytail answered. Spencer didn't give him the opportunity to retreat back into the cockpit, but rather grabbed his collar and led him back to the rest of us.

"We need more information, and since I can't beat it out of Mr. Smith, you will have to do," said Spencer in a voice that made me shudder.

A nervous Ponytail, encountering four angry faces, seemingly made the decision to try and help, or at least give the impression of helping. "What do you want to know?" he asked. His eyes darted around the plane as if an exit would immediately present itself.

"To start with, why are we going to Africa?" shouted Alex, getting into Ponytail's face. One look from Spencer sent Alex sitting back into his seat. Spencer wanted to direct the questions.

Ponytail stared at Alex and then at Spencer before answering. "You heard Mr. Smith, to see if there are parallels in the cases between Australia and Africa," he answered nervously. Spencer stared deep into his eyes and let the uncomfortable silence hang in the air. It was a long, full thirty seconds before Ponytail continued. "Okay, I'll tell you something I shouldn't: you aren't the first group we had tracking this. The first group was comprised of four scientists with a background in prion diseases. We lost contact with them twenty-four hours before you guys were recruited. They didn't turn up anything. You guys did, and for that reason alone, Mr. Smith sees value in having you continue. I don't know what he hopes to accomplish by your involvement, I really don't. You met the guy. He doesn't explain his reasoning to anyone, even me. Until he decides that you no longer have value in this mission, you're stuck."

"Tell me what happened to the other group on the boat that *disappeared*," demanded Spencer.

"We don't know—honestly."

Even I could tell he was lying, or at least not revealing everything. Spencer's right fist clenched and he stood and towered over the frail man as though he was going to hit him. Ponytail sunk into his seat and raised his hands to divert an impending punch.

"Then tell me what you do know," said Spencer with a suddenly gentle tone. The change had a distinct unsettling effect. Ponytail was becoming unnerved, which I think was Spencer's intention. He was good at this.

"I've already gone out on a limb by telling you anything," Ponytail pleaded. "He is always listening." A look from Spencer let him know he was not going to get away without giving us more information. "Okay, okay. Their boat left the dock at eight a.m. We were tracking it out to the reef via satellite. The boat was bugged, so we heard everything that was said. No one approached the boat, and no one got off. There was no abnormal chatter on the radio. No one said anything out of the ordinary on the trip, just a long, boring discussion about protein-based diseases. I think that's why Mr. Smith has been impressed with you guys. So far, you have thought about things from a new perspective. Bringing in local resources, finding another animal infected with the prion. Believe it or not, all that helps us narrow down the list of suspects.

"Back to what happened to the boat please," urged Spencer.

"The boat was checked ten minutes before departure, and no explosives were on board. However, the boat never reached the reef. About ten minutes before they arrived, we heard an explosion. We don't know how or why, but the boat sank in a matter of seconds. Mr. Smith came to the conclusion it could have been an accident."

"Do you still think that?" said Spencer with sarcasm.

"Can I go back to the cockpit now?" said Ponytail, uncomfortable with his position. Spencer thought about it for a bit, but then moved out of his way.

"Do you believe that guy?" asked Nell in an aggravated tone.

Spencer simply put a single finger to his lips and looked up. We all got the message. There was no more discussion to be had with big brother listening and likely watching. We were heading to Africa.

We all shut our eyes and tried to get a bit of sleep. I drifted off in an instant and dreamed of dark shadows and eyes peering in the night. We landed two hours later at Kilimanjaro Airport. It was morning, but again, I had lost track of what day of the week it was. I didn't bother asking, since at this point, it really made no difference. I wished I had my phone, a line to connect to my kids. Based on the way Alex was holding his phone up in the air, I doubted we'd get service anyway.

Tanzania was much cooler than I thought it would be. The day was crystal clear, and we could see snow on top of Kilimanjaro in the distance. Because it rose so high, I guessed it remained capped in every season. Nell, Alex, and I sat down on a bench outside the terminal, near the runway. Spencer curtly told us to stay put before disappearing into the building.

The sun felt alive on my face as I surveyed the surroundings. The airport itself was small, with a single runway. A small jet descended, landed, and came to a stop in the middle of the runway. The ground crew efficiently pushed a metal stairway to the side of the plane and signaled to the cockpit that it was safe to open the door. As the people disembarked, they were directed into the one-story, yellow building, surrounded by colorful shrubs. The construction appeared to be from the 1960s or earlier, with no significant updates. A little lizard scurried by our feet, and Alex lifted both feet off the ground as if the little guy was going to attack. I found this amusing and chuckled, which brought a curious stare from both Alex and Nell.

"What could you possibly find funny in this situation?" asked Alex.

"Nothing," I responded, not wanting to get into it.

Spencer appeared from the door and waved us in, so we grabbed our bags and walked inside the airport, which was white and very clean, almost like a hospital ward. Several small restaurants had short lines. Most people were eating burgers and fries at elevated tables surrounded by bar stools. Apparently, you can get burgers and fries anywhere in the world. A long line of people waited at immigration, but a uniformed officer waved Spencer and the three of us through. Several people gave us dirty looks.

We proceeded to exit through the front entrance of the airport. "We need to take a prop plane to get to where we're going," explained Spencer, "so we'll drive to a local airport."

"Why can't we take the jet?" asked Alex.

"You'll see when we get there," grinned Spencer.

We piled into a roomy Toyota Land Cruiser, driven by a local. The ride took only twenty minutes, but it was scenic. Coffee plantations lined the road on both sides and stretched for miles through rolling hills. I sighted several black-and-white monkeys in the higher trees, eating some sort of fruit, and the air was fragrant, if dusty.

We arrived at the tiny Arusha Airport. Single and double prop planes sat parked along its single runway, reminiscent of cab stands at US airports.

Spencer again asked us to wait in the parking lot and entered the terminal. "Why do we have to wait like children while he goes inside?" asked Alex with annoyance.

A few minutes later, Spencer motioned us inside. "What is going on?" I asked.

"Military protection 101," responded Spencer. "No one can sabotage a vehicle or replace a pilot with one of their own if you don't make any plans in advance. Being unpredictable and random can make all the difference in the world."

"Then how can you ever know that anything will be available?" Nell asked.

"Discretionary spending fund," answered Spencer with a smile. "At least Mr. Smith is good for something, if not information. If you have the cash, you never have a problem finding transportation. Besides, I can be very persuasive if I want to be." He playfully elbowed me in the ribs, and I pretended it didn't hurt.

The plane was a six-seater that smelled like soil after the rains. We clambered into the back, and Spencer took the copilot seat in the front. With the flip of several switches by the pilot, the two propellers revved, and we were on our way. The noise of the prop did not allow for conversation, but at least there were no noise-canceling headphones conducting the voice of Mr. Smith. I looked out the window to try and get a sense of our bearings. Kilimanjaro remained visible for the first fifteen minutes of the flight before fading from view into the morning sky.

Civilization itself faded away. The plane was traveling at a low altitude, so the ground was clearly visible. Roads and buildings could be seen for a short while until the landscape melted into what appeared to be dry shrubs and low hills for as far as I could see. Not a soul—human or animal—interrupted the monotonous flow of earth below.

After about an hour, the plane began its descent. Now an azure river with obvious white rapids in sections wound through the landscape, and the ground had become greener, as if someone had just sprinkled vibrant colors from the sky.

The ground seemed alive, moving in places, until I realized thousands and thousands of dark-colored animals were moving in unison across the plain. Wildebeests. So many creatures congregated at the side of the river, they obliterated the ground, and patches of dust were the only evidence of the earth. I imagined the sound and the vibrations that would be created by thousands of hooves pounding the dry ground simultaneously. The great migration—seeing it had been on my bucket list for years. This almost incomprehensible mass of animals, roaming for hundreds of miles, searched for greener grass and the hope of more nutritious feed for their young.

Of course, with the herd came the predators. As we descended, I could start to make out individual animals with short horns and massive shoulders. I had stepped back in time. Is this what the world was like before people started to carve it up with roads and towns and pollution and masses of humanity in cities? What a sight it would have been to see the great plains of the United States a few hundred years ago, where the buffalo ruled.

The runway came into view. We were only a few hundred feet from the ground now, and I understood why Spencer chuckled at the thought of landing the jet here. The runway looked no longer than the length of a high-school track, and the landing area was nothing but a grass field—in the middle of which a herd of zebras grazed. I found myself moving my legs forward and pushing my feet into an imaginary brake. I gripped the arm rests of the seat and watched my knuckles turn white. The zebras still did not move as the tires of the plane touched the ground. I glanced at the pilot, who was not overly concerned as his craft bore down on the animals. How much damage would a zebra do to a moving plane? When we were merely feet from the animals, they galloped to the side of the runway. They gazed back at the plane, and I swear, if animals could look annoyed, they certainly did. Our flight ended near a shed with one dirty window. The terminal. The engine shut down and we began to hear normal sounds. Spencer announced, "We're here. Let's get out."

"I really don't want to be in this environment," said Alex. "I'm much more of a city-sidewalk kind of guy. I don't suppose there's any way that Mr. Smith will allow me back to the United States?" he continued. "I don't need the jet. I'd be happy to fly commercial and make all the arrangements myself. I'll take my chances with a lawsuit if I have to, but this is nerve-racking. We're in the exact middle of nowhere."

"Don't worry. I heard the tents are very nice," replied Spencer.

"Tents!" exploded Alex. "I don't think so."

"You could always sleep under the stars if you want," replied Spencer, "but a lot of things wouldn't give a second thought to eating you out here."

Realizing no other option would present itself, Alex responded, "Fine, but Mr. Smith is in for a whopper of a lawsuit when I get back to the city. I know most of the finest lawyers in the area and--"

Spencer, Nell, and I had already deboarded, and Alex realized there was no one listening to him anymore. We watched him climb out of the plane, tentatively alighting onto the grass below. Being very close to the equator, the weather here was remarkably different than it had been in the shadow of Kilimanjaro. The sun had climbed into its late-morning position, heating the air to the mid-nineties, without a wisp of breeze.

A truck pulled up and two women got out. The passenger approached us wearing a red robe that covered both shoulders and hung below her knees. Her tightly braided hair matched braided earrings extending below her shoulders. She carried a long walking stick and a beaming smile. With a heavy accent, she introduced herself as Zawadi. The driver was dressed in a khaki-colored, button-down shirt with a matching hat and green cargo shorts. "I'm Sarah," she said. She saw my face light up and raised a friendly eyebrow.

"That's also my daughter's name."

"It's a good name," she proclaimed with a smile.

The truck looked like a long pickup truck with the cab removed. A tan canopy held up with four metal poles extended the length of the vehicle. The windshield was folded down onto the hood. In the back were three rows of cushioned stadium chairs, which provided a great vantage point to see out of the vehicle. On the side of the doors, a silhouetted logo depicted an acacia tree, a sunset, and a strolling giraffe. Below the beautiful picture it said *Wild Africa*. Zawadi grabbed our bags and threw them into the back of the truck like they were weightless, ignoring our attempts to help.

"Let's go," Sarah said. "I understand you want to see the area where the hyena attacks occurred. That wouldn't be my first choice of what to see around here, but you guys are calling the shots."

Sarah transitioned into the role of tour guide as we left the airport. She had been doing this for the last ten years, originally hailing from the outskirts of London. She came to Africa as a Peace Corps volunteer right after college and immediately fell in love with the continent. She had gone back to London for a year after the volunteer experience, since her parents wanted her to take over the family business, a bakery, and lead the fourth generation of owners. "Since the time I could walk, I spent every free hour working in the shop, and I never liked it," she explained. Even though her entire family, including her two younger sisters, loved it, it got to the point that the smell of baking bread, which most people find so wonderful, actually made her sick to her stomach. She found herself waking up every morning, miserable, at four a.m. to get to work so people could have fresh bread and rolls before their day started.

She longed for the open skies and freedom of living in Africa. Sara had gotten so depressed that she started taking medication until she came to the realization the city life and the family business were slowly choking her. She told her parents she was moving to Africa. Unfortunately, they did not take it well, and she had not spoken to her family in ten years. She sent Christmas cards every year but, sadly, never received replies.

Her enthusiasm for the hard choice she made, however, showed. Sarah spoke with such passion about the land she had left her previous life for. We could not help but be drawn into her life story and love for Africa. As she casually pointed out various plants and nesting sites, I found her knowledge of the area impressive. She knew the unmarked winding roads like the back of her hand. None of the roads were paved, and to even call them roads in some areas was a stretch. At first, I was disappointed with how few animals we had seen.

I had almost forgotten Zawadi was in the car, since Sarah was so engaging. Suddenly, Zawadi sat up straight and didn't seem to shift her eyes to either side, but out of nowhere she said, "There is a pride of lions to the left."

Our heads all turned in unison as Sarah slowed the car. I did not see anything. Sarah carefully pulled the car off the dirt road and onto an area of knee-deep grass. The car crept quietly along until we came to a full stop. About a hundred yards away in the shade of a small tree, six adult lions slept in the grass. Eight cubs played around the adults and occasionally jumped on one of the female lions. We watched in awe as these animals remained unaware of our presence. To see life go on and to simply be observing an unspoiled moment of pure nature took my breath away.

Spencer interrupted the magic.

"We're not here to see the wildlife. Let's move on, shall we?"

Sarah looked hurt, and I couldn't help but be disappointed. As we slowly backed onto the dirt road and pulled away, it struck me: we had not seen another person or even the signs of another person since we deplaned.

"We'll need to cross the river," said Zawadi. "The sixth bridge is the closest, and the wildebeests have been massing on the banks all morning. If we are lucky, we may catch a crossing." I grinned. I guess you can't take the safari guide out of these two, despite Spencer.

Several minutes before we got to the river, I began remembering a class called *ambulatory*, which was required in veterinary school. We students were meant to learn about the management of farms with large numbers of dairy cattle and the basics of herd health. Because of the logistics of the course, only three students were enrolled at a time, and the class was offered throughout the year. Everyone wanted to take it in the fall or spring, before it got too cold or too hot. Unfortunately, I was assigned the class in the heat of early August. I still recall coming home and having to strip down to my underwear in front of our condo since the smells associated with this experience were so foul my wife would not permit me in the house with my clothes on. Some days, the stink was so intense that Julia pleaded with me to hose off in the garden before entering to shower. Perhaps it was this past experience, but I definitely smelled the herd before I was able to see anything.

Next came the flying insects. Without warning, a horde of flies buzz-bombed the truck. We rounded the corner and went down a small hill toward the sixth bridge—which really wasn't a bridge. It was a cement structure across the river with multiple, rusted, eight-foot steel pipes underneath to allow for the passage of water. In the center of the cement, the water was high enough that it was passing over the bridge as well. We slowed down as the water rose near the tops of the tires. The landscape to the left of the bridge was a sight to behold. Thousands of wildebeests and zebras had massed on the steep banks. In the river I could see crocodiles swimming back and forth, almost willing the herd into the water. Further upstream, hippopotamuses were wallowing in the shallows of the river.

"Did you know that a group of hippos is actually called a *bloat*?" asked Sarah to the group.

"They are going to go," said Zawadi, still staring straight ahead.

All at once, the entire herd of wildebeests charged down the steep embankment and entered the water, as if someone turned on a faucet of animals. I noted their coordinated, normal motions. The front of the herd could not have turned back if they wanted to. Animals poured down the banks of the river, trampling the smaller, slower ones, each with fear in their eyes and one goal; get to the other side as quickly as possible. Not all of the herd made it, but most did. A few of the ones that got pushed to the sides were singled out by the crocodiles in the river. Their massive tails thrashed as their jaws clamped on to the nearest prey. Nature was ferocious, but all was as it should be. As the quickest in the herd reached the far side of the riverbank and scrambled up the other side, Sarah pulled the truck further along the bridge, far enough forward so we were no longer in the water but were able to watch the spectacle. She glanced at Spencer as if to ask if this was okay, but even Spencer was mesmerized by the thundering sea of mammals. The crossing went on for at least twenty minutes without slowing down.

"How many are there?" I asked Sarah.

"In a moderate-sized crossing like this, probably fifty thousand, but some consist of a few hundred thousand," she answered in a perfect tour guide voice. "This is one of the sites that people come from all over the world to see. Worth the price of admission, right?" she asked with a playful smile.

Sarah eventually put the car into gear and we crossed the remainder of the bridge and up the steep embankment on the other side. She turned the car along the river and we drove slowly, watching the stream of wildebeest risking their lives for the promise of greener pastures. The herd enveloped us as we drove upstream through their path along the far side of the river. The animals enshrouded the truck as if they didn't even notice we were there. The survivors of the passage were already enjoying the rich, green grass on this side of the river.

"The attack occurred about two miles upstream on this side of the river," said Sarah. "We need to be cautious. Authorities have told tours to avoid this area, even though the hyenas were killed, and no others have been spotted acting in an aggressive manner."

"Where are they?" I asked.

"Where are who?" responded Sarah.

"The bodies of the killed animals," I asked.

"I don't know, but we can ask when we get to camp. They were probably incinerated or buried."

"Does this thing have sides that can be put up?" asked Alex motioning to the truck.

"Afraid not," said Sarah. "That is why we have Zawadi."

"What is she going to do if something tries to jump in here, hit it with her stick?" asked Alex.

"She won't have to," responded Sarah. "She will let me know if anything dangerous gets close, so we can avoid it."

"How can she do that?" asked Nell.

"The same way she knew about the lions in the tall grass off the road and that the wildebeests were going to cross," explained Sarah. "I can't explain it, but some people are so in tune with the world out here, they can sense things. They have developed that close a relationship with this world."

"That's bullshit," said Alex. "Is there even a gun in this truck?"

"Let me ask you a question, Alex," said Sarah. "If I let you out of the truck right now and asked you to take a walk, even with a gun, how long do you think you would live?"

"Ten minutes?"

"*If* you were lucky," agreed Sarah. "A gun wouldn't help. You can't fight things out here; you need to avoid them. The Maasai tribe, of which Zawadi is a member, has been living in this environment for at least the last three hundred years. They walk around with nothing but a wood staff to protect themselves. They shepherd herds of goats across the plains. Their ancestors have lived on this land for God knows how long. The oldest known fossil of a human was found not far from here, dating back over three million years. Zawadi could get out of the truck right now, and if I picked her up a week later, she'd be fine."

"I'm not sure I believe you," muttered Alex.

"I can't fix that. But people like you and me don't get nature the way she does. For most of the planet, development and the constant need to consume destroys the world around us. People don't live *in* nature but rather take steps to avoid it. That is a recent development in the history of humankind. You have to believe me when I say having Zawadi sit next to me is much, much safer than having any gun."

Throughout this conversation, Zawadi sat with her eyes straight forward and didn't say a word.

"We're almost at the spot of the hyena attack," said Sarah.

Nell asked, "How did it unfold?"

"Two hyenas stalked the van, much like the one we're in now, which slowed for the tourists to get a better look. Before now, hyena attacks on vans were unheard of. One animal jumped up and bit the arm of a middle-aged woman sitting in the rear," Sarah explained.

This caused all of us to scoot toward the center of the truck and pull our arms away from the sides of the vehicle.

"The hyena latched on," Sarah continued, "pulling the woman out of her seat. Her husband grabbed her and managed to dump a full bottle of beer into the hyena's mouth and nose, causing it to let go for a second, allowing the husband to pull his wife back in. In the process, the husband got severely scratched on his hand. They were both airlifted to a hospital in Kenya, but I don't know what happened to them. Rangers were called in to try and find the hyenas that did this. I thought it was a fool's errand, since packs of hyenas are known to roam for miles at a time. But the two were found right near where the attack had occurred. They were rolling in the grass, unable to walk for more than a few steps without falling over. They were shot in the head and taken away by the rangers."

"Have any other incidents been reported?" I asked.

"None. The community around here is small, and if anything out of the ordinary had occurred, we would know about it. I've never known a hyena to be so bold around people in the middle of the day," replied Sarah. "This area is huge with tourists. People come from all over the world to see the great migration. If animals attacked people in trucks, the safaris would be permanently shut down."

"Hyenas are scavengers," Zawadi said in her accented English. "They hunt mostly at night and will travel in a pack, but they prefer to steal prey from the cats that kill, especially cheetahs. The smaller cats are no match for a group of hyenas. They will bring down prey and then lose their meal to the scavengers. Hyenas are not smart. They will eat the tires off cars occasionally. This woman is lucky the hyena did not take her arm clean off. A hyena can crush large stones with its jaws, if it wants to. When confronted during the day, they simply run away. A hyena wants nothing to do with people. Some attacks on people have been reported over the years, but always at night and always with a pack. This activity now is unheard of in a healthy animal. There was something wrong with those two. There is talk of evil spirits in the grasslands. Something has disrupted the balance of nature." Zawadi went back to staring straight ahead, her eyes not straying to the right or to the left. "There are no hyenas near here now, but I am uneasy. Something is not right."

"Did you say the husband was merely scratched? Not actually bitten?" asked Alex. "That must be a mistake."

"That's what we were told, but I wasn't there," answered Sarah.

We drove around in concentric circles in the immediate area for the next hour and found nothing amiss. All the animals we saw were behaving as they should.

"I'm a bit embarrassed to ask, but how does someone go to the bathroom around here?" said Nell with a nervous chuckle.

"We'll go to the picnic area," said Sarah. "That will be the safest. It's near here."

Alarm bells went off in my head. The origin of both outbreaks being so close to picnic areas? It couldn't be a coincidence. Even though the two outbreaks were seven thousand miles and a full ocean away from each other, the source of each was near where tour groups congregated to eat food.

The "picnic area" was just a field overlooking the Mara River. The view was spectacular, but there were no tables or facilities.

"And the bathrooms are . . .?" asked Nell.

"Boys on the driver's side and girls on the passenger's side is the way we typically do things," answered Sarah. "Give Zawadi five minutes to make sure things are safe."

Without a word Zawadi got out of the truck and walked the perimeter of the field. At one point she stared into a line of trees for a full minute without moving as the wind blew through her robes. She moved effortlessly and made no sound. It was almost as if she floated an inch above the ground.

"There are a few big cats in the far distance, but they are moving away from us," she said when she got back to the truck. "The wind is blowing our scent in the other direction."

I wondered if this was a good thing or a bad thing, but Sarah was already getting out of the truck.

When we got back in the truck, I asked Sarah, "So who uses this area?"

"A lot of the tours that come through stop here, because it's as safe as you can get on the Serengeti and a nice area to set up a table and eat lunch."

"Would a scavenger come through here and eat the trash?" I asked.

"No trash," said Sarah. "The companies that are allowed to use the land understand the concept of leaving nothing behind. If a company didn't follow the rules, they wouldn't be allowed back next season."

"If something *were* left behind, would a hyena eat it?" I rephrased my question.

"A hyena would eat anything it finds, including something deliberately left behind, if I get the point of your question."

Spencer immediately pulled out his phone.

"There's no cellular service for miles," said Sarah.

"This phone doesn't need cellular service," he said, stepping out of the car, moving to beyond earshot, keeping his eyes along the edges of the picnic area. I wasn't sure if he was watching for animals or people or both. He soon jumped back into the truck.

"How many camps are in this area?" Spencer asked Sarah.

"About two hundred camps are stationed along both sides of the river."

"This is the first solid lead we've had," said Spencer with a bit of excitement in his voice. "Mr. Smith is going to cross-reference groups between Queensland and here to see if any tour groups have followed this path. If anything is to be found, he'll find it. It shouldn't take him long, as it's got to be a short list."

The sun began to set over the horizon, and the sky turned a stunning shade of orange. The acacia trees in the fading light looked exactly like the logo on the side of the truck. A herd of elephants walked by in the distance, silhouetted by the setting sun. It was magical.

Sarah, ever the tour guide, turned back and said, "Do you know what a herd of elephants is called? A *memory*," she said with a distant smile.

As the jeep bumped along the road in the setting sun, Nell leaned over to get a better view of the sunset from my side of the van. She put her hand on my shoulder as she leaned in closer. I found myself enjoying her proximity until the spell was broken by Alex.

"Can we get out of this country now? I think we've done more than enough for Mr. Smith, and I want to go home."

Nell leaned back to her side of the truck, leaving me disappointed. I felt like an embarrassed high schooler with a crush. What was wrong with me? This was so out of character.

"Bush pilots don't fly at night," responded Spencer. "None of the grass landing strips have lights, and if something went wrong, it would be game over. We'll stay at Sarah's camp tonight and hopefully fly out first thing in the morning."

Sarah told us on the way that none of the camps were allowed to have permanent structures. Because they mostly followed the migration, they needed to be mobile. Again, she told us no one leaves any trace behind—all were subject to inspection by and approval from the government.

When we got to the camp, I was surprised to turn around and see Zawadi disappearing into the fading light. We hadn't even said goodbye, no less thanked her.

Chapter 13

WE FOLLOWED SARAH INTO THE camp, where two guards with what looked like AK-47s stood guard. Spencer held their gaze for much longer than I did.

"That is Puce and Erick. Both with the Tanzania rangers. We invite them to stay in the camp whenever they want," explained Sarah, with a friendly wave to the two men, and they smiled and waved back.

"That's some serious hardware they're carrying," remarked Spencer.

"It would barely slow down a charging elephant or even a smaller rhinoceros or hippo, for that matter," answered Sarah. "The guns are not for the animals. The rangers are almost as proficient as Zawadi at reading and predicting animal behavior. The guns are to discourage poachers. Unfortunately, there are still people out here who try to make a living by killing endangered animals. Such people aren't discouraged by harsh language or fines, but an AK-47 will typically do the trick. Also, people from the camps aren't allowed out after dark without a ranger escort. If the rangers find someone on the roads, it's typically bad news. Since most poachers have no qualms about firing on the authorities, it's essential to be able to outgun the opponent. The park rangers have learned that the hard way, but they are very effective at what they do and are passionate about protecting the animals within the preserve."

Sarah's camp was beautiful. The entire area could not have been more than an acre. Chains of white lights hung from several of the trees, which provided enough illumination to walk around the interior of the camp. A spacious, central tent offered a bar and dining area, which contained a round table able to seat sixteen. The bar area included several couches surrounding a fireplace. An open campfire also burned in the center of the camp, with chairs all around. Off to the side of the main shelter, another big tent seemed to be for those who worked at the camp. They scurried in and out with supplies. And behind this were four more tents, each with a string of dim lights connecting them to the other enclosures along a crude path. In the distance I heard the hum of a generator. I caught the faint smell of meat cooking with a few aromas I couldn't identify.

Sarah introduced us to a new guide, who led us to our tent at the northwest side of the camp. Its ceiling was over nine feet high, and the interior felt immense, with three distinct spaces defined within the canvas-enclosed area. On either end was a bedroom containing two beds covered in colorful blankets; each pair of bunks shared a single nightstand between them. There was a separate bathroom area with a toilet and a shower for each of the bedrooms. A common room separated the bedrooms, furnished with two couches around a rectangular table. The wooden floors—like a large pallet—provided for solid footing throughout. The entire structure was enclosed with screens covered by thick canvas, which could be brought down for privacy. Each of the end bedrooms was separated from the common area with the same thick canvas. Pictures of animals commonly seen on safari hung on the "walls" from thick ropes attached to the poles supporting the canvas.

Our bags had already been brought to the tent. Nell's bag and mine were to the right; Spencer's and Alex's were on the left.

The guide followed us into the tent and invited us to sit down on the couches in the common area.

"You should know about a few rules in the camp, designed for your safety," he said with a cheerful smile. "First, please do not leave the tents after dark without an escort. The camp is fairly safe at night, but you never know what lurks in the shadows, as I'm sure you'll hear tonight."

I raised an eyebrow, not knowing what he meant by that.

"If you need an escort, you'll find two flashlights in each side tent on the nightstand. Go to the entrance of the tent and wave the flashlight at the main tent. Someone stays awake all night, and they'll come immediately. They're here for your service, so don't hesitate to signal. You'll also find an airhorn in each nightstand drawer. In case of an emergency, blast the horn, and people will come running."

"What do you mean by an emergency?" asked Alex.

"Don't worry, sir, the horns are seldom needed," he said, flashing Alex a reassuring look.

"The fact that they are here at all is extremely alarming to me," responded Alex.

"I assure you, we're well protected here. Just shine the lights when you're ready to be collected for dinner. Please don't drink the water by the sinks. It's for washing only. It won't kill you, but some of our guests have experienced gastrointestinal upset. Drink the bottled water on the other side of the sink—that's quite safe."

The guide headed out, and we walked to our separate tents.

"I think I need to change out of these dusty clothes," said Nell, closing the canvas. "Do you mind closing your eyes?"

"I'll wait in the common room," I offered.

"I'm not fourteen. Close your eyes for a minute while I get changed."

It only took her thirty seconds to get on a new shirt and jeans. "You can open your eyes now," she said.

In the dim light, I would be lying if I didn't admit to myself that she was stunning. Again, her plain, almost drab attire served to set off her natural beauty. I tried not to stare as she brushed out her hair.

"I think I have about an inch of dust covering everything," she said.

"I need to change as well." My clothes smelled of dust, and I could taste the dirt on my lips. I walked to the bathroom to wash my face and hands in the water by the sink.

"John," Nell said, from right behind me. "I think we got off on the wrong foot."

"What do you mean?" I asked, knowing full well she had been intentionally cold the first several times we had spoken.

"I'm used to dealing with men who end up being complete asses," she continued. "Iciness has become my default mode. But I can tell you have a kind heart, so for the way I treated you, I'm sorry."

"Don't give it a second thought," I said, taking a short step toward her.

"Is everyone decent in here?" came Spencer's voice from outside the tent door.

"Yep," I responded, cursing the interruption. "Come right on in."

Spencer and Alex came in. "I'm getting us out of here at first light," said Spencer, maintaining his military tone. "This place is beyond beautiful, but we are too vulnerable, from too many possible threats."

"Amen to that," muttered Alex. "Give me Manhattan any day."

Spencer continued, "Mr. Smith will move heaven and earth, now that he has a solid lead to try and uncover what is going on. He is grateful for your assistance."

"Did he say that?" I asked.

"No, I'm afraid not. If you're expecting a thank you from that guy, you'll be waiting a long time." He put his hands out, palms up, in a gesture of uselessness. "So, is everyone ready for dinner?"

"In a second," I responded as the three others walked into the common area and I put on a fresh shirt and pants. "Ready," I announced as I joined them.

Spencer flashed the lights, and within seconds a guide appeared. We walked as a group to the commissary. The night air was cool, with a slight breeze.

Based on the empty glasses and the half-eaten rolls I spotted around the communal table, the other guests had been waiting for us. I suddenly realized how hungry I was and couldn't remember when I had last eaten. Ten people around the table were on safari from England. These evidently were two families whose parents were old college friends. All the kids obviously knew one another as they joked and chatted throughout the introductions. Spencer introduced us as colleagues from a tech company on a retreat together. He used our real first names but did not offer any last names. The last two seats at the table were filled by younger women with infectious smiles who were the safari guides for the ten. They talked with the families like old friends. Most of the conversation recounted the most exciting animals seen that day. The guides offered interesting facts about all the encounters and kept the conversations light and entertaining. They were good at their jobs. One tour had been lucky enough to see a mother and baby rhinoceros run right in front of the car. The other family had spent the day at the river, marveling at the giant herds crossing and the hungry crocodiles waiting in the river.

Family-style platters were brought to the table and passed around. I salivated as the food and smells swirled by, and I took hearty helpings of a thick lamb stew, white rice, and various roasted vegetables. I could not remember the last time I feasted on a more fulfilling spread. Sarah walked around the table and offered glasses of wine to each of the guests. It was a French Burgundy that went perfectly with the meal.

We said little during supper, but the two families discussed Brexit, and their talk became heated. Fortunately, dessert—a lovely chocolate cake with a scoop of creamy vanilla ice cream—broke up the argument.

Following dinner, Sara invited us all into the bar for after-dinner drinks. The kids opted to sit around the outdoor fire. The sides of the tent were pulled up, and a cool night breeze blew through. While the others gathered at the bar, I stepped outside. The night sky was as clear and pure as any I had ever seen. The three-quarters moon cast an eerie shadow across the visible camp. The stars were so bright that the fantastic spill of the Milky Way Galaxy sparkled. I inhaled deeply, enjoying a contentedness I hadn't felt in days.

Stepping back inside, I spied a bottle of Macallan 25 at the fully stocked bar. Knowing I'd regret it, I asked for a glass, and Sarah poured generously into a thick-bottomed glass. Nell asked for white wine, and the two of us gravitated to the fireplace, which I was glad to see had a metal chimney to conduct the smoke well above the tent. The chill in the night air was a stark contrast to the oppressive heat of the day.

We both gazed outside, admiring the stars, listening to the night noises. Insects, chirping and bird noises, and the voices of others carried through the stillness. From a distance, a sudden roar seemed to make the tent shudder.

"That's a male lion," said Sarah. "Most likely about a half mile off."

Nell grabbed my forearm and gave it a gentle squeeze. Spencer and Alex left the bar to join us by the fireside.

"How close do they come to the camp?" Alex called to Sarah, apprehensively looking up from his martini.

"We've once or twice seen them walk through camp at night," she replied, "but they try to avoid people. We keep the lights on, and there's really nothing for them here. The action is all out there." She waved her hand to indicate everywhere but here.

"How many people do you have watching the camp?" asked Spencer. He had selected a light beer, but it didn't appear he was actually drinking any.

"Two always sit and watch the four tents from here. I found when I posted only one, they'd be asleep in the morning."

"Are they armed?" asked Spencer.

"We have two rifles in the camp, but the people watching the tents don't carry them, if that's what you are asking," answered Sarah. "Animals *are* predictable, and we have never had a problem in the camp," she said with a reassuring smile.

"Animals are predictable," I offered as reassurance, forgetting for a minute I was supposed to be a tech executive on a retreat and not a veterinarian. No one seemed to notice.

We four were out of earshot from the others, and Spencer muttered. "It's not the animals I was thinking about."

"You can't possibly think there are people out here with malicious intent," I said. "No one could possibly know we're here."

"As I've said, it's my job to assume bad people are everywhere, even in the middle of nowhere."

"I'm as cautious as they come," said Alex, "but we *are* pretty far off the grid."

"I'll relax when we're back on the plane tomorrow," said Spencer. "Until then, I'd prefer we head back to the tent. My vote is that we stick together as a group. Dawn comes early, and we're taking the first flight out."

I glanced at the pictures above the fireplace. Most of the pictures were of guests of the camp, sitting in this very room with happy smiles. A few were guests in the back of the safari vehicles. In the corner was a young girl with a bright orange hat and an infectious smile sitting on the top of a truck with elephants in the background. It took a minute before it hit me. "That's Ella," I exclaimed.

"Who?" asked Spencer, at once very interested.

Sarah had overheard and walked toward us. "How do you know Ella?" she asked curiously.

"It doesn't matter," I responded a little too quickly, and I could tell Sarah was a bit offended. "When was this taken?"

"A little over a week ago. Ella comes to this camp at least twice a year with tours. Her mother runs an upscale touring company. Her daughter's a doll, and all the guests take to her. I think she could run one of the tours by herself, given all she knows of this area." Another guest summoned Sarah back to the bar.

"It can't be a coincidence," I said. "The same girl in two different, very remote parts of the world where outbreaks have occurred? This must be the link Mr. Smith is searching for."

I filled Spencer and Alex in on the details of our encounter with Ella on the beach.

"Are you suggesting this ten-year-old is an international terrorist killing animals on safaris?" countered Alex, slightly slurring his words as he sipped on his second martini.

I ignored him and gave Spencer a nod. "It's got to be somehow related."

Spencer excused himself for several minutes and made a call. When he got back, he filled us in on the call. "Mr. Smith will track this down. If there is any connection, we'll soon know."

We all finished our drinks, and Spencer put his untouched beer on the counter. Sarah walked us back to our tent herself and wished us a good night. We sat down in the main tent around the center table and sank into the soft couches. Spencer waited for Sarah to round the corner on her way back to the main tent before he spoke.

"We're as safe as we can be out here, but I don't like to take chances. I can't exactly walk the perimeter of the camp safely, so if you need anything tonight, give a shout. The positive news is that we're close together here, and they have guards watching the camp. I managed to sneak in a quick talk with one of them right after dinner, when people were heading to the bar. I requested special precautions, saying our tech company was being targeted by an extremist group. I'm not sure if he believed me, but my talk should produce the desired effect. If anyone unknown wanders into the camp, hopefully they will immediately perceive it as a threat. And if the guards raise an alarm, I'll be ready." He reached behind his shirt and pulled out a small Glock. "Again, we leave at sunup. Our pilot will be waiting at the airfield to bring us back to Arusha. Have a good night," he offered, heading to his tent. Alex followed on his heels.

"Shall we?" said Nell as she got up and walked to our tent.

The light was dim, and it was challenging to see in the bathroom as I brushed my teeth and prepared for bed. From the shower area came a soft thump. I must have jumped a foot into the air. In the dim light, I made out the largest bullfrog I have ever seen, disappearing under the wooden slats that made up the floor. I returned to the bedroom. Nell sat on the corner of her bed, brushing her long hair. My God, she was beautiful.

"Be careful when you use the bathroom," I said. "A giant bullfrog lives in there."

"Is that code for something?" Nell replied with a wink.

"No, there *is* a frog in the bathroom. Though it's no threat to us," I said awkwardly.

Nell got up from the bed and took a step toward me. I stepped right to allow her into the bathroom as she stepped left. Suddenly we were face to face and locked eyes for a few seconds.

"What?" I asked curiously.

"I'm wondering," said Nell, leaning in and giving me a kiss. It was the softest kiss I had ever experienced, as if her lips were barely touching mine. I leaned in and gently wrapped my arms around her perfect waist. Her kiss became more passionate, and we were in a full embrace now as the sounds of the night faded away. All I was aware of was her. Her mouth tasted of sweet wine, and I wondered if mine tasted of scotch. She smelled softly of perfume or perhaps just smelled like a woman. It had been so long since I had been this close to a woman in this way. Nell subtly changed position, and her hair brushed against my cheek. My hand moved up to the back of her head as I pulled her even closer.

In an instant, something changed. She pulled away and stepped back. Her cheeks were red, and I thought her eyes were tearing up in the dim light.

"I'm sorry," she said, so softly that it was barely audible. "I thought I wanted this, but I'm not quite sure I'm ready."

I stood in confusion, trying to adjust to this new mood.

"It's only that I don't do one-night stands, and we only met each other a few days ago."

Had it only been a few days? So much had happened.

"I don't want you to be mad or disappointed or frustrated or . . ." The tears in her eyes were no longer subtle. "I really like you and would love to get to know you, but I can't be with you physically. Not yet, at least."

Now *I* stepped back, sensing she longed for a bit of space. "I don't mind," I lied. I wanted so much to hold her. "Watch out for the frog," I said, diffusing the tension of the moment.

She laughed nervously and wiped her eyes and proceeded to the bathroom, pulling the canvas door closed.

I let out a deep sigh, walked to my bed, and sat down, unsure of what to do now. I decided to lie down and pulled the thick, colorful blanket over me. I had taken off my boots and socks but decided to sleep in my clothes. I was staring at the ceiling when Nell came out of the bathroom.

"Please don't hate me," she said with a pleading stare.

"I don't hate you—couldn't hate you."

"I really do want to get to know you."

"Perhaps we could go out to dinner when we get back."

"Did you just ask me out?" she said in a playful tone. "Where would you take me?"

"Let's see," I said, relaxing. "What do I know about you and how would that translate to a date?" I pondered that, staring at the roof of the tent, pretending to consider multiple options. After a short while, I looked at her and smiled. "I think I would take you to Mongolian Barbeque and then to Polyesters Night Club."

"What?" she said with eyes wide open. "Isn't Polyesters the place where everyone dresses like they're in a seventies John Travolta movie? Why would you make that choice?"

"That's the place. Based on what I know about you, I thought it would be a perfect evening."

"I'm not sure you are very good at reading women."

"Well, I'm guessing most men would say a nice French restaurant and then to the museum," I said.

Her eyes lit up. "That sounds more like my style," said Nell.

"Nope," I said playfully. "Too boring. That's for a fifth date."

"Wow! Aren't you a bit confident?" said Nell, now fully relaxing and laying down in her bed with her head propped up by her hands. "Already planning a fifth date."

"Actually," I boasted, "I already planned out the first ten. I like to keep things open after that. You know, too much planning takes the spontaneity out of things."

"I haven't even said yes to the first date yet."

"How much time do you need to decide?" I asked.

"Give me until next Friday," she said.

"I don't even know what day today is."

"Neither do I!" She laughed, and the sound was musical. She sat up on the bed and pulled her legs to her chest, stretching her back. She relaxed and sat back with her legs crossed and her arms folded on her lap.

The sound registered before anything else: a soft ping, almost like air being forced through a narrow tube. I saw a black mark appear on Nell's pillow, and feathers being thrown up, and slowly falling toward the bed. Strangely, I thought to myself, timing is everything. If she had not sat up, she would have feathers all over her hair. It took a split second longer to figure out what had happened. I think Nell realized it at the exact same time. That was a gunshot.

"Help!" I screamed, as loud as I could, regretting it instantly as I again heard the ping and felt a bullet rush by the side of my face. "Get down," I whispered to Nell.

She was already on the floor, and she put her finger to her lips. We crouched in the corner and made ourselves as small as we could. I slipped on my boots, and Nell mirrored my actions. Why had Spencer not come running?

Two more pings rang out and black circles formed in the center of each of our beds. The holes in the thick canvas told me that the shots had come from the center of the camp. Where were the guards? Where the hell was Spencer? Two more pings rang out and holes appeared in the canvas just above where we were crouched. I knew they could not see us, but I wasn't sure that mattered. They had guns and we had nothing.

Two more pings rang out, and now I could hear footsteps approaching. A deafening explosion boomed from the other side of the tent as Spencer returned fire. The footsteps stopped. At least they now knew it would not be as simple as walking up and shooting us in the head. Two more pings and two more holes, this time five feet to our right. They only had to guess correctly once.

A second explosion from Spencer's tent, followed by five quick pings. How long would this standoff last? We were sitting ducks, waiting for the gunman to "guess" right. "We need to leave," I whispered into Nell's ear.

"And go where?"

"Away from the lights, into the dark."

"Not a good idea," she said as two more pings and two more holes this time in the boards of the floor two feet from us.

"Come with me," I pleaded, as I carefully picked up the canvas, praying it would not make a sound. The wood on the floor of the tent allowed Nell to silently wriggle under the canvas. Not a sound was made as her feet disappeared out of the tent. Her hand appeared, and she held up the canvas for me as two black holes appeared where we were just sitting.

The silvery moonlight allowed us to see through the brush to several trees about fifty feet away. I pointed toward the area I thought we should retreat to, and Nell gave a small nod of approval. She grabbed my hand as we headed toward the cover of the trees, crouching low.

Nell squeezed my hand so tight that it hurt, but I realized I was squeezing hers as hard, and the terror of what was happening started to sink in. We made it to the trees, and the glow of the lights from the camp allowed us to see the outline of the tents. We could not hear the pings anymore, but there was one more loud explosion from Spencer's tent and then nothing as we saw the shadowy silhouette of six figures with long guns walking around the corners of the tents. The three who entered our side quickly came out of the tent and peered into the darkness where we were standing. I was reasonably certain they couldn't see us, but we shrank lower into the brush. I could feel her trembling next to me.

"I'm scared," she whispered into my ear.

"I am too," I responded, trying to sound brave but failing terribly.

"What should we do?" she asked. I risked a glance toward the camp and saw three beams of light spaced about twenty yards apart slowly making their way toward our hiding spot.

"We can't stay here," I said. Still holding hands, we set out walking away from the camp. Two more loud explosions echoed in the night. I prayed Spencer and Alex were okay, but I needed to focus on us.

The moon provided some light, but the grass was tall and the ground was uneven. Thick bushes with long, nasty spikes every several yards made walking slow and perilous. Creatures in the dark scurried away every several minutes, each time making my heart pound into my chest. Even though the night was alive with sounds and we were trying to be careful, every stick that cracked or every mound of dirt that crunched seemed to set off sound waves leading our pursuers to our location. The flashlight beams behind us followed our path as if our pursuers knew where we had stepped.

"Do you have your cell phone with you?" I whispered. She pulled it out, shielding the light from the screen with her shirt.

"Yes, I do, but there hasn't been a signal since we landed."

"I'm worried they might be able to track it. Leave it here," I said. The adrenaline coursing through my veins made it difficult to keep my voice at a whisper. I wanted to scream and run with every fiber of my being.

She nodded, tossed her phone, and we moved another fifty yards deeper into the thicket, up a slight incline so we were able to see in all directions through the eerie moonlight. Four flashlights now pierced the night, relentlessly getting closer to where we hid. The light stopped about where Nell had left her phone, and for several seconds none of them moved. I thought I heard hushed whispering, but I couldn't make out what they were saying or even if they were speaking English. I grabbed Nell's hand and took a step backward, tripping over a large termite mound and landing on my back with an audible *oomph* as the wind was knocked out of me. Ten feet ahead of us something large crashed through the brush, attracting the light of the flashlights, which now scanned back and forth, ruthlessly pursuing us. The beams approached us at an accelerated rate, bouncing up and down across the rugged landscape. They were running toward us.

"They are going to find us or something is going to eat us out here," whispered Nell to me in a shaky voice. My hand was hurting again, but nothing could make me release her hand.

Too scared to move, we cowered in the tall grass. Time—and our options—were running out.

Chapter 14

I ALMOST SCREAMED OUT LOUD AS a figure appeared out of nowhere, right beside us. I had not heard a thing.

"Make no sound," whispered Zawadi. The breath I'd been unconsciously holding escaped, but I thankfully kept it quiet. Zawadi stared straight ahead into the night. Were her eyes closed?!

"You are being pursued by four men," she said. "They all have guns but are clumsy and awkward. You need to follow me. I am going to lead them to the river."

"Isn't that dangerous?" Nell asked, as softly as she could.

"For them, yes. Very," responded Zawadi. "That is why we are going there."

"What about Alex and Spencer?" I asked.

"I don't know," Zawadi responded without changing expression. "People were going to help, but I don't know if they got there in time." She turned away from us. "Move now."

Zawadi's sandaled feet covered the ground swiftly. I felt like a child as I tried to keep up with her. Still holding on to each other, Nell and I stumbled through the thick brush, making more noise than I cared to. Every fifty feet or so she stopped and changed directions slightly. We were still being pursued, but the distance was greater now. I could see the wide arcs of the flashlights and hear our pursuers crashing through the brush.

"It won't be long now," said Zawadi in a whisper as she dropped one knee to the ground and stared straight ahead. After a minute she stood up and ripped a small piece of her red robe off and hung it at eye level on a thorny bush. Without a sound she walked off to the left. We followed closely behind.

The walking became easier, as though we were on a crude path. But our break had allowed the men following us to get closer, and I could hear them talking more clearly now. Based on their excited voices, I guessed they had just found the piece of robe Zawadi had left for them.

A blood-curdling scream came moments later. Then a chorus of shrieks. I almost cried out myself—the sound was of pure torture. Nell's fingernails dug into the skin of my hand as the shrieks went on for about thirty seconds. Then there was an eerie silence. Even the sounds of the birds and night insects ceased. Thirty seconds later, the Serengeti awoke again, as if nothing had happened.

"They won't be pursuing us anymore," said Zawadi. "I doubt they are alive."

"What happened?" I asked, not sure I wanted to know.

"The men following us do not belong out here," answered Zawadi in a philosophical voice. "This is not their place. They probably thought guns would keep them safe, but you can't shoot what you can't see."

"So what happened to them?" asked Nell in a voice slightly louder than a whisper.

Zawadi put a finger to her lips before answering in a barely audible whisper. "Nature is balanced, and they did not belong. We can't disrupt the balance, or we will not belong, and nature will do what nature does." She moved forward without a sound, and we did our best to mimic her motions and move silently through the night.

We walked for a full hour in the darkness, occasionally stopping and listening and changing directions. No more flashlights pursued us. The moon was directly overhead now, and if not for the terror of being in this raw, wild, and dangerous environment, the night was actually beautiful.

I had no frame of reference to determine where we were heading but blindly followed Zawadi's instinctual understanding of this world. Now and then, something scurried away from our path. Zawadi never flinched, but I nearly jumped out of my skin each time.

The sound of the river first developed as a faint disturbance in the night sounds, which I was growing accustomed to. Progressively, though, the water's thunder drowned out all other noises. We stepped out from the grass of the crude path we had been on and our feet hit gravel. We were on a dirt road. Zawadi looked down the road toward the river for a full thirty seconds before speaking—quietly.

"Six men arrived at the camp soon after you walked to your tent. They came in a ranger vehicle, but it was wrong, unlike any other ranger vehicle I have seen. The men walked to the main tent and quickly and quietly overpowered the two guards. Then the gunfire began. I led several of the employees to a safe spot I know and returned to help you two."

"Did you see Spencer or Alex?" I asked.

"No. But the two men who split off from the four pursuing you were closing in on their tent. I fear for their safety. But we don't know if the camp is safe, so I can't lead you back."

"What are our options?" asked Nell.

"The rangers use this road, but I am not sure if we can trust any vehicle that drives by."

"Can we shelter near here, somewhere?" My voice sounded tired and weak, even to me.

"Even my people are sometimes killed by a predator out here." Despite her words, Zawadi's voice was calm and decisive. "No, the safest place to wait for a vehicle is on the bridge to our left. But if the vehicle has the same men that came to the camp to kill you, then there will be no place to go. To jump into the water is certain death."

It was an impossible choice. Wait for a vehicle which may contain those who would kill us, or stay in the wild and take our chances. "How many roads lead to the camp where we are staying?" I asked, still at a whisper.

"Four lead to the camp. We stand on the road least used."

"My vote would be to wait on the bridge," I said, with obvious hesitation.

"I agree," said Nell, with a confidence that surprised me.

"Why do you think that the bridge would be the right choice?" I asked.

"Hey! I'm agreeing with you," replied Nell.

"I guess I'm just not sure," I said.

"The men who followed us are injured or dead," reasoned Nell. "The two men back at the camp had Spencer to deal with. In a fight, I would put my money on him any day. I think we have a good chance that all six are out of commission, which means that Spencer and Alex are likely fine." This last sentence was uttered with hope rather than confidence.

"God willing," I muttered.

Zawadi said, "I do not sense an army out here searching for us. They sent six to get four. I am sure they expected to kill us with minimal difficulty and then disappear into the night. We have dealt with six. If any are left, they most likely will regroup, to develop a new strategy. The bridge is the safest place. Come." She gave a small nod and headed down the road toward the bridge.

The river generated a slight mist, and through the moonlight, ghostly shadows danced on the surface. Combined with shadowy banks, the river appeared to be in a deep cavern. We settled on the edge of the cement bridge and watched the water flow through the huge pipes below us, mesmerized. Nell snuggled closer to me, and I put my arm around her shoulder. She was shivering. It wasn't exactly cold, but the adrenaline of being pursued and almost killed was ebbing. Our grim reality was gaining the upper hand.

I felt like I was in a trance, with part of my mind shut down. Zawadi stood erect in the center of the bridge and stared into the darkness. I wondered what she saw, felt, and heard. I followed her gaze and saw nothing but black. Time seemed to stand still, as still as she was.

The sound of the water was soothing, and I found myself struggling to keep my eyes open. Did I fall asleep? I was confused and cursed myself for having that scotch.

"Someone is coming," said Zawadi. It took another minute before I saw the headlights bouncing along the far side of the river. The vehicle had a spotlight that oscillated left and right, until it abruptly turned off. We only had moments before the truck would turn toward the bridge, and we would be seen.

"Are you sure about this plan?" I asked Nell.

"No."

"Not a great time for uncertainty," I responded, standing up.

I could feel my entire body tense up. The headlights swung toward us as the vehicle turned onto the bridge, moving at a crawl. And there we were, illuminated. Three defenseless people at the edge of the world.

Zawadi stood her ground in the center of the bridge, making it impossible for the truck to pass. It stopped ten feet from her. I had to shield my eyes from the glare of the headlights and saw Nell doing the same. Zawadi still stared straight ahead.

"*Jambo*," a voice cried out in the night. For the first time since meeting her, I saw Zawadi's body language change. Our sentinel relaxed, and she started to talk to the two rangers from the vehicle in a language I did not understand. Several times I heard the driver use Zawadi's name. They occasionally laughed like old friends.

It was clear we had made the right decision, and Nell and I walked toward the vehicle. The rangers motioned for us to get into the back and offered us warm tea. Sarah's camp had called for help on the radio about an hour ago. These park rangers were responding to the call but had few details beyond that.

We made our way slowly down the road toward the camp. The rangers would sporadically turn the spotlight to the left or the right of the truck, but it was unclear what they were searching for. Nell and I talked nervously in the back and sipped on warm tea, which had an amazing calming effect, though we shared an unspoken dread about what we would find back at the camp.

All the lights were on in to the camp, and there was a flurry of activity in the central tent. People ran in and out of all of the tents. Another ranger vehicle was parked at the entrance, and the same two park rangers we had seen before nervously looked around with their AK-47s held at their sides. They relaxed upon recognizing us. Sarah ran up and gave Nell a giant hug.

"I am so relieved you both are okay," she said. "We feared the worst."

"How are the others in camp?" Nell asked anxiously.

"Not good, I'm afraid. The two scouts watching the grounds were shot. One was killed, and we can't stop the bleeding on the other."

"Spencer and Alex?" asked Nell.

"Both are injured, but I think they'll be all right. Spencer shot and killed one of the gunmen. If not for him, I suspect things would have gotten a lot worse. We managed to get our two rifles and just shot at the remaining gunman's feet. That was enough for him, and he ran to his truck and sped out."

Nell and I walked into the main tent. The two families were curled up on the couches. The parents sat with blank faces staring into the fire as the kids dozed. A woman who was bleeding from an abdominal wound lay stretched out on the dining room table. In the corner, a white sheet, stained red with blood, covered what I assume was the second scout. Alex was tending to the woman on the table, applying a wrap to her abdomen. His own right calf also was wrapped tightly, and he winced when he put weight on that leg. Spencer stood in a corner, his left arm tied to his chest with a makeshift sling. He spoke on his phone, engaged in what appeared to be a heated exchange. I would hate to be on the receiving end of that phone call. His face, paradoxically, was pale gray. His shirt showed blood stains on the front and back. They both ran to us as soon as they saw us enter the tent.

"Oh, thank God," said Spencer. "Why did you run off?" he asked.

"Because we didn't want to get shot, like you two!"

"How did you make it back?" asked Alex.

"Zawadi," answered Nell. "If not for her, we would both be dead. The men chasing us were bearing down, and she led us safely back here."

"What happened to the men chasing you?" asked Spencer, scanning the perimeter of the camp again.

"We don't know." I filled in the group on what had happened. Alex visibly shuddered when I described the screams we heard.

Spencer promptly took charge of the camp. He closed the sides of the main tent and spread people out along the floor. Pillows and blankets were brought in from the sleeping tents, and the park rangers with their AK-47s were posted outside along the four sides of the tent. He arranged for the guides to walk the perimeter of the camp at intervals, with an armed escort. If someone was going to try and attack the camp again, it would not be so easy.

I told Spencer our theory of people tracking Nell's cell phone. He didn't seem convinced but nevertheless persuaded Alex to hand over his phone. When he smashed the phone on the ground and threw the pieces into the fire, Alex looked as though he'd lost a family member. He retreated to a corner of the tent, and I actually felt sorry for him.

I had never felt so tired, and I was having trouble keeping my eyes open. I laid down in a dim corner of the tent with a pillow and a blanket. From the other side of the tent, I caught Alex's surprise when Nell laid down right behind me and wrapped her arm around my shoulder.

"Don't say a word," she said, as I felt the contours of her body match mine.

I felt warm breath on the back of my neck as her breathing pattern became regular and slow. Despite the terrible night, I felt supremely content.

That night I dreamt I was a young child, lying down in the woods by a small running creek. The earth was warm, and a soft breeze blew just above my body. All was silent except for the running water. I had dreamt this scenario in the past, but not for many years. I now understood it to be my place of peace and well-being.

In the morning, Nell had not changed position, even a little. I didn't want to move and was perfectly happy to stay still. The sky brightened, and a few people were milling about, stretching. I smelled strong coffee and bacon. Though I knew I had only slept a few hours, I felt fully refreshed, for the first time in a very long time. I even smiled.

I spied Spencer, sitting in the west corner of the tent, eyes closed, while the sun cast shadows behind him. I thought he was asleep until he brought a cup to his mouth and took a small sip. I suspected he hadn't slept at all last night.

Nell's arm remained draped around me, and her body was warm and snug against my back. I closed my eyes for a brief second before the spell was broken by Sarah.

She walked into the tent and announced that breakfast would be ready in five minutes. I heard a universal groan as people began to sit up. The sides of the tents were lifted, and I could see three separate tables were set behind the main tent with perfectly white tablecloths and seemingly expensive china. The blood had been cleaned, and it was as though last night's events had never occurred.

Alex's leg wound turned out to be minor, suffered when Spencer pulled him off his bed and sent him flying into a corner of the tent. It was scratched and bruised, but he was already walking without a limp, and appeared even chipper in the early light.

Spencer's wound was a bit more serious. A bullet struck his left shoulder, ripping away some skin, but not causing any significant muscle or bone damage. I offered to place a few sutures to close the wound, but he politely refused. "I'm not a dog," he said. I ignored his attempt at humor.

The man Spencer killed had no identification.

We learned at breakfast that the woman with the abdominal wound had been driven to a nearby airfield and taken by helicopter to a hospital in Kenya. She had been operated on and was stable. Thank God. Also, the scouts had gone to the place where we heard the men scream, but all they found were several blood trails, no bodies.

I overheard Sarah talking to one of the families, promising them a full refund and an invitation to come back any time they wanted to finish their trip. She was doing her best to be upbeat and positive, but the expressions on the guests' faces were stone cold. Their return trip seemed unlikely.

When she got to our table, her warm expression soured. "This entire episode may have ruined me," she said in an accusatory tone, out of character to her warm outgoing personality.

"Word will never get out," said Spencer with reassurance.

"With all due respect, I think what happened at my camp is because of you four, and I don't buy for a second that you are on a company retreat. Who brings an illegal handgun into a foreign country and is able to defend himself against six armed assailants?" she glared at Spencer. He met her gaze with a blank expression and didn't say a word. "I won't go so far as saying it's your fault, but this camp is my life. This is all I have, and I fear it's all over." She looked like she was about to cry.

"Can we help?" I asked.

"Reviews, both positive and negative, define this business, and there is no way that last night's series of events will remain out of the news or out of reviews. The internet is a cruel place, and once the trolls take hold of a story like this, it will destroy me." She glanced around the camp. "I can't leave this place.

I won't," she said, now shedding a tear and swiftly wiping it away.

Spencer replied gently, "My boss has a vested interest in keeping this story from becoming public. If I'm being honest, I have to admit he doesn't really care about your business. But he will keep things secret because it's in his best interest. Even if that were not true, I would persuade him to prevent any of this from coming out."

"A gun battle played out in the middle of a safari vacation camp," Sarah said in a grim monotone. "Two of my employees were shot, and one was killed. An unidentified dead body remains in my camp. I know this is a third-world country, but we still have a press, not to mention guests and employees who saw the entire thing. There is no way this story *doesn't* become public."

"You have to trust me," replied Spencer, placing a comforting hand on Sarah's shoulder.

She pulled away. "I don't trust you," answered Sarah coldly. "No one controls the press or the internet. People can write whatever they want. That's how it works."

"*He* does control the internet and the press," said Spencer, not defining who "he" was. "That's not how it's supposed to work, but it is the reality of the world we live in. Powerful people can manipulate anything they want to."

Sarah remained unconvinced, but the host in her ultimately won over. She politely wished us well. Our bags were already packed into one of the safari trucks, and we all piled in. I couldn't help but notice an armed park ranger sat in the passenger's seat, and Spencer's Glock sat on his lap. Zawadi was not in the camp this morning, and Sarah explained she had gone out at first light for a long walk and would likely not be back for hours. Nell and I were both upset that we didn't have the opportunity to express our gratitude, but Sarah promised to pass things along.

"Zawadi doesn't believe in saying goodbye," explained Sarah. "She just never has. It's not part of her culture to bid anyone farewell."

Chapter 15

THE TRIP TO THE AIRPORT was blessedly uneventful, and a small plane awaited on the grass runway. Once we were in the air, Spencer put away his Glock and closed his eyes. He had refused to let any of us tend to his wound and promised that he was fine. According to him, this happened all the time, and this wound was minor compared to others he had sustained in his career.

The trip back to Arusha was quicker than I remembered. Before long, we were waved through customs at the Kilimanjaro Airport, again sustaining several dirty looks, and finally we were back onboard the jet. We took our seats and put on the noise-canceling headphones.

Mr. Smith's voice came across the headphones, almost as if he were sitting at the table with us. As creepy as ever. Ponytail was nowhere to be seen.

"Ella's full name is Ella Montgomery. Her mother, Carolyn, owns and runs the company Off the Grid Tours. They are an elite, ultra-high-end touring company for wealthy clients. The company has a reputation for giving the client exactly what they want. I don't know where they get permission for some of the things they have done, but they have guided tours in North Korea, Africa, Australia, and even restricted religious sites in the Middle East. She somehow managed a tour in a small sub to the *Titanic* for two wealthy history buffs. And guess where

Montgomery's company is based?" Before any of us could answer, he said, "Memphis, Tennessee. But it doesn't fit."

"What doesn't fit?" asked Spencer. "These must be the people we're after."

"A single mother and her child running a tour company doesn't fit the profile of international bioterrorists," continued Mr. Smith. "I looked into their background and found nothing abnormal in any post on social media. They don't visit radical web sites, they don't communicate with any known extremist groups, and even their private and company bank accounts don't indicate great influxes or outlays of cash. The company does well, but the Montgomerys are not even millionaires. When at home, they live in a small suburban house on ten acres in Montana and go to church on Sundays."

I was a bit terrified by how complete a picture Mr. Smith had on these people, in only a matter of hours. Do people really leave such an obvious digital fingerprint in every aspect of their lives? Big brother *is* watching.

"Why don't we bring them in for questioning?" asked Spencer. "Where are they right now?"

"I don't think that is a wise idea," answered Mr. Smith with a calculated tone. "If they are not behind this prion, they are either knowingly or unknowingly involved."

"How can you be unknowingly involved?" I asked.

Mr. Smith didn't bother to answer my question, and I knew asking again wouldn't change the outcome. "If they are being used," continued Mr. Smith, "we need to know by whom and for what purpose. This prion has not been used on humans anywhere except in Memphis. The other outbreaks were so off the grid that they were probably intended to go unnoticed. I suspect something more sinister is at play here," continued Mr. Smith.

I doubted Mr. Smith was telling us everything he knew, but I was getting used to that feeling.

"I want to catch up with the Montgomerys and observe everything about them before I decide how to manage things."

I felt the plane slowly being pushed back from the terminal toward the airstrip.

"There is no way to observe the Montgomerys where they are right now. No street cameras, traffic cameras, or even cell phones that work. We only have satellite surveillance, which has its limits."

The plane started accelerating, and the chairs swiveled forward in the now-familiar process of takeoff.

"So where are the Montgomerys?" asked Spencer, annoyance edging his question.

"Don't worry," said Mr. Smith. "You will catch up with them when you get to Ecuador."

"Ecuador has plenty of cameras," countered Spencer, as the plane started its dramatic, upward trajectory.

"But none in the Galapagos Islands," responded Mr. Smith.

"I am *not* going to the Galapagos!" shouted Alex into the hidden microphones. Mr. Smith, of course, did not respond, and the plane screamed toward South America. I exchanged a worried but resigned glance with Nell.

When the plane leveled out, a haggard Ponytail came out of the cockpit. I couldn't help but think he looked as though he had aged a year. He had circles under his eyes and a heaviness to his face. He seemed to veer away from Spencer as he walked toward us and took a seat. In his hand was a folder for each of us with information about the Galapagos Islands. The thoroughness of the information in the folder suggested that the decision to send us to another exotic location had been made well before we climbed on board. I wondered if it had been made even before the attack on our lives.

The island chain is owned by Ecuador and comprises eighteen larger islands with hundreds of smaller ones, more accurately described as rocks that jut above the ocean. The entire area covers over seventeen hundred square miles, north and south of the equator, and is located over five hundred miles from the coast of South America. The islands arose from the floor of the Pacific and were all volcanic at various stages of development.

Unique ocean currents in the area keep the water hovering at about sixty degrees or colder, even though the location on the equator provides a more tropical land environment.

The Galapagos Islands are closely regulated, and only a limited number of people and boats are allowed, to preserve the unique environment. Darwin made the islands famous by his writings on evolution. He actually demonstrated evolution in action by documenting differing stages of development in similar species between differently aged islands. Over time, ninety-seven percent of the land in the area became a national park that people were not permitted to ever develop. The other three percent was inhabited by people native to the Galapagos. The islands are popular among ecotourists who can afford to go, and like all other places we had been to in the last several days, is very much in the middle of nowhere.

Smith's data stated Off the Grid Tours was anchored in a cove on the coast of Genovesa Island. The had chartered a forty-person boat for four days, although the manifest showed only ten guests on board. The crew, including Ella and Carolyn Montgomery, also numbered ten. The names of all were recorded with the exception of one person, labeled "guest." This caught my eye, and I asked Ponytail about the unknown passenger.

According to him, Mr. Smith was looking into the identity of this person, but as of now, it remained unknown. The boat had a permit to go snorkeling in the morning and to hike on the island in the afternoon. Our jet was scheduled to land on Santa Cruz Island, and from there, we were to take a boat to Genovesa to intercept the Montgomery's charter. We were scheduled to arrive at the island shortly after lunch.

At this point, we were all getting used to the strain of the ultrafast jet on our bodies, and Ponytail had retreated back to the cockpit. Alex continued to protest the trip, but we all agreed that this was above and beyond what we had committed to do, but there was no response over the headphones.

Spencer had been curiously quiet the entire trip. He sat back with his eyes closed. He might've been sleeping or was more hurt than he let on, but either way, I decided the best strategy was to let him be. We landed and were ushered to the docks in a tour bus that could easily accommodate sixty passengers. Even though the trip took a mere twenty minutes, I could not help but notice Spencer sat through the entire trip, again with his eyes closed. For a guy so good at keeping watch, this behavior was strangely out of character.

Our charter was a seventy-foot, sleek touring boat with four cabins designed to accommodate up to a dozen guests. An inflatable Zodiac with an outboard motor sat on the front deck.

We climbed aboard and were underway in a matter of minutes. The crew consisted of a captain and a first mate. Although our boat was fast, it would still take over four hours to reach Genovesa, explained the captain. A weather system in the area would make the trip a bit rough. And since the arrangements were made post-haste, they couldn't staff a full crew, so we'd have to fend for ourselves. Accordingly, we found cold, bottled water behind the bar. We sipped from the bottles and watched the magnificent frigatebirds hover above the back of the boat, gliding effortlessly in the air currents.

"So, what are we planning on doing when we get to Genovesa?" asked Alex.

"We're being used," said Spencer abruptly. This caught our attention and we all turned to him for an explanation. He took a deep breath and motioned us all into a tight circle where we could talk quietly. For a moment he looked as though he was contemplating something, and then nothing but resolve showed on his face.

"We are a team, right?" he started. Nods all around. "I know you were all coerced to be here, and I was ordered, but we are being used as pawns in a much larger game. There is no way anyone could have followed us from Australia to the Serengeti. We are in a plane that can circle the globe faster than most people can get from DC to Boston."

We all nodded in unison as Spencer continued his explanation. "The people who attacked us were in park ranger vehicles, in park ranger uniforms, and knew the camp. That type of prep work doesn't happen in a matter of hours. I think they were already there for the hyena attacks, probably assuming their presence would never be noticed due to the remote location. When we showed up—conveniently herded into the camp—they viewed it as another opportunity to eliminate the competition. That we're so close on their heels makes us a threat to them. It was too tempting an opportunity to pass up, but they missed."

"Well, mostly," I said, pointing to Spencer's sling.

He ignored me. "Since we have managed to put a few pieces of this puzzle together, we will be seen as an ongoing threat and whoever is behind this will continue to try and eliminate us. Mr. Smith knows this and is trying to use it to his advantage, possibly at the cost of our lives."

"Goddamn that man!" Alex burst out.

"Now that I have time to objectively review this entire mission, I suspect whoever sabotaged our diving gear in Australia also was there before us and knew what we were doing before we even landed. That suggests someone within our operational circle, someone with nearly unlimited resources, is involved."

"Another Mr. Smith?" I asked dubiously.

"Let's try to think like a Mr. Smith," continued Spencer with a heavy sigh. "I had counted on our speed in getting places and the covert nature of what we were doing to protect us. That was a serious miscalculation on my part and led to someone getting killed. We could have all been killed. We were lucky. Looking forward, we have to assume that whoever is behind this is expecting us. Mr. Smith must have come to the same conclusion. He could make this a military operation and overwhelm the boat that the Montgomerys are on, yet he's sending us. Why?"

We all shrugged our shoulders. It didn't make a lot of sense.

"Think in terms of an end-game strategy," continued Spencer. "You three are doctors. What would happen to the world if this prion got out on a massive scale?"

The question hung in the air. We had been tasked with investigating local outbreaks, but I don't think any of us truly contemplated a wide-scale pandemic, until now. Each of us knew how devastating that outcome would be.

Spencer continued, "Mr. Smith is trained to look at information and figure out worst-case scenarios. In the grand scheme of things, four lives are disposable. In a way, he wants us to fail."

"Are you saying he wants us to be killed?" asked Nell, the color draining from her face.

"No," answered Spencer. "Not to be killed, but to be bait for whoever is behind this so they can be exposed. You three are seen as a threat. Every time someone surfaces to try and kill us, a trail emerges, even if that trail is hard to follow. Mr. Smith is putting together a complicated puzzle, and each little piece of information makes the overall picture a bit more complete. I'm certain Mr. Smith gained information from the encounter in Australia and then again from the encounter in Africa. It just has not yet led back to the person behind all of this. If Mr. Smith thought the Montgomerys were behind everything, they would already be dead. If he thought they knew who was behind it, they would be at Guantanamo Bay, being waterboarded. He needs us to reveal the next little piece that fits into his puzzle."

Nell and Alex stared at the floor. I felt as though I was going to throw up.

"Can we turn around and go back to the plane?" I asked, almost ashamed to ask the question out loud, even though we were all thinking it.

"If that is what the group decides, I will support it," said Spencer. "Please know this is not a decision I take lightly. For me to even utter those words would be grounds for dishonorable discharge from the military, as well as a likely court martial, but I will do it rather than put you three unwillingly further into harm's way."

The last statement hung in the air. The waves gently rocked the boat, and the only sound was the hull crashing into oncoming waves. There was no land visible in any direction, and the tropical sun suddenly irritated my eyes as we all contemplated our next decision. Do we turn back or continue to try and help?

"I vote we move forward and do what we can to help prevent a catastrophe," said Alex, with sudden resolve. Nell and I both looked at him with surprise. Spencer's reaction revealed admiration.

"Okay, I get it," continued Alex. "I know I'm a pompous ass. I know what people think of me. I'm not stupid. I've been through lots of relationships in my life, and if you ask any of my exes, they will have a lot to say about how self-centered and narcissistic I can be. But I'm also a doctor and a neurologist. I have seen the devastation of neurological diseases my entire life. The reason I spent so much time in the hospital in Australia is that people were dying, and I was unable to prevent it. I have never felt so helpless in my entire career. And now we believe this can happen on a massive scale? If I can do anything to try and stop that from happening, and I turn my back on that responsibility . . ." He shook his head, contemplating it. "I will never be able to look at myself in the mirror again. Let's do what we can. But just to be clear, I am still planning on suing Mr. Smith for every nickel he's worth when we get back."

I couldn't help but smile at that last part. Alex was at least staying partially true to form. Nell and I also agreed to continue on. How could we not?

Spencer let out a long breath. In reality, I suspected he was anticipating we would turn back, and he would be left to face the consequences alone. The relief in his face was obvious. Only then did I realize what Spencer had risked by offering us an out. This would have been the end of his entire career.

"Now that the decision to continue is firm, we need to come up with a strategy that will not get us killed," Spencer said with a smile. "We need to assume that whoever is trying to prevent us from uncovering anything knows where we are right now and where we're heading. This knowledge gives us the upper hand, but only if we use it to our advantage. Let's talk to the captain."

Spencer walked to the bridge and after a short conversation, the copilot took the wheel and the captain joined us on deck.

"Please tell us about Genovesa Island," asked Spencer.

The captain's eyes lit up. "Oh, this island is one of my favorites. The island is also known as bird island, and it's one of the best places in the world to observe the red-footed boobies and--"

Spencer cut him off. "That's not what I meant. Where do boats dock, and where do people go to hike?"

Appearing a bit offended the captain continued. "All the boats dock in Great Darwin Bay, which is an expansive, protected bay with a relatively narrow channel going in. There's really no other place to set anchor for the night without risking pretty extreme seasickness."

"How many boats are typically in the bay?" asked Spencer.

The captain continued, "Great Darwin Bay is almost a mile wide. The area could easily accommodate over a hundred boats, but usually only three or four are anchored at any given time. The government of Ecuador strictly limits the number of people who are allowed into the Galapagos."

"And where do people go to hike?" asked Spencer.

"There is only one place people are allowed to go. Hikers start on a narrow landing and immediately go up a steep set of stairs built into a cliff called the Prince Philips Staircase. Once at the top, the trail goes around to several nesting sites. Visitors are not permitted to go off the trail."

"Two questions," asked Spencer. "Is the Prince Phillips Staircase the only way up? And once you get to the top, is it wide open?"

The captain quickly replied. "Yes to both questions. The staircase is the only way to get to the top, since the island is essentially a wide open lovely plateau surrounded by steep cliffs on all sides. The views from the top are spectacular, and the bird life is unparalleled."

"Do you have charts of the island?" asked Spencer.

"Yes I do, but we keep them on the walls for decorative display," answered the captain. "I used to love the feeling of using paper charts for navigation. There was just something about it that made sea travel romantic. Everything is electronic these days, and it feels almost artificial."

"Last question for now," said Spencer. "Did you radio anyone our position or where we were going?"

"Our sailing plan and the hiking permit were filed with the Ecuador government, as is the regulation," responded the captain. "Other than that, no, I have not contacted anyone."

"Good," said Spencer, nodding. "Please keep it that way."

The captain excused himself and headed back to the bridge. Spencer grabbed a topographical map off of the wall, removed the frame, and spread it out in front of us.

"My initial plan was to pull into the bay and watch from afar or perhaps even follow them on the hike, observing from a safe distance," sighed Spencer. "I suspect that is exactly what they are expecting us to do."

"Who are they?" asked Alex.

"I don't know. That's for Mr. Smith to figure out," responded Spencer. "The Prince Philips Staircase is a perfect place to stage an ambush. This place is remote. It would be easy to pick an elevated position along the top of the staircase and wait. If I was designing a place to attack someone, this is where I would do it, as there are no crowds, and you can see people coming from a long way off. Even if some of the group decided not to go on the hike, the boat is in a large bay with only one exit, so they pick off anyone remaining behind by ambushing the exit area.

This entire island is basically like a trap designed to covertly eliminate an enemy."

"If what you say is true, to go into the bay is not going to end well for us," I reasoned.

"Yes," Spencer muttered, almost to himself, reviewing in his head the plan he contemplated. "It needs to look like we're going into the bay for an afternoon hike. Deception is the key. If there are people who wish us harm, they will set up on the Prince Philips Staircase. It's their only strategy, so we can assume that's what they'll do. All we need is an entry point that isn't so obvious." He traced the map with his hands. "This island is surrounded by cliffs. We have four hours until we're scheduled to take the hike. Thanks to the Ecuadorian government, we know where and when the Montgomerys are going to be on the top of Genovesa Island. If we get to the island in two and a half hours, we should have enough time."

"Enough time for what?" I asked.

"Enough time to finally get the upper hand," responded Spencer. "I have some planning to do," he muttered as he grabbed his phone and walked away.

I turned to Nell and Alex, and the concern on their faces was obvious. We sat around in a tight circle on the deck.

"Let's review what we know and see if there's anything else we can uncover," suggested Nell. "We know animals have been infected with prions, and we suspect the infections occurred at or near picnic areas where Off the Grid Tours have been. The human infections have been direct results of animal interaction, and that could not have been predicted."

"So we're chasing someone on high-end ecotours who wants to kill the wildlife?" asked Alex. "That doesn't make any sense. Do you think we're going to find a villain with a poison dart gun, shooting at iguanas?"

"Perhaps we're looking at this the wrong way," I suggested. "Let's assume for a second that someone is developing a biological weapon that works across species and causes rapid, fatal disease. You need to test this, so what do you do?"

"You infect lab mice or rats in a controlled environment and observe them to see what happens," replied Nell.

"I agree," I responded. "Now, let's imagine the lab tests are a success—mice die and so do monkeys. Next I'd want to know how contagious this thing is."

"You could release it to a population of wild animals or people, and see what happens," responded Alex, sitting at attention.

"But if you want all of this to be top secret?" I continued.

"Then I'd travel to remote parts of the world and release it where no one is likely to take notice," answered Alex while rubbing his goatee. "The wilds of the world are the perfect test tube. The areas are obscure enough and the species of animals are diverse enough that it could provide someone a glimpse into how this prion would behave if it were released on a massive scale. No one could possibly make the connection that animals in Queensland and Africa were getting sick. In fact, very few people would care. The local communities would care, but it would not make significant news, unless it was so contagious that people got sick."

He was on a roll. "But one could argue that the people who got sick were accidental. Someone infects animals in a picnic area on the Daintree. A team observes the effects until all the animals die. Perhaps they were careless and didn't collect the bodies or wanted to see what would happen next, but a tourist discovers a bunch of dead marsupials and tells the authorities. The authorities know it would affect the tourist trade if a bunch of rotting corpses turned up near a picnic area, so they dispose of the animals in the easiest way possible and the animals are tossed in the river. The crocodiles enjoy a free snack, essentially go crazy, and attack tourists on the Great Barrier Reef. It makes the news, but it isn't a giant international incident. Same thing in Africa. Someone leaves something tasty for a hyena and stays to observe the effects. There would be no way to predict that a person would be attacked, but even if that happened, who would take notice? These are wild animals that crazy people go to watch in their native environment—I'd guess stuff like this happens several times a year. A tourist getting bitten in Africa would not have caught Mr. Smith's attention had he not been focused on a specific set of symptoms. The only reason we went to Africa is because Mr. Smith was looking for that specific scenario. If Spencer is right, and those who attacked us in Africa were already there, they were most likely there to observe the effects of the prion and not us. We were in the classic wrong place at the wrong time."

The logical conclusion was staring us in the face. This was not random, it was calculated. Whoever was behind it all had conducted experiments toward a specific, disastrous outcome. And it was likely more experiments would be carried out until the prion was modified exactly to meet some catastrophic end. I shuddered at the thought.

Spencer reappeared. "Mr. Smith is having the navy send down a Cyclone-class patrol ship," said Spencer. "It's still several hours away, but it will be close enough to provide support if we need it, when the time comes."

"Hmph. That's subtle," said Alex.

"The ship will stay about forty-five miles off the coast of Genovesa. That should be far enough out that it won't appear on the radar of the ships in the bay. So we have backup. Next, based on satellite imaging, there is a small beach on the northwest side of the island outside of the bay that can provide a landing spot for a Zodiac without being seen. We can hike up the back of the island, well away from the bay and the established trail. Based on the topography of the island, we should be able to make it to the plateau, where we will have the upper hand. But one thing still bothers me." Spencer paused and winced, trying to remove the sling from his arm.

"Can we please examine your shoulder?" asked Nell. "You know we're doctors?"

"No, you cannot."

Alex, unconcerned about Spencer's shoulder, said, "Per favor, comandante, what's been bothering you, besides people trying to kill us, that is?"

"People try to kill me all the time," responded Spencer.

"It's a fresh experience for me," I offered. "And not one I would like to continue having."

"What bothers me is that the people behind this are so elusive," continued Spencer, ignoring our commentary. "I have been involved in missions throughout the world, and it has always been clear who you are fighting. You may not know where they are, and it's hard to understand the motivation at times, but the who is usually the easiest to uncover. Any mission typically starts with the who and then moves on to the where and then, sometimes, finally the why. Not knowing the *who* is unnerving."

Chapter 16

THE NEXT HOUR CONSISTED OF reviewing the plan and getting the Zodiac ready. Spencer had briefed the captain and co-captain on what he was planning. They were reluctant to do anything that would get them into trouble, and there was no question the government did not allow landings on an island at a point other than what was strictly regulated. After a long discussion followed by several phone calls, including one from the head of the governing council of Ecuador, the two pilots agreed. They would drop us off just before the entrance to Great Darwin Bay and then continue into the bay and drop anchor. Spencer stressed that the boat remain near the entrance, and if any boat were to approach them, the two were to leave immediately and return to port at top speeds.

The basis of the plan was simple. We would get to the top of the Prince Philips Staircase before the Montgomery group was supposed to start their hike. If there was to be an ambush, we would be on the higher ground, and no one would be looking up for someone on the top of an uninhabited island. The trick would be getting to the top in time.

For the illusion to work, Spencer had the captain radio in updates on an open channel. He would confirm the time of the hike with the government, citing a discrepancy in the permit as a reason for the call. If anyone was listening, it should convince them that we were preparing to reach the bottom of the Prince Philips Staircase at the same time as the Montgomery group.

Thanks to Mr. Smith and the marvels of satellites, we knew two large tour boats currently lay anchored in Great Darwin Bay, and their positions were well away from the entrance. If the Montgomerys were directly involved, the guests on their ship would set up an ambush. If they were not involved, then the other ship held bad actors who could be traced back to a person or organization. The value in what we were doing was clear, but we couldn't ignore the risk. Each of us hoped we were wrong about everything, and the ships held nothing but high-end ecotourists, keen on having a wonderful afternoon walking with the birds. Unfortunately, none of us believed it to be true.

We arrived at Genovesa on time. Launching the Zodiac off of the boat was surprisingly easy. The small craft was lifted by a crane and gently lowered over the side. The entire process took less than ten minutes.

Climbing on board was a bit more challenging. Some of the bigger swells were up to eight feet, which gently lifted both crafts but caused the Zodiac to bump off the side of the bigger boat. After several minutes of trying to time the jump between crafts, we were all safely on the smaller boat. We pushed away, and Spencer manned the outboard motor to direct the Zodiac toward the island as the captain sailed the touring boat to the entrance of the bay.

The seas were rough as we approached the northwest side of the island. We could see the entrance to the bay was about half a mile ahead. The Zodiac was tossed around like a toy in a giant tub as the waves swelled the closer we got to the cliffs. The four of us clung to the sides and tried not to get thrown into the chilly water. I started to doubt the plan as we watched the waves crash against the rough cliff walls. I saw no place where we could land the boat without being smashed against the jagged rocks, much less climb to the top.

Based on the satellite images of the island, we expected to find a sliver of land with a small sandy beach and a twenty-foot rock wall to climb to get to the plateau. Spencer maneuvered the boat so we were only about twenty-five feet from the shore, at a distance just beyond where the waves were breaking. With every wave, the Zodiac listed to the side about thirty degrees, creating the illusion we were about to flip over, before flattening out. I was starting to feel nauseous and was about to suggest that perhaps we should come up with a plan B.

As we crested an abnormally high wave, I finally saw the point we were aiming for. The sand beach was not a beach at all, but rather a section of gravelly rock where a portion of the cliff had collapsed. Luckily, the area still provided a potential landing point where we would not be destroyed by the surf. The timing would have to be perfect.

The waves pounded the shore as if they were trying to pulverize the island with each deafening crash. Spencer waited for a wave to recede and then gunned the engine and rode the next wave directly onto the rocks. A wave crashed around us and dropped the boat directly onto the rocks with no pity for the bottom of the boat or the outboard engine, which I assumed had been crushed as the engine sputtered and died. We all bounced around the rubber craft, which thankfully cushioned the blow. Peering over the side, I could see the boat was on solid land. Seconds later, another wave crashed and nearly dislodged the boat and pulled us back out to sea.

"We need to get out now!" shouted Spencer, even before the wave completely receded. "Grab the side and pull," he commanded as we attempted to drag the small craft a bit higher before the next wave clawed at us. I gazed out at the ocean and noticed a small group of sea lions observing us with curious amusement from the rough surf. It took several minutes and a lot of colorful language, with waves occasionally rising to the level of our knees, but we succeeded in beaching the boat above the reach of the surf.

Scaling the rock wall was our next challenge. The rocks were wet and slippery, and going was slow. At several points in the ascent, each one of us slipped on the sharp rocks and sustained a cut or bruise. Spencer was especially struggling with his injured arm. Upon cresting the peak of the cliff, I was struck by the sounds of tens of thousands of birds, seeming to be all screeching as one. Their sheer number was unlike anything I had ever seen. The ground was almost completely white with bird droppings, and the top of the island smelled of rotting fish. Out in the distance, the entrance of the bay could be seen. The waves crashed against the cliffs at either edge of the bay, but the water in the bay appeared as smooth as glass from this height. From our vantage point, we could see our boat as it entered the massive bay and headed toward the far shoreline. There were two other boats moored, and they sat so still, they could have been a painting.

We reviewed the plan one final time. Spencer and Alex would go to the top of the Prince Philips Staircase and wait in the shadows. Nell and I waited back one hundred feet or so in the bushes, on the off chance that someone would approach from any other direction. Mr. Smith would monitor the satellite feed and alert us on Spencer's satellite phone if anyone approached.

We had an hour left to make it to the top of the Staircase. Walking was easy on the plateau, since the ground was mostly hardened dirt with small pebbles and low-lying shrubs, few and far between. It was difficult not to be completely consumed by the beauty of this place. A remarkable number of frigatebirds, red footed boobies, and gulls swooped up and down the sheer cliffs, continually creating a flurry of motion. Their bright colors were a stark contrast to the dark volcanic rocks. The birds were fearless and made no attempt to fly away, even when we were within inches of them. Several times, we had to step over a nest as the mother looked up with apparent curiosity or just paid no attention. They made no attempt to flee from our presence. This was their world.

It took us half an hour to get to the staircase, and we cautiously approached the top of the stairs, encountering no one. Spencer's assessment of the area was spot on. Built into a ravine in the rocks, the wooden staircase led one hundred feet down to the calm waters of the bay. Book-casing the steps were a sheer cliff on one side and on the other, massive, uneven rocks formed by centuries of decay. I spotted several small caves that could provide easy hiding spots, mere inches from the stairs. Even without military training, I knew an assailant could easily, without warning, hide and attack someone on their way up.

Spencer set up Alex in a small cavity in the rocks, twenty feet from the top of the staircase. For Nell and me, he pointed out the best cover in the brush. "If anyone approaches from the rear, wait until they are at the staircase, and then scream, so I can hear you. I'll just have to be certain to take care of the threat," Spencer instructed. He then chose his own station to the left of the stairs, in an area of rock which jutted out past the edge of the cliff. He could see down almost the entire length of the staircase, but I doubted anyone could see him from below. From our respective positions, we would be invisible unless someone was close enough to touch us.

Nell and I retreated into the brush. "I hope Spencer's wrong, and no one's coming to kill us," I said to Nell nervously.

Time stood still, and I could hear my own heart pumping in my ears. Birds enveloped us in our hiding spot, squawking noisily and hopping from rock to rock. I imagined the noise giving our hiding spot away and immediately realized how absurd the thought was. I wanted to talk to Nell, but couldn't think of anything to say. I was so out of my element here.

Spencer's phone must have rung, as I saw him retrieve it and put it to his ear and nod. He spoke briefly and then signaled to us to stay low and out of sight as he crouched lower in his hiding spot and disappeared from our view. This was it.

Soon we would know. It was nerve-racking not to know what Spencer could see as the minutes ticked slowly by.

After an eternity, I heard faint pinging sounds, reminding me of the shots in Africa. None of the birds moved, but I couldn't help but duck down lower in the brush where we were hiding and grabbed Nell's arm. One look told me she was as nervous as I was. I found myself trembling, but Nell took my hand from her forearm and enclosed it in hers, calming my nerves.

Finally we saw Alex and Spencer coming to collect us. As we all walked back toward the stairs, Alex blurted, "This was real. Someone was trying to kill us, but Spencer killed them first."

"Smith alerted me when a Zodiac departed one of the boats, with three men aboard," said Spencer. "Two men jumped off when they got to the bottom of the staircase, and the third steered the Zodiac back to the larger boat. The men were dressed in black and moved cautiously as they ascended the staircase. They checked out the rocks on both sides, but seemed unconcerned as they took time occasionally to stop and talk."

"It's surreal," I said. "This is a world in which I previously have no experience. And I don't want any more."

"Me too," said Nell. "But I do want to hear everything."

Spencer continued. "About three-quarters of the way up, both men climbed over the rails of the stairs and disappeared behind a boulder that would completely block them from being seen by anyone walking up. Each drew small pistols with silencers, leveled them down the stairs, and waited."

Alex, whose adrenaline was spiking, burst in. "They never even bothered to look up the stairs, or they would have seen Spencer as he crept out of his hiding place and took aim. They were perfectly exposed to the higher ground. Spencer fired, twice, dropping both men within seconds. Even from where I was, I could see the small holes in the backs of their heads where the Glock had done its terrible job."

"I used a silencer," said Spencer to Nell and me, "so you may not have heard anything."

"We heard pings," I responded, "but we didn't know from whose gun."

We reached the top of the staircase. It took Spencer only a few minutes to walk down to the bodies and frisk them. They carried no identifying information. He dragged each one behind the rock where they fell, all the while being careful not to be seen from the water—or by anyone else walking up the stairs.

"This should buy us some time," Spencer reasoned. "The men were most likely instructed to stay hidden until we came up the staircase. However, they had radios. Hopefully they weren't instructed to check in regularly."

"Can we use the radios?" Alex asked.

"No. They're protected with a code, useless to us. But these could help us." He held up the assassins' two guns.

"Count me out," said Nell. "I appreciate all you've done for us, Spencer, but I've lived by an anti-gun principle for a long time, and recent events have not persuaded me otherwise."

"I'll carry one," I said. "But show me how to work the safety."

Alex just put his hand out for the other, and Spencer gave us a brief demonstration of the safety and trigger mechanisms. We slipped the surprisingly compact guns into our pockets and waited.

Spencer's phone apparently vibrated, as he retrieved it from a pocket and listened. "Roger that," he said and slipped it back in his pocket. "Two more Zodiacs are headed to the staircase, this time from the Montgomery boat. We can now shadow the Montgomerys without being noticed."

Nell, Alex, and I would join the back of the Montgomery tour and observe without being seen. Spencer would trail far back on the trail, in case anyone else approached from behind. With our boat still stationed near the entrance of the bay, it appeared as though we were all still waiting on board. The illusion was working, for now.

We waited behind some low-lying shrubbery about a hundred feet off the trail. From where we crouched in the dirt, we could observe the top of the staircase without being seen. All that could be heard were the relentless cries of the sea birds enveloping the island. I put my hand down on a rock and looked into a shallow crevice immediately to the left of where we were hiding. I gasped to see a Galapagos short-eared owl five feet away. He stared without blinking and showed no fear, despite our proximity. I pointed him out to the others and the tension broke as we all admired this magnificent bird.

Some minutes later, ten guests with cameras appeared at the top of the staircase. Either these were the best disguises in history or these people were truly tourists. The average age of the guests must have been seventy-five, and they required about a ten-minute picture break at the top of the staircase, to catch their breath. Leading the group was a very high-energy, gregarious girl with an orange hat—Ella. Trailing behind and enjoying it all was a tall woman wearing an Off the Grid Tours T-shirt. She was about forty years old with two long, graying pigtails in braids. She was holding the hand of a stout, middle-aged man with obvious signs of Down Syndrome. Every once in a while, he burst out laughing at something Ella said. As the tour passed by, we crept out from our hiding place and casually walked up the path. We were close enough to hear Ella describe the nesting habits of the short-eared owl. She hoped the group would be lucky enough to see one. "How ironic," I whispered to Nell.

We should have been paying closer attention, because as we rounded a bend on the path, we nearly bumped into some stragglers at the back of the group. The plan was to stay far enough behind that we would not been seen. It was too late for that as we made eye contact with the two women in the back, who gave us warm smiles. "You can walk on past if you want," said an elderly woman who leaned on a long walking stick. "Don't let us hold you up."

Not knowing what to do, Alex walked past the group with a comment about how beautiful the view was, and we followed suit. Several steps later, we caught up with the rest of the seniors, who had made another stop. Ella was going on about how the red-billed tropic bird was by far her favorite because the beak was actually more orange than red. She stopped mid-sentence and said, "Miss Nell! Is that you?"

Ella was staring directly at the three of us. I silently cursed under my breath for being so careless as to catch up with the group. So much for a covert operation. I tried to read the faces, all turned toward us now. Most were a bit confused, others resumed taking pictures of the surroundings. I detected no malice in any expression.

The woman with the gray pigtails walked up to us and, with a very polite but curious tone, introduced herself. "I'm Carolyn Montgomery, and this is my twin brother, Timmy."

Timmy walked up to Nell and gave her a big hug. "You're pretty," he said.

Nell, a bit flustered, managed to respond, "And you are very handsome."

Timmy glowed as he went back and held his sister's hand.

"And how do you know my daughter Ella?" she asked. Not quite threatening, but in the way that a mother might question a stranger in a playground.

"We met on a beach in Australia, a few days ago," I offered. I thought of saying it's a small world, but somehow, being in the same remote location several continents away seemed more than a coincidence.

Carolyn didn't look satisfied, but Ella broke the tension when she again started the tour, leading the group toward the cliffs and the incredible nesting sites of the red-footed boobies. We all walked casually toward the far side of the island, occasionally taking breaks for pictures or for Ella to point out a specific bird. Carolyn kept eying the three of us and twice stopped and turned, as if she was going to say something, before rethinking and continuing her walk behind the tour group while holding her brother's hand.

I turned to say something to Nell when, out of the corner of my eye, I saw what appeared to be Timmy dropping pellets onto the ground. It was subtle and fleeting. The first time I wasn't sure it had even happened, until he did it again.

I grabbed Nell's wrist and whispered. "Could you please go get Spencer and bring him up here?" She gave me a curious look and then, without a word, turned around and walked back the way we had come.

It didn't take long. Thirty seconds later, Nell reappeared with Spencer in tow. Carolyn now glared at the four of us. She stopped and turned to us, trailing her group by about twenty yards. She whispered something to Timmy, dropped his hand, and walked toward us. I saw Spencer's entire body tense as his right hand slid into his pocket.

"Easy," I whispered to him.

"I don't know what's going on here," started Carolyn, keeping her voice low, out of earshot from the tour as the group continued to move forward. "No one bumps into another person by accident in Australia and then in the Galapagos. We were supposed to be the only group on this island today. I double-checked this morning. Each member in my group pays a lot of money to be out here with no one else, and I don't like that my daughter has met you people, and I have no idea who you are."

Spencer visibly relaxed as he realized the only threat here was a chewing out by the coordinator of a tour. Just then his phone rang, and he put it to his ear and turned away.

"That's impossible," exclaimed Carolyn. "The nearest cell tower is a hundred miles away."

"I understand, sir," said Spencer into the phone. He hung up, and turned back to us, pausing. I knew he was considering his options.

"They are coming," said Spencer. "Two Zodiacs have started loading from the assailant's boat. Mr. Smith already radioed our boat and instructed them to retreat out to sea. I don't know how, but they know we are here. The jig is up. We don't have much time." He spoke to Carolyn, firmly. "You need to come with us."

"Come with who?" answered Carolyn. "Where? Nothing's up here but birds."

"I am sorry, and if I'm wrong, I'll apologize again. But you, Ella, and Timmy are coming with us," responded Spencer taking the tone of a military drill sergeant.

"Like hell we are!" barked Carolyn, stepping in front of Spencer and blocking his path to Ella and Timmy. "You have no right to--" Her face turned white at the site of the gun coming out of Spencer's pocket. "Please don't hurt Ella or Timmy, I beg you." Her face was turning whiter, and her hands shook badly, as though she was having a mild seizure. "Oh God, oh God, what could you possibly want? I have nothing out here. No money. What do you want?"

Carolyn was having a full-blown panic attack. This was not a master criminal. Nell grabbed Carolyn's forearm and that seemed to calm her down a little bit.

"We're here to protect you, not to hurt you. You have to trust us," Nell pleaded with Carolyn.

"I don't," answered Carolyn. "Protect us from what?"

The question hung in the air and remained unanswered as we walked forward toward the tour.

"What about the ten seniors?" I asked Spencer.

"No way we can help them, and they are not a threat to whoever is coming," snapped Spencer. "There would be no reason to harm them." He looked at me and then back at the path toward the staircase making calculations in his head. "In fact, we can use them to our advantage, if we act now."

I wanted to ask a dozen questions, but Spencer was already again hurrying ahead.

"I don't know how much more of this I can stand," muttered Alex.

We caught up to the group. At the sight of her frightened mother, Ella ran over and hugged her leg.

"Is everything okay, Mom?" she asked.

Timmy grabbed Carolyn's hand, which calmed her down. The color returned to her face, and she said with a calm and strength I found surprising, "Timmy, Ella, everything is fine."

Her turnaround from frantic to balanced in a matter of seconds was astounding. Perhaps the result of years of caring for a brother with Down Syndrome while being a single mother and running a company. Her tour group was already forming a circle around us.

"Listen up, everyone," said Spencer, the gun now back in his right pocket. With his left hand, he held up his phone as a prop, saying, "I just got word from the weather service that a hurricane is headed to the island at a very fast speed. We need to get you all back down as quickly as possible. Please head out the same way you came, and a boat will pick you up. John will lead you to the stairs."

Several of the seniors gazed up at the bright-blue sky with obvious doubt.

I shot Spencer a hard stare, meant to communicate I was not comfortable walking toward danger.

He gave me a reassuring look that did nothing to calm my anxiety. He leaned in and said in a whisper only I could hear, "Lead them to the top of the staircase as fast as you can. As soon as they are on the stairs, run like hell back to us. We won't be far."

I saw no way to get out of this, and it was clear Spencer had made up his mind. I held up my hand, and in as commanding a voice as I could muster, asked the group to start heading down the path. The reluctance was obvious, but eventually all the tour group began shuffling their feet in the right direction.

"Do you have a radio to the boat?" asked Spencer quietly to Carolyn.

"Yes, I do," she replied icily.

"Call them and tell them to send the Zodiac, please," commanded Spencer.

Carolyn hesitated until Spencer's hand again went into his right pocket. She gave him a scowl but called the Zodiac to pick up the group. The captain seemed confused but agreed to send the boat right away. Spencer took the radio, turned it off, and pocketed it and his phone. He motioned for Carolyn to walk ahead.

"I need to go with the tour group--" she protested.

"You can't. You and your family are not safe. None of us remaining on this plateau are. Men are coming up here to kill these three," he pointed to us, "and they won't spare the rest of us."

"But why? Who are you?" Carolyn asked us.

Spencer remained in charge. "They're scientists, and I'll explain more as soon as we're secure. Right now, we need to figure out how to evade these men. Sending the seniors down the stairs will buy some time, but we need to hide and wait for the calvary to arrive. There are too many coming for anything else to be successful. It's the safest plan," said Spencer.

I listened to the plan being hatched in real time, as long as I could, before jogging off to catch up with the tour group. It only took about ten seconds. I was sure I didn't like this plan, as I headed down the path with this painfully slow group. Several stopped to gather around a waved albatross that had landed—the magnificent bird must have stood at least three feet high. In different circumstances, I would have admired the sight, but my heart was beating out of my chest, and I could feel beads of sweat dripping down my back. I walked up to the group, willing them to continue quickly. I helplessly wrung my hands together as I imagined armed soldiers charging down the path at us with guns drawn.

"Hurry, please. This is a really dangerous weather system," I announced as officially as I could. Again the seniors gazed upon the blue sky and murmured objections to their afternoon hike being cut short. "I know it doesn't look like it yet, but the storm is approaching at over sixty miles an hour, and the wind speeds are over one hundred miles an hour near the eye," I lied. "It will be here in about thirty minutes, and you all need to be back on the boat by then, or it may become impossible to use the Zodiacs." At that moment, the wind picked up ever so slightly, as if on cue. That got their attention, and the group collectively sensed an imaginary danger. The front of the group picked up their pace heading to the stairs as I breathed a quick sigh of relief.

"Are they coming?" asked the nearest senior, taking one last picture and motioning down the path to where the Montgomerys were.

"Another group is up ahead, whose radio is out. We need to warn them so they don't get stranded up here. We'll all catch up with you shortly. Your safety is our top priority."

The man seemed to believe me and started to walk away.

I ran to the front of the group of seniors who had just arrived at the top of the steep narrow stairs. I felt elation that there was not a group of assassins running up the stairs with guns drawn. We had made it in time; Spencer knew what he was doing. The first of the seniors started down the stairs holding onto the rails the entire time. The stairs were too narrow for anyone to come up while this slow moving group descended.

Down below, a Zodiac with a driver with an Off the Grid T-shirt pulled up to the landing at the bottom of the stairs, and I gave him a friendly wave. He waved back with confusion on his face, not knowing who I was and why the tour was ending so abruptly.

In the distance, two Zodiacs filled with men approached the staircase. The landing was being blocked by the Montgomery's driver who held up a finger to indicate to the latter two boats that it would be a minute. There was no way to pull up with the stairs full and the narrow landing blocked. For a second, I thought they might cause trouble, but the late-coming Zodiacs backed away and waited their turn.

"Please, take your time going down the stairs," I called out to the last of Carolyn's tour, as she was taking one step at a time resting several seconds before placing the next foot down and holding onto the rail for dear life.

"At my age, I always take my time," she said with a warm smile.

Let's hope so, I thought, turning and running at a full sprint. It took about ten minutes to catch up to the group. They were heading to the center of the island, along the only path available. I filled Spencer in on the what I estimated to be about a dozen men coming for us.

"We have about ten minutes until Carolyn's group is down the stairs and the two other Zodiacs can unload," I reported.

Spencer took a moment, calculating our options. "There's no way to get all of us down into our Zodiac with the amount of time we have," he said. "And I can't ambush two boatloads of men. We need to find a place to hide."

Glancing around the plateau, I didn't see much in the way of options.

"Did you say 'hide'?" asked Ella beaming.

"Do you know a good hiding spot?" asked Nell, trying to conceal the panic in her voice.

"I am always the best at hide-and-seek," boasted Ella. "People can never find me. One time we played right here on this island while the adults were looking at birds. There was a group of ten kids, and no one could find me. I didn't come out until they all gave up."

"Can you show us your hiding spot?" asked Nell.

"Only if you promise not to show anyone else. I wouldn't want to spoil a spot this special," said Ella.

"I don't like this one bit," Carolyn whispered to Spencer, who had taken up position right behind her with his hand still in his pocket.

"If I wanted to hurt you or your family, that would have already happened. But men who will harm all of us are about to storm this island," said Spencer in a calm voice. "You have to trust me."

"I reluctantly have to do what you say," corrected Carolyn. "Because you have a gun, and my daughter and brother need me. But I don't trust you."

"At this point, I'll take what I can get," said Spencer, looking behind us with concern.

Ella took Nell's hand and skipped down the trail. Timmy followed them, and I kept a close watch on Timmy and his pellets.

Several hundred feet from the end, she veered off toward the cliffs where the majority of the birds were nesting. It only took five minutes to get to Ella's hiding spot. Just at the edge of the cliff was a deep ravine in the rocks. I didn't see a way to safely get down into the ravine, but Ella pointed and said, "My spot is right here."

My heart sank, and I saw the despair in the other's faces. We had wasted precious time and now were cornered into a position with a cliff behind us. There was no way to go but back toward the staircase. I pictured the last of the seniors getting onto the Zodiac and the men with guns racing up the stairs and my heart sank. Even with three guns and Spencer on our side, we could not possibly defend ourselves against the armed squad that was coming.

"There is no way down," said Nell, her voice cracking. Alex seemed struck dumb.

"Not from this side, but there is a hidden way down," said Ella with a devious smile. "Come on, I'll show you."

We approached the far side of the ravine. Spencer appeared increasingly nervous, as he kept looking back along the path we had come. We were putting a lot of faith in a ten-year-old girl, and our options were swiftly running out. If this plan failed, we'd be in desperate trouble. At the end of the ravine, the rocks formed what appeared like a series of steps, each about two feet lower than the other.

"See," said Ella triumphantly. "Can we go down, Mom?" she asked with pleading eyes. Carolyn looked at Spencer, and after an agonizing five seconds said, "Yes dear, we can all go down."

"Cool," responded Ella, already jumping down the first two ledges. Nell followed Ella as she disappeared from sight. Carolyn helped her brother down the steps, followed by Alex, and then finally Spencer and me.

Within the ravine, it was about ten degrees cooler, since the afternoon sun hadn't warmed the rocks. After about ten steps, we came to a ledge that was recessed from the top of the cliff, now twenty feet above us. The ledge was about twenty feet by three feet. Ella was already sitting on the edge with her feet hanging down. She was absolutely right. There was no way to tell from above that this ledge existed, due to the outcropping. To the left, a solid wall of rock curved out to the sea; to the right, the cliff was more jagged, and I could see where I thought our Zodiac must be in the distance. Marine iguanas sunned themselves on crevices too small for more than one or two of these odd, black-and-red scaly creatures.

Nell sat down next to Ella, and they admired the awesome view of the ocean and raw wilderness of the rock. Timmy immediately sat down next to Nell. It was obvious he was infatuated with her.

I joined the others, who were standing—in confrontation.

"I want an explanation of what's going on and why you've kidnapped my family," said Carolyn. Though she whispered, her resolve was firm. The sounds of the waves crashing below and the distant shrieking of birds made it difficult to speak in whispers, but at least Timmy, Ella, and Nell would not hear what we were saying.

Spencer filled Carolyn in about the prion and the last several days of our travels. He left out some of the details, but essentially told her enough to get his point across. What was going on was deadly serious, and people were dying. The expression on Carolyn's face changed from hate and fury to confusion and horror.

When Spencer told her about the outbreak in Memphis, she looked down and shifted weight from leg to leg.

"The tour company is stationed in Memphis, and we have a small house in the suburbs, where Timmy lives," admitted Carolyn.

"Ella told us she lives in Montana," I said with a questioning tone.

"Ella's father died when she was very young," answered Carolyn. "He had a small ten-acre ranch he left for Ella in his will. We live there most of the time when we are not visiting my brother or touring around the world. She always refers to the ranch as her home. In fact, even though she is only ten, she technically owns it."

"Then why is the company stationed in Memphis?" I asked.

"Better taxes," responded Carolyn matter-of-factly. "Besides, Timmy lives in the house we grew up in and is able to maintain a job at a restaurant in the city. He functions at a high-enough level to be on his own most of the time. He can take the bus to his job and the grocery store. Ella and I are in Memphis frequently, so we can check in on him regularly, but he loves his independence. He's so proud of living on his own." Carolyn brightened as she looked at her brother before turning back to Spencer. "We have nothing to do with any of this. I can understand your confusion, since we have been to places where animals have gotten sick, but that's just a coincidence. I want to know who is coming after you, and how you plan to safely get me and my family off this island."

"It's frankly too much of a coincidence that the outbreaks have followed you around the world," answered Spencer. "At this point, I don't know if you are being used or are a part of this, but you are going nowhere until we find some answers. And just so you know, I'm not sure that the men coming to kill us are actually after us or *you*." Carolyn shuddered at this last statement, but didn't break Spencer's stare. She was a strong woman.

"If you think we are international bioterrorists, why are you telling me all this rather than just shooting me?" asked Carolyn in a sarcastic tone.

"If you want to know the truth, I think you're being used," replied Spencer. "I think someone is using your brother." With this, Carolyn took a menacing step toward Spencer. For a second, I thought she was going to hit him. Spencer did not back down one bit.

"What do you mean using my brother?" asked Carolyn, with venom dripping in her voice.

"Go ask your brother what's in his left pocket," I urged, as gently as I could.

"And why would I do that?" responded Carolyn now turning her glare at me.

"Because I saw him dropping pellets on the ground. And if I'm right, what he's dropping is food laced with a deadly prion," I responded, matching her stare.

"I'm not getting Timmy involved in any of this," replied Carolyn.

"Then I'll ask him," said Spencer, losing his patience and dropping his hand into his pocket with the gun.

Carolyn stepped in front of Spencer and placed both hands on his chest. She was prepared to protect her brother at all costs. I suspect she had been doing it her entire life.

Spencer hesitated, but he took a small step forward, pushing Carolyn out of the way as if she wasn't even there.

Carolyn took this besting in stride. "Okay, I'll ask him, and you will see you have the wrong people," said Carolyn, softening her tone. Spencer gave her a single nod, and we all stood within earshot as she walked over to her twin brother.

Timmy was talking to Nell. Carolyn gently put her hand on Timmy's shoulder and asked him to stand up and come over and talk to the group.

"Timmy," she said with a gentle tone, "What is in your left pocket?"

Looking uncomfortable, Timmy gazed down at his feet, shifting his weight. "I think we need to go back up with the birds now," Timmy said.

"Timmy," continued Carolyn, "You need to tell me what is in your pocket."

"I can't," responded Timmy, turning a light shade of pink in his face. "I promised."

"You need to tell me," continued Carolyn in a gentle tone.

"He'll be mad," responded Timmy. "He was already really mad at me once because I didn't do a good job at following the rules. He said he would punish Ella if I didn't follow the rules again." Tears pooled in Timmy's eyes.

Carolyn persisted, possessing a practiced patience that must have come from a lifetime of caring for him. "Timmy, you need to tell me what is in your pocket," she repeated.

He seemed to consider saying something, but then averted his eyes in silence.

Carolyn shifted tactics. "Timmy, do you remember when you had a pet mouse in the box in your closet when we were kids?"

Timmy smiled. "Do you mean Marvin?"

"Yes, I mean Marvin," responded Carolyn. "Do you remember when I found out you had Marvin, and Mom and Dad didn't know?"

"Yes, I remember," said Timmy.

"I kept it a secret, just between the two of us, so you know I can keep a secret," said Carolyn. He pondered this for a minute while the rest of us did our best to appear like we weren't listening.

"I have medicine in my pocket," said Timmy finally. "The doctor gave it to me to help save the animals from getting sick. I'm not supposed to tell anyone about the medicine since it's an experiment," Timmy continued. "I have to wash my hands for five minutes every time after I touch it," continued Timmy. "The doctor got mad because I touched it and went to work and forgot to wash my hands one time."

"When was that?" asked Carolyn, as a tear rolling down her cheek, leaving a track where the dust from the hike was washed aside. I knew she was breaking, inside, but her outward demeanor remained a rock. Her brother didn't seem to notice the tear.

"I was working at the barbeque, and I wasn't supposed to touch the medicine unless I was on a trip, but I wanted to see what this batch looked like," said Timmy. "I only touched it for a second, and then I had to go to work. I was late for the bus, so I had to run, and I didn't have time to wash my hands. The doctor got mad because some people got the medicine. He said that shouldn't have happened yet."

The word *yet* sent a shock down my spine. Carolyn continued, more tears flowing now. "What is the doctor's name?"

"I'm not supposed to know his name," continued Timmy.

"But you do?" asked Carolyn.

"One time, a worker gave me the medicine while I was on an adventure with you to see the panda bears, and while I was with him, he got a call," explained Timmy with proud excitement. "I heard, even though I wasn't supposed to hear. I think the man on the phone was the doctor and the worker called him Roger. I usually got the medicine from home, except that one time. You need to keep it a secret," pleaded Timmy looking around as if someone might hear. "We need to help the animals, and the medicine will make them better. That's what they told me. Can I sit with Nell now? She's pretty."

"Yes," said Carolyn, "You can sit with Nell now." Carolyn put her head into her hands, and her whole posture sunk inward. "I can't believe this. He doesn't know any better. I know he thinks he is helping the animals. I take him on the trips and take great lengths to protect him. I keep his name off paperwork when I can. He loves the trips, and he adores Ella. He's innocent, you have to believe me. Someone has been using my brother to kill animals."

"No," I said, putting my hand on her shoulder, "not to kill animals but to test a deadly disease."

"Why?" asked Carolyn.

"We don't know why yet," answered Spencer, "But once we determine who is behind this, I intend to find out."

Spencer walked away to the edge of the ledge and spoke on the phone for several minutes, in a hushed tone, before clicking off. He looked up the way we had come, and then down over the ledge, letting out a deep breath before speaking to the group.

"According to Mr. Smith, fifteen men are on the island searching for us. They found our Zodiac, so an escape is out of the question. They are searching the island inch by inch, but none of the men are near the north shore, where we are, yet. We have time, but I'm not sure how much. I filled in Mr. Smith on what we know so far. So, there is nothing to do but wait and hope Ella is as good at hide-and-seek as she says she is."

"What about the navy ship off the coast?" I asked.

"Technically, we are on foreign soil, and no one from this new squad has even taken a shot in our direction," explained Spencer. "To send in troops would be an act of war if the people searching the island end up being citizens of Ecuador. That is not a risk the US military is willing to take, so we wait."

I ambled to an edge, taking in the vista, trying not to think. Nell got up and walked over to me.

"Yes is the answer," she said with a smile.

"What is the question?" I asked.

"You asked me out," she said with a playful pout. "Don't you even remember?"

"Of course I remember. But that was a while ago." My mind was racing, and I was thinking about how we could get off this island. I looked at Nell, and her warm smile made me completely forget the danger we were in.

"It was only yesterday, believe it or not. So I've made up my mind to go on a date with you, though I'm still not sure about your choice of venue."

"I guess that's negotiable," I said softly, returning her smile and trying not to fall too hard for this woman I had just met. There was no doubt she exerted an incredible pull on me that I had not experienced in years. I felt lost as I stared into her perfect eyes. She broke the connection first and gazed out across the ocean. The waves broke over the rocks below in a rhythmic pattern as we stood in silence, enjoying the moment.

The sun had come over the ridge and was now shining on the cold rock we were trapped on. It felt good, and the temperature seemed to rise about ten degrees. I watched the waves crashing against the cliffs below. The rock face appeared perfectly smooth and wet with the constant spray from the sea. I walked to the outer ledge we stood upon, to look up toward the plateau above. The bright sun made it hard to see anything but the sea birds dancing in playful flight along the upper ledge.

Nell's hand brushed against mine. Without hesitation, I grabbed it, and our fingers interlocked. I thought to myself, there is really no place I would rather be than on an island in the middle of the Pacific with this woman. The spell was broken by the sound of Spencer's satellite phone. He listened for a short time and hung up without saying anything.

"They're coming this way," Spencer said, pulling his gun out of his pocket. He briefly scanned along the ledge for what must have been the hundredth time. There was no place to go. The ledge dropped off at least fifty feet to the ocean below, and the waves crashing against the rocks made any attempt to jump into the ocean suicide. The path we had taken down the rocks to get to our current hiding place was narrow and opened to the plateau above where fifteen men were searching for us. I found myself wishing the navy had agreed to send in the cavalry.

"Get everyone as far back from the ledge as you can," said Spencer as he eyed the narrow path down to our hiding spot. "There is a chance they won't be able to find this spot." Alex and Nell grabbed Ella and Timmy and pulled them back from the ledge.

"What's going on?" asked Carolyn as she joined the group against the rock wall.

"People are coming," I whispered. "Please stress to Timmy and Ella that they need to stay absolutely silent."

Alex and I took positions behind Spencer, one to either side. We awkwardly held our guns, but Spencer cautioned, "Avoid firing as long as possible, preferably only if I'm down. I want to minimize ricochet accidents in here."

We stared up the narrow entrance to our hiding spot. Spencer fixed his gun at a spot halfway up the rocks. Several seconds later, shadows appeared along the ravine leading down.

"They're here," whispered Spencer.

"Let's hope they can't figure out how to get down," I added in a whisper.

Chapter 17

WE WERE NOT SO LUCKY. The first man appeared, along the narrow rock channel, gun drawn. Before he could utter a word, Spencer fired a single shot into the man's chest. Even with the suppressor, the sound of the gunshot echoed along the rocks for several seconds. Carolyn grabbed Ella and shielded her body with her own as the young girl started crying. Timmy brought his knees up to his chest and rocked back and forth as the echo of the gunshot faded.

"We're in trouble," said Spencer as the shadows retreated.

"Can we hold them off?" I asked.

Spencer crept up to the body of the man he'd shot. He retrieved a strange-looking gun with a long suppressor attached to the barrel and tucked it into his waistband.

"Not for very long," he replied. "They're regrouping as we speak, and they will probably come from multiple directions."

"There's only one path down here," Alex said.

"If they have ropes or any type of weapon other than guns, then we're extremely exposed," he replied.

"We can't jump," I said, reading his mind as he looked over the cliff to the crashing waves below.

"I'm weighing all options." Spencer's commanding tone returned. "We need to get everyone into the ravine and off the ledge, *now.*"

"I don't understand," I responded.

"Follow orders," he commanded, shoving me toward the ravine.

The others followed. It was a tight fit, but we all crammed between the two rock spurs and waited. Several seconds later, I heard a strange sound from the cliff above. Looking up, three men appeared, rappelling down ropes in front of the ledge we had just occupied. Bullets randomly sprayed the rocks from automatic weapons, creating little dimples where seconds ago, Carolyn had cradled Ella in a motherly embrace.

Spencer fired three shots with terrifying efficiency, and the three men fell into the crashing ocean below. The ropes dangled from the cliffs as the echoes of the shots stung our ears in the narrow ravine.

"They'll come again soon," said Spencer. "Alex, John, cover me—unload on anything that moves from above." He ran out to the ledge and grabbed the three ropes, cutting them with a knife he produced from an ankle holster and hurried back to the ravine. He handed the ropes to Alex and ordered him to tie them into one long rope, as he tied the other end around Ella's waist.

"Grab hold," he ordered Carolyn. "As soon as you reach a spot to stand, untie yourselves and tug twice on the rope." He turned to Alex and me. "Lower them off the cliff, as quickly as you can."

Exchanging desperate glances, we set our guns on safety and followed orders.

Spencer eyed the area above the rock ledge and the ravine as he prompted us to hurry. After lowering the rope for about a minute, the weight was suddenly gone and a quick glimpse over the edge told me Carolyn had managed to find a foothold about five feet from the water. She tugged twice on the rope, and we pulled it to the top rapidly. We wasted no time in tying Timmy to the end of the rope. Alex told Nell to grab the rope as well.

"It's too much weight," she protested.

"Grab on!" Alex insisted, and we lowered them down the rock face. The strain was incredible as Alex and I wedged ourselves between the rocks for leverage.

A shot rang out from above, and the rock splintered about three feet from our heads. A blind shot, but Spencer returned fire. We were running out of time. Two more shots rang out, rocks splintered, and multiple shadows appeared above us. Spencer fired a shot that sent rocks flying upward, and the shadows retreated.

After an eternity, the weight lifted from the rope. Another quick glance told me Timmy and Nell had reached the bottom, and Carolyn and Ella had managed to shimmy their way about twenty feet to the right, where the cliff had crumbled and there was better footing.

Alex was pulling the rope back up while I grabbed for my gun. I fumbled with the safety as the full assault unfolded.

Three men from the top of the ravine appeared, spraying gunfire all around us. Spencer returned fire, and I saw one assailant's head snap back as he fell deeper into the ravine. I had always heard that in times of extreme stress, the world seems to slow down. It was something I had never experienced until now. Turning to my left, I briefly made eye contact with Alex, a split second before a bullet ripped into the side of his head. I knew he died in that instant. My head whipped to my right, and I saw Spencer keel over and swiftly recover, as a bright red circle appeared in his side.

"We need to go!" he screamed, ignoring his injury.

I fired blindly behind him, as more men appeared, and he grabbed my hand and pulled me over the edge into an abyss.

The fall to the water below seemed to take several seconds as I looked up to the bright sun on the cliffs above. I felt the sting of making contact with the water before its coldness enveloped me. All went black for several seconds, and I couldn't determine which way was up.

The powerful force of the breaking waves tore at my body and tumbled me as if I were in a washing machine. I rolled several times before I managed to figure out which way was up. Swimming to the surface, I inhaled a quick breath into my burning lungs, in time before the ferocity of the next huge swell to throw me into an inevitable collision with the sheer rock face. I tried to turn my legs toward the shore as I braced for impact.

I felt the pain of my right knee hyperextending and my entire body was pulled sideways and dragged along the sharp crags before the water mercifully receded. The pain was overwhelming, and for a moment, I thought I would lose consciousness. As the water subsided, I only had seconds before the next surge smashed me into the rocks again. Summoning all my remaining strength and channeling my skills as a former competitive swimmer, I knifed through the water, away from the cliff.

The next wave pulled me underwater, rolling again in the relentless surf. I braced myself, but the impact never came. When the water subsided, I was dangerously close to the jagged outcropping, but I had avoided contact. Fueled by the hope I could get out of this yet, I furiously dug for deeper water away from the cliffs. This time, I made it out past the breaking waves to the relative safety of deeper water. Looking toward the shore, in a mixed patch of sand and rock, I saw Nell huddled behind a large boulder, hiding her body from the men on the high cliffs above.

Some of them were aiming guns in my general direction, but I didn't think they had seen me yet. I ducked under, holding my breath until I thought my lungs would combust. I had no idea what had happened to my gun, just that I no longer had it. When I surfaced, there were no men to be seen up on the cliffs. Scanning around I saw Spencer, twenty yards away, floating on his stomach with his face in the water. I swam to him, feeling my knee swelling even in the cold water. When I got to him, I turned him over and did my best to keep his head above the water. He was unconscious, and I wasn't sure if he was alive.

Desperately scanning the shore, I spotted a small area where the waves were blocked by a natural stone pillar, offshore. Hauling Spencer along as best I could, I felt the exhaustion from the cold starting to set in. I heard Spencer cough as sea water spewed out of his mouth. He continued to gag and cough as I tried to drag his dead weight toward the shore, aiming for the rock pillar—a struggle that went on endlessly.

By the time I got to the scraggly edge of the rocky shore, I could barely move my arms. Finding a hold, I grabbed at the rock with my free hand and supported Spencer's weight as best I could. Even though the waves were smaller, each one that hit felt like I was being pummeled, as if I were a heavy bag at a boxing gym. I could no longer feel my legs at all, and my grip kept slipping. I was running out of time.

Should I let go of Spencer and try to pull myself up, I wondered, immediately ashamed I had even had that thought. This man saved my life twice now. With resolve, I pushed the thought out of my head. Whatever happens to him, happens to both of us, I concluded. I owe him my life, and if I must pay that debt today, then so be it.

A crashing breaker ripped my grip from the rock, and we both slipped below the water before I was able to regain hold. I pulled us both up high enough to be safe for a few more seconds, until the next wave. I looked up to the cliff, half expecting to see faces and guns pointing down.

"They will keep coming. We have to keep moving," said Spencer in a weak voice.

"I thought you were dead."

"Then why didn't you let go?"

"We're in some trouble here, buddy. Do you have any ideas?"

"Yes, my plan is to not sink below the water again," responded Spencer. "That sucked."

Without warning, a strong hand grabbed my wrist. It was so unexpected that I screamed. I turned to see Timmy, balanced along a semi-flat space of rock, leaning over and reaching out.

"Grab Spencer first," I pleaded with Timmy.

"Okay, I will," he said with a bright smile as he pulled Spencer out of the water with surprising ease. Once Spencer was out of the water, Timmy grabbed under my arms and hoisted me onto the rock. He was incredibly strong and dragged me onto the rocks like I was a paperweight.

"Thanks, Timmy. We owe you," I said. Spencer and I collapsed into the rocks to catch our breath.

Nell, Carolyn, and Ella came into view, and I saw room enough to join them on the gravelly shore. "Timmy has always been a strong boy," boasted Carolyn.

"Where's Alex?" asked Nell, looking around, panicked.

My head sagged between my shoulders. I couldn't bring my face up to meet hers. She walked closer and knelt down, repeating her question. I slowly lifted my gaze, with tears forming at the corners of my eyes. "Killed. There was nothing we could do. They came at us so fast."

"Are you sure?" asked Nell, also tearing up.

"I'm sure," I responded, frustrated at our impossible situation and furious at myself for not being able to do more. Nell walked over to Spencer and tried to inspect his wound. He pushed her gently away.

"This needs to be attended to, you're still bleeding," said Nell.

"Later," said Spencer, struggling to sit up. "My phone; check my pocket, I need my phone." Both guns were gone, but luckily, the phone was in a zippered pocket and miraculously still worked. Spencer dialed quickly. He was almost screaming as he explained our situation to the voice on the other end.

"It's going to be close," said Spencer without explanation.

I didn't need to ask. Reinforcements were on their way, but would they get here in time? The patch of shore we occupied was surrounded by the cliffs, open only to the crashing surf. This time there truly was no place to hide.

The first Zodiac appeared from around the edge of the cliff on the right, followed by a second. I grabbed Nell's hand. Ella was sitting on Carolyn's lap staring out at the ocean in terror as the boats drew near. I counted four men on each boat. Three leveled automatic weapons in our direction, while the fourth operated the outboard. They were in no hurry, apparently knowing we had no way to defend ourselves. Each of their faces lacked emotion. Might they spare Carolyn, Ella, and Timmy?

Suddenly, the automatic weapons that had been focused on us now pointed at the sky. Looking up the cliff, all I saw were the beautiful tails of the red-billed tropic birds. And then I heard it. A large helicopter materialized from just above the cliff. The down draft from the huge rotors sent small rocks showering all around us.

The men in the boats fired their weapons at the helicopter, but it was no use. What followed could only be described as a slaughter. The helicopter returned fire, and the boats seemed to eject small sections of rubber as the bullets ripped into them, the men, and the surrounding water. The attack only lasted a few seconds, but when it was done, nothing remained of the men sent to kill us.

Our small unit was unscathed, though traumatized into a frozen silence. I closed my eyes to the sickening shade of red in the water. All I could hear were Carolyn's sobs rising above the crashing surf. I kept my eyes closed, to no avail. The vision of the men being ripped apart from a merciless hail of bullets was seared into my consciousness.

Chapter 18

IT TOOK ABOUT AN HOUR for the navy ship to arrive and send boats to shore to get us. They needed to load Spencer in a stretcher and stabilize my swollen knee, but the sailors were nothing but efficient. Despite the pounding surf, the small landing party was able to load us into small boats from the rocky shore. The trip to the Cyclone patrol ship only took a few minutes in the high-powered boats. Before long, we were all safely aboard the ship.

On deck, two men with hazmat suits approached Timmy and, to his horror, made him take off his pants and hand them over before washing him down with what smelled like bleach. The men retrieved the pellets from Timmy's pocket and placed them in a double sealed plastic container which they carried as though it might explode.

Carolyn pleaded with an officer to return Timmy, Ella, and her to the tour boat, but all requests were declined, and the three were ushered below deck.

"What about Alex," I pleaded with the officer on the deck. "He was killed, and his body is still on the island."

All I got in return was "We'll handle it."

Spencer was taken to the sick bay to treat his wounds, and I noticed he was no longer resisting treatment. Nell and I were shown to the cafeteria and given warm coffee. It tasted like it had been brewed three weeks ago, but surprisingly, I did feel better after drinking the inky liquid.

"I can't believe Alex is gone," said Nell, choking back tears. "How could this have happened?" I gently grabbed her hand, but she pulled back. "This is surreal. We should not be here. Everything has gone way too far, and now Alex is dead. I can't believe it."

A small man dressed in jeans and a tan button-down shirt entered the cafeteria and approached our table. "I need you two to come and sit with Timmy as we question him," he demanded. "He refuses to answer anything, and just keeps repeating himself, asking for his sister and Ella. When we explained that's not going to happen, he started asking for Nell. That's you, right?"

He didn't wait for an answer before walking out and down the hall. He walked so fast we practically had to jog to keep up. After walking through multiple corridors, we came to a small door, which he opened and motioned for us to walk inside. I had to duck to prevent hitting my head.

Timmy didn't even look up as we walked in. He was now dressed in a jumpsuit which seemed about two sizes too small. He was in emotional distress. All the walls of the tiny cabin were metal, which caused an artificial ringing any time the naval officer raised his voice—essentially every time he asked a question. We sat on hard metal chairs that were the only objects in the room, and it was uncomfortably warm. The naval officer paced back and forth. Timmy had tear stains on his cheeks and refused to answer any question he was asked by the naval officer and kept burying his head into his hands. After about ten minutes of berating, the officer stormed out of the room and slammed the door. A loud click let us know the door was being locked behind him. As soon as the door slammed shut, Timmy burst into tears.

"Why is he angry at me?" asked Timmy between sobs. "He doesn't even know me."

Nell knelt down in front of Timmy and smiled warmly. He stopped his sobs and returned a weak smile.

"Do you know why that man is so mad, Timmy?" asked Nell. "I think he probably didn't get a good breakfast and is feeling hungry. Don't you get angry when you're hungry?"

Timmy nodded but didn't say a word.

"What's your favorite food?" she asked.

"I like barbeque, like the type they serve where I work."

"What do you do at the restaurant?" asked Nell.

"I have a really important job," replied Timmy, looking up with obvious pride. "I fill the water as soon as people come in, and whenever the glasses get low. People get very thirsty when they eat barbeque, so I always have glasses to fill. I also bring the empty trays to the kitchen so they don't pile up. That's important, since people like to stay when the dishes are there, and they leave when the dishes are cleared. My boss says he makes more money when people leave right away, so that more people can come in."

"Is that where you met the doctor?" asked Nell.

Timmy nodded slightly and used the back of his sleeve to wipe his nose before responding. "He came in to eat by himself, and I filled his glass right away. He talked to me and even knew my name, that's why I remember him. Most people don't say anything, or they just say thank you, but he looked at me and talked to me."

"What did he say to you?" asked Nell with a gentle soft voice.

"He asked me if I like animals. I told him, of course I do. My sister takes me all over the world for free to see animals, and all I have to do is help on the tours."

"What a great job," I said.

Timmy was perking up. "The man said animals all over the world were getting sick, but no one was supposed to know, otherwise people would panic. He mentioned he had secret medicine, and that I could help cure the animals, but I couldn't tell anyone, not even Carolyn or Ella. And do you know what he did then?"

"What did he do, Timmy?" asked Nell.

Timmy glanced nervously left and right before leaning in toward Nell and whispering, "He gave me a one-hundred dollar bill. I'm not supposed to take money from people, but he said it was okay because he was a doctor, and it was for helping him and not related to the restaurant. He said it was okay," said Timmy again, somewhat uncertain. "Do you think it was okay?" he asked Nell.

"Yes, it was okay," said Nell, putting a reassuring hand on Timmy's shoulder.

"When did he give you the medicine?" I asked.

Timmy remained hesitant. Nell placed her other hand gently under Timmy's chin to raise his head so he was forced to look at her. "It's okay, Timmy. John and I are your friends, and friends can keep secrets."

With this, Timmy relaxed his shoulders a bit and leaned forward. "The doctor was always too busy to bring the medicine, so someone else would deliver it. He usually brought it to my house and left it in the mailbox the day before I would go on a trip. The medicine was a little different each time, and that's why I liked to see it, but I always washed my hands for five-minutes after," he said with a proud smile. "I even set a timer, so I knew it was five minutes. Except the one time I forgot, and the doctor got mad," he added almost as an afterthought.

"If it wasn't the doctor, who brought you the medicine?" I asked.

"I don't know his name," responded Timmy.

"Can you tell me what he looked like?" I asked.

"He had a long, gray ponytail," answered Timmy.

I exchanged concerned glances with Nell as Timmy continued. "I wasn't supposed to see him. He always left the medicine in my mailbox like the postman had delivered it. He left it in the middle of the night. But I don't always sleep well and sometimes I like to play on the computer. One night I was excited because we were going to see penguins at the South Pole the next day, so I couldn't sleep, and I saw a man with a gray ponytail drop it off in my mailbox. I know it was him because I checked right afterward, and the medicine was there."

"Thanks, Timmy," said Nell. "You have really been a big help." He smiled at her.

The door clicked open, and the navy officer walked in with a phone and, without a word, handed it to me. I stepped outside the hot room and was not surprised to hear the voice of Mr. Smith on the other end.

"Nice job," he said, almost sounding genuine. I didn't bother asking how he had heard the conversation. Nell gave Timmy a reassuring smile and told him everything was going to be okay before following me out of the room. The door closed behind us with an audible click, leaving Timmy alone in the room.

"You know that Alex was killed, and we almost died!" I yelled, with emotion I had been bottling up for far too long. Nell leaned into me, and I held up the phone so we could both hear what Mr. Smith was saying.

"Yes, I know, and for that I am sorry," he responded. "No one was supposed to get hurt."

"And do you know that your assistant is behind all of this?" I asked with an accusatory tone.

"I'm looking into it right now, but just because he wears his hair in a ponytail, doesn't make him the same man Timmy was talking about." His voice lacked conviction.

"Sure," I said with as much sarcasm as I could muster.

"I called as a courtesy," continued Mr. Smith. "This is not something I am in the habit of doing, but given the circumstances, I think I owe you and Nell an explanation. So I'm going to give you information, classified information, so please don't discuss it with anyone other than Nell. I assure you, that if you do, I will know, and there will be consequences."

I didn't bother to ask what he meant by consequences.

"The boat with your assailants was apprehended," he continued. "Those left alive did not reveal their employer, but they are being aggressively questioned as we speak. Also, you are not the first team I have sent to investigate these outbreaks. We now know the outbreaks have been going on for at least a year in various parts of the world. At first, I sent a group of scientists to investigate an outbreak in Iran, but they found nothing and were all dead in a matter of days from a variety of suspicious accidents. After that, the trail went cold for several months, until a group of animals got sick in the Sichuan Province in China. I sent a group of military operatives under the guise of tourists to investigate, but they were killed in a massive explosion before uncovering anything.

"The outbreaks again stopped until the report of abnormal behavior in Australia. As you already know, the first group I sent to Australia was killed when their boat sank. So you were recruited. The four of you were not chosen at random. There were specific reasons each of you was recruited. Based on where we are today, I chose wisely. I sent you four with two goals in mind. First, to gather information about the prion and how the disease progressed, and second, to be watched so that a suspected internal traitor might be revealed."

"So we were being used as bait?" I exploded, not believing the words I was hearing. "We should have been told, so we knew the risks involved."

"If I told you, you wouldn't have gone," replied Mr. Smith with no emotion. "Each outbreak has been progressively more deadly. Someone with unparalleled expertise is manipulating this prion to become more and more dangerous. Judging from the events of the last several days, they have almost perfected their work. Intelligence indicates something massive and terrible is about to happen, and I need to stop it. I believe time is essential, and for the first time since this all started, I have a real trail to follow. That is because of you four. I am truly sorry Alex died, but if I can stop a global catastrophe, then I have made the right decision."

"That was not your choice to make," I argued. "You should have told us what was going on, what was at stake, so we could have made a choice with all the information in hand." I looked at Nell, unsure what else to say. My blood was boiling at being used in this way, and based on Nell's clenched fists and the rage in her expression, she felt the same way.

"I'm afraid it was my decision to make," replied Mr. Smith calmly. His tranquil voice only added to my agitation. "It is my job to protect the common good, and yes, sometimes at the expense of an individual. This is the closest to an apology you will ever get from me doing my job. I need Timmy, Carolyn, and Ella back in the States as soon as possible. They may have more information that can help."

"Can I suggest that you have someone other than an aggressive naval officer question them?" I uttered. "They're decent people who don't deserve to be treated as criminals."

"You can suggest anything you want," said Mr. Smith and hung up abruptly.

I couldn't believe what just happened. This couldn't be the way the United States government operated. I paced back and forth in the small hallway, feeling helpless and angry. There were no words I could utter that made any sense. I wound up and threw the small phone against the floor and watched it shatter into hundreds of shards of metal and plastic.

We were led to small cabins and given clean clothes. The boat was heading back to Santa Cruz, but the trip would take a couple of hours.

As I parted from Nell, I asked, "Are you okay?"

She frowned and nodded wordlessly.

"I'll meet you in the medical bay when you're ready. I'm going to shower and get into those clean clothes." She pressed my hands in hers and went on to her cabin.

The warm water felt refreshing as it washed over me and sent all the dust and sand swirling down the drain. Although I was still furious, I felt better afterwards.

I had to ask three people before finally finding the medical bay. Spencer was sitting up in bed with a bandage on his abdomen and an IV in his arm. He held up a single finger as he talked into his phone. Nell sat in a small chair to the left of the bed and gave me a frustrated smile as I took a seat on the other side of the bed.

Spencer hung up and said, "From what I hear, Mr. Smith filled you two in on what has transpired?" We both nodded but said nothing. Spencer sat back in the bed and cringed as he changed position.

"Does this happen a lot?" asked Nell softly.

"Do you mean me getting used or getting shot?" asked Spencer with a grin.

"Well, actually both," continued Nell.

"The easy question to answer is that I have been shot twice before," said Spencer. "Luckily, both were glancing blows, requiring minimal care. This is certainly the worst I've been banged up. As for being used, I'm in the military, so I'm used every day of my life. The difference is that, in all the previous missions, I knew what I was up against. While I've been in fights all over the world, this time was different. The last few days have tested my faith in the system. I was just on the phone with my commanding officer, discussing my potential resignation." He sounded angry.

"Because of us?" Nell asked.

"No, of course not. My point is, I never again want to be put in a circumstance where my team's failure is treated as a success by others. We were all bait in a complicated game. For me, that's okay, as long as I know I am bait. Sometimes it's the mission's goal to lure people in closer, so that the kill shot is easier to take. And it's always been military versus military. But you three, being civilians—it wasn't right. Information was withheld that made failure practically inevitable.

"It made Alex's death predictable," I murmured.

"Precisely. So I was quite clear to my boss that this will be my last mission under these circumstances. He's discussing it with others higher up the chain of command. I suspect I'll either be given a medal or be sent packing. A hero or a goat—when it's hard to tell the difference, then it's time for a change."

After a silence, Nell said, "Being a civilian, I can only imagine your disillusionment with the military. But I think I speak for John as well when I say I'll never again trust in my government the way I used to. I think that's an injury we all share. And I'm so angry that it hurts."

The ship pulled into port at Santa Cruz, and we disembarked to the dock. Carolyn, Timmy, and Ella were allowed to come with us, under Spencer's custody. We clambered ashore, and the sailors unceremoniously pulled away, without a word.

"What's going to happen now?" Carolyn asked Spencer.

"We've got a jet that's going to take us all back to the United States," responded Spencer.

"I've heard *that* before," I muttered to Nell.

"Yeah, I'll believe it when I see it," she replied.

Spencer continued filling in Carolyn. "I'm told your tour group was informed there was an accident at Genovesa, and Timmy needed to be airlifted out." He chuckled. "They were confused when the killer storm didn't materialize, but the fact that their tour would continue with a local guide seemed to satisfy them."

Carolyn appeared relieved by this explanation but persisted. "That's not what I meant. What is going to happen to Ella, Timmy, and me when we get back to the United States?"

Spencer looked her square in the eyes as he answered. "I'm being honest when I say I have absolutely no idea. I've filed a report in which I state the three of you have been nothing but cooperative throughout the entire incident, and that you were unknowingly used. I included how Timmy saved our lives when he pulled us out of the water. While it's likely you'll be questioned, it'll just be for gathering information—nothing accusatory. Simply be honest and helpful, and I'm guessing they'll let you go. The people who make these decisions have a much higher pay grade than me, but they're after big fish here, not you three."

A small van was waiting at the end of the dock to return us to the airport. Spencer insisted he was well enough to walk on his own, but after several steps, he casually placed his hand on my shoulder for balance.

Spencer settled in a seat on one side of the aisle with a painful groan, and closed his eyes.

Carolyn, taking a seat beside him, said softly, "Thank you, Spencer, thank you for everything." To my surprise, she leaned over and gently kissed him on the cheek.

He opened his eyes, a bit taken aback. "What was that for?"

"For saving our lives," responded Carolyn. "You didn't need to lower the three of us first. You could have left us on that ledge. You're a good man, and trust me, I'm an excellent judge of character."

When we arrived at the airport, Ponytail was nowhere to be seen. I wondered if he had fled or was in some cell somewhere, being questioned under bright lights. After climbing on board, Spencer insisted on searching every square inch of the plane, including patting down both pilots. At first they resisted, but a look from Spencer told them it was not optional. The search took several minutes, thankfully turning up nothing.

We took our seats in the back of the plane. Carolyn sat between Ella and Timmy. She made sure Ella was fastened in tightly, helped Timmy, and then strapped in herself. Ella chattered excitedly, never having been in a craft like this one.

"This is a very high-speed jet, Ella," Nell explained. "But it's incredibly loud. Use those headphone to protect your ears against the noise." Ella thought the headphones were really neat, but Carolyn and Timmy did not seem so sure.

The plane jolted as it was pushed back onto the runway. The powerful engines started revving up and creating a familiar vibration. When the seats rotated forward without warning as the plane accelerated, Ella squealed with delight. Carolyn and Timmy weren't enjoying the experience quite as much.

The ride back to the United States was only supposed to take two hours. After we leveled off, the seats predictably turned, and the table rose.

Mr. Smith's voice came over the headphones. "Spencer, Nelly, and John," he began. "You can hear me, but the others can't. I need you to confirm something. It is essential you do this as efficiently as possible. There is a picture that I sent to you. I need Timmy to identify whether or not this is the doctor he met in Memphis."

Spencer reached to the side of his seat and grabbed a tablet, probably an iPad. "Timmy--" he started. Timmy looked up.

Nell grabbed his leg and shook her head. Spencer nodded knowingly and gave up control.

"Do you like the plane, Timmy?" Nell said, smiling warmly.

"I don't like the way it makes my body feel," he responded, grabbing his stomach.

"I know. It's a little rough. But my tummy is returning to normal. Is yours?"

He nodded. Carolyn watched suspiciously but didn't say a word.

"I'm glad." Nell casually took the tablet from Spencer and turned toward Timmy. "You remember that I'm a scientist, right?"

He smiled and nodded again.

"Well, I've been doing some research on famous doctors," she stated with a straightforward tone.

"Really?" said Timmy, more interested in her than the tablet she was holding.

"I think I may have found your doctor," she continued. "This man is an important doctor. He helps rare animals from all over the world. It was in the news that he's been saving animals with the help of some secret assistants."

Carolyn shot Nell a dirty look but still said nothing.

"Can I show you his picture?"

"It's in the news now?" asked Timmy. "So it's no longer a secret?"

"Yes," Nell answered, "otherwise how would I know?"

He pondered the question a minute before smiling. "Okay, you can show me his picture."

Nell turned over the tablet and immediately, Timmy's face lit up. "Yep, that's the doctor," he beamed. "I told you he was saving animals all over the world. And I helped!"

The intercom clicked off and none of us could hear what Timmy was saying, although his lips kept moving. Nell smiled broadly and mouthed "thank you," to Timmy.

I looked at the picture and vaguely recognized the man. Below the image was the name Raj Bakshii. As Nell scrolled down the information, Spencer, Nell, and I read that Raj was the richest man in India and the twelfth-richest man in the world. He made his fortune in telecommunications and owned an empire, including pharmaceutical companies and multiple shipping companies. Below the bio was a link to a speech Raj had made over seven years ago. My heart sank when I saw the title of the speech: "Radical Solutions to Global Overpopulation."

Nell hit *play*, and Raj Bakshii's voice filled our headphones. Carolyn, Timmy, and Ella had picked up magazines from the sides of their seats and read quietly. It was clear that the speech was not being transmitted over their headphones. In the first few minutes of the video, Raj talked about his childhood in New Delhi. He spoke about how disease filled the city streets, and how his family struggled to find food. Many nights he would go to sleep hungry. His younger sister died as a young girl from typhus. The next several minutes he talked about the limited supply of farmable land in the world and the dwindling freshwater supply.

The video turned dark as he went on to talk about the inevitable destruction of the world due to overpopulation, with a current world population of eight and a half billion; within twenty years, that number would surpass nine billion. Raj made his points with the help of giant graphs projected behind him, which cast him in an eerie silhouette of pink and green. His utter conviction was intense, even on the small computer screen. Nine billion, he argued, is the point of no return, exceeding what the planet could sustain. Passing that threshold would not just lead to regional problems but would also result in massive, global starvation and war. Food and other resources would become so scarce that humans would die in immense numbers. Moreover, the predictable hoarding of resources by rich nations would accelerate the perpetuation of the problems. No one would be spared from the terrible impending global catastrophe.

The camera panned to the audience, as they hung on his every word. People nodded in agreement and, at times, applauded his most extreme predictions. Raj painted a picture of a world so bleak that suicide would be a pleasant escape. My stomach felt as though I might be sick from hearing his words and the cheering crowd, who regarded him as a savior. The only logical solution, he concluded, would be to preemptively stop this calamity before it occurred. The last few seconds of the video panned across the crowd, as Raj concluded, "Even now, I have a team working on a solution capable of delivering this salvation. Only through dramatic decreases in the world population will catastrophe be avoided." They were giving him a standing ovation. How could so many people agree with mass extermination of large populations?

In the next split second, an image appeared on the edge of the screen and disappeared. Bile rushed up my esophagus, and I thought I was going to be sick. I must have imagined it.

The screen went blank, and we all continued to stare for several seconds before Nell broke the silence. "Now that we know who is behind this, what will happen?" she asked.

"Mr. Smith will bring the wrath of God down on this man," responded Spencer. "He needed a target, and we provided him the target. That's all he wanted from us. Our job is done."

I wasn't paying attention. I needed to know if what I thought I saw was real. As casually as I could, I grabbed the tablet from Spencer and started to replay the video. "Why would you watch that terrible speech again?" asked Nell.

"I need to see something," I responded, trying desperately not to show my agitation. I fast forwarded the video to the end, where the crowd was cheering. It took three tries to pause the video at precisely the right spot. The image was a bit grainy and it was off to the side, but there in the crowd, joining in the wild cheering, was my old friend David Fowler. I slumped in my seat and the tablet fell to the floor.

"What's wrong?" asked Spencer.

I was unsure of what to do. Was it possible David was involved in all of this? We had been friends, but other than the casual weekend get together, I can't say we spent significant time together in the last fifteen years. I knew that if I told Spencer what I had seen, big brother would also know, and the repercussions to David would be dramatic and swift. Did this video prove anything? I had a choice to make. I weighed my options. Nell looked at me curiously. The greater good, I thought. *Find the source.* I made a choice, and I hoped it did not destroy an innocent man.

"My friend David is in that crowd," I responded to Spencer.

"In the video?" asked Spencer.

I nodded, feeling defeated. The silence was deafening. No response from the unseen wizard. Did he already know David was on that video? Was this a test of my loyalty? Did he even hear what I had said? There was no way to know. I put my head between my legs and quietly cried.

Chapter 19

W E LANDED NORTH OF PHILADELPHIA, just as night was falling. We all deplaned, exchanging goodbyes, but fell silent when we encountered several armed guards on the tarmac. I was afraid they were going to take us all into custody, but they only ushered Carolyn, Timmy, and Ella into the back of a Suburban and shut the doors, without saying a word. I asked one of the men where the family was being taken and was met with silence. The black SUV quickly drove away.

"What happens now?" asked Nell.

"Now, we go home," answered Spencer as he slowly walked away from the plane toward the entrance of the base.

"Mr. Smith is pretty useless at this stage, isn't he?" I asked with frustration.

"Yep," answered Spencer.

"Anyone want to share an Uber?" asked Nell.

"Sure," I answered. "Where to?" The lights of Philadelphia were visible in the distance and she pointed toward them.

"I know a great French restaurant in Philadelphia," she said.

"I'll catch up with you two later," said Spencer, continuing toward the entrance.

"Not a chance," answered Nell. "No way we're going into a big city without a babysitter. Besides, you're the only one with a phone, remember?"

"I've been shot twice in the last two days," said Spencer. "I need to sleep for a month, and then try and figure out my life."

"You can't do that on an empty stomach," I reasoned. He pondered this for a minute and smiled, pulling out his phone and summoning a car.

The Uber got us there in under fifteen minutes. The restaurant was located along the famed restaurant row in the middle of downtown Philadelphia. Luckily, there was a table available for three, and we took our seats in the back. We each declined the waiter's offer to get us drinks. I was afraid I'd fall asleep before the meal came. Spencer and I both decided on the beef bourguignon, and Nell went with the coq au vin. It had to be one of the best meals I ever had. We kept the conversation light and tried not to recount any of the horrors we had encountered over the last several days.

The waiter walked over as we finished and offered dessert menus. He turned to Spencer, "Sir, are you feeling unwell?"

In the dim light of the restaurant, Nell and I hadn't noticed how pale he had become.

"I'm fine," Spencer insisted although the slur of his words suggested otherwise.

Alarmed, I said, "We need to get him checked out."

After a quick conversation with the maître d', we determined an excellent VA hospital was just several blocks from the restaurant. It took Spencer two tries to stand up, and we staggered out of the restaurant, supporting him under each arm. He no longer was trying to insist he was fine, and we hailed a cab and piled in the back. The hospital was only a five-minute ride, but by the time we got there, Nell had to run in to get a wheelchair to roll a barely conscious Spencer into the waiting room.

He was immediately taken to the back for treatment, leaving Nell and me to fill out some of the basic paperwork. The waiting room was like all other hospitals, with a TV in the corner playing news with no volume. The chairs were hard plastic and especially cold. There were no others waiting to be seen, and I was puzzled that every now and then the receptionist scowled in our general direction.

Several minutes passed before a nurse came out to lead us into the bay where Spencer was being treated. The nurse must have only been five feet tall and was nearly about as wide. Spencer had an IV in his arm and was already starting to look better. He grinned as we walked in.

"Your friend has two gunshot wounds, and he is reluctant to tell us how this came to be," the nurse's dirty look made the receptionist seem like an amateur. "These wounds didn't just happen, which begs the question what have you been up to." She glared at us with eyes that could pierce through metal.

"We just finished dinner and Spencer started to go pale--" Nell started explaining.

But the nurse erupted. "You took a man to dinner with two gunshot wounds before taking him to the hospital!" she screamed. "Are you two completely insane? He needs treatment right now. If something happens to him, you two will be held accountable and could even be convicted of manslaughter."

"He *has* already been treated," I said, though this fact only enraged the nurse further. I caught a glimpse of Spencer snickering to himself in the corner.

"He obviously hasn't been treated appropriately, otherwise he wouldn't be here needing emergency resuscitation."

Spencer was now laughing out loud. The nurse shot him a death stare. He said,

"You two better leave now. I'll be okay—check in with me tomorrow."

The nurse continued to sputter as Nell and I backed out of the room, hurrying toward the exit. As we walked down the driveway, the nurse appeared at the emergency room door and continued to yell at us at the top of her lungs, confirming that Spencer really was stable enough to be left alone. I thought she was going to call the police as we walked away from the hospital and back toward downtown.

The cool night air was refreshing, but exhaustion was setting in. "I need to crash," I uttered as we walked toward downtown.

"Me too," said Nell.

For the first time, I noticed the bags forming under her eyes. "Do I look as tired as you?" I asked.

"If I look like death, then the answer is yes," she answered.

My knee was still in a brace, and whatever they had given me for pain had worn off hours ago. I hobbled down the street as Nell put her arm through mine.

"I am going to get a hotel room for us to share tonight," said Nell. "But to be clear, it is only because I think we are both too tired to make it home."

"Wow!" I joked. "Aren't we still on our first date? You're moving pretty fast."

"Dinner with Spencer doesn't count as a date," she responded as she playfully punched me in the side. I tried not to wince, as the light blow sent waves of pain throughout my body.

We found a place not far from the hospital, and Nell got us a room with a king bed. The room was nice and clean and overlooked Rittenhouse Square. I took a long shower and let the water rinse over me as I contemplated the last few days. I imagined Mr. Smith tracking down an army of villains in my head. I wondered what was happening with my friend David. This all must be a misunderstanding. Perhaps it wasn't even David in the video. I tried to shut out the horrible thoughts that kept creeping into my head. I walked out and announced, "The bathroom is free," but Nell was already fast asleep in the bed. I crawled under the covers on the other side of the bed, being careful not to wake her and swiftly fell into a deep, dreamless sleep.

It was after 11:00 a.m. when the hotel phone rang. We had both been asleep for over thirteen hours by my estimation, and it took a bit to clear the cobwebs from my head. I answered the phone to the voice of Mr. Smith. "Good morning, John."

"You are a creepy stalker," I said into the earpiece. "I thought we were done."

"You are done, but I am not," he responded. "Before you turn on the news, I want you to know that Mr. Bakshii had targeted fifty-three cities. We tracked crates shipped from his companies in all parts of the world and intercepted all but three. Whatever happens in the next several days would have happened in fifty-three cities if it were not for your team. Even though the world will never know or appreciate what you and your team have done, you have saved a great many lives, and I am grateful." The line went dead.

"Who was that?" asked Nell in a sleepy voice, with a large stretch.

"Believe it or not, it was Mr. Smith," I answered, no longer surprised by his ability to track exactly where we were at all times. The thought made me a bit unnerved.

"How the hell did he—never mind," she said trailing off.

I grabbed the remote from the counter and turned on the news, dreading what I might see. The stories were typical for a big city. It was supposed to rain tomorrow, there was a shooting in West Philly, but no one was killed. Traffic on 676 was terrible due to an overturned tractor trailer. I clicked the television off with relief. Perhaps Mr. Smith was wrong. No global calamity was unfolding. For a second I wondered if the last several days had just been a bad dream. Nell broke me out the trance.

"Let's check on Spencer," said Nell as she rolled over and gave me a kiss on the cheek.

"Can we stop by a store on the way?" I asked. "I need a new phone." To my surprise, my knee felt a bit better today, but it was still terribly swollen, and I needed the brace I had gotten from the ship to walk without pain. There was an Apple store several blocks from the hotel, and I managed to pick up a new I-phone in no time.

Thanks to the magic of an Apple ID and automatic updating, in several minutes, my new phone booted up and was indistinguishable from the one I had lost. As soon as the little computer device connected to the network, the phone started dinging excessively. I groaned when I saw I had sixty new text messages and over one thousand emails.

"Popular boy," said Nell with a wink. She was bright and perky and absolutely gorgeous in the morning sun.

"Would rather not be," I muttered under my breath scrolling through the texts, as Nell purchased a phone of her own. Most of the messages were work related, none were from the kids, and two were from Hank, wondering when I was going to pick up my dog. Nothing here that couldn't wait.

It was a beautiful morning, so we decided to walk to the hospital. The city streets were bustling with activity, and several times our bags bumped into someone rushing by without drawing attention. I couldn't help but notice the contrast between the city and the recent places we had been. The air here smelled of exhaust and dirt. The morning sun was bright, but there was a dull haze hanging over the city like a low-lying cloud. Nature was being choked out by civilization, and I let out a deep sigh.

As we approached the hospital I turned to Nell. "You don't think that Nurse Ratched is still on duty, do you?" I uttered with concern. "I really don't want to get yelled at again."

"She can't be," reasoned Nell. "It's been well over twelve hours since we dropped him off."

All the same, we slipped into the emergency room like teenagers sneaking into a college party. I peered around the corner into the waiting room. The room was empty and the receptionist behind the desk was not familiar. She had a smile on her face, talking into her phone and reviewing her clipboard. "Coast is clear," I whispered, rounding the corner into the waiting room. We walked up to the receptionist and waited for her to finish her phone call. According to the tag clipped on her white sweater, her name was Joy.

"How can I help you two this fine morning?" she asked in an upbeat tone. I couldn't help but notice the change in attitude between the nighttime and daytime staff.

"We are hoping for an update on a friend who came in last night," asked Nell.

"Are you family members?" Joy asked.

"No, but we are close friends, and we dropped him off," reasoned Nell.

"I'm sorry, but we can't give updates to anyone other than family members," replied Joy firmly.

"We just need to make sure he's okay," I persisted. "His name is Spencer Rose, and he came in with two gunshot wounds late last night." With that last statement, Joy's eyes widened.

"You two are the ones who chose to get a bite to eat at a quaint French restaurant before bringing Spencer in to treat his bullet wounds," Joy said with a chuckle.

"That would be us," answered Nell.

"The entire hospital was talking about you three last night," continued Joy. "You guys are infamous around here. In fact, the nurse who triaged Spencer last night insisted we should call the police and have you two arrested. In all fairness, she is having a bad week. It's fortunate that Spencer is charming. He even had her laughing about the entire situation by the end of the night. How was the food?"

"What food?" asked Nell.

"The French food," responded Joy. "Any food worth eating with bullet holes in you has to be special. I'll go check on him. Please have a seat."

While we waited, I couldn't help but notice several people poked their heads out the doors to get a glimpse of us. I swear one of them actually took our picture on her phone before disappearing behind the doors again. We were celebrities, but not for a good reason.

"I guess we could have handled last night a bit better in retrospect," said Nell, her face turning slightly red.

"He knew what he was doing. I blame Spencer," I joked.

"Besides, the food was spectacular."

"Better than the hospital food would have been," said Spencer, now standing behind us. We both jumped up and turned around. "Remind me to never let you take guard if we're in a dangerous situation again. It's way too easy to sneak up on you." He was grinning from ear to ear and looked human again.

"I never plan on being in a dangerous situation again," I said, fully relieved to see he was feeling better. Spencer's arm was in a sling, and I could see a bandage on his shoulder under his shirt.

"All patched up?" I asked.

"Certainly feeling better now," he responded. "Let's get the hell out of here before they ask any more questions about how I got shot. Last night was more of an interrogation than a treatment," Spencer joked. "How's the knee?"

"Feeling better today," I said cheerfully. "I'm surprised; I could have sworn I ruptured my ACL when it happened, but now I'm not sure."

"Get it checked out," said Spencer.

"I'm not taking medical advice from you," I joked, walking toward the door.

Nell did not move. Her eyes were glued to a television in the corner of the waiting room. The sound was off, but the ticker at the bottom of the screen read: "Hundreds sick with unidentified neurological disease in Mumbai."

"This can't be the . . ." Nell didn't finish her thought. She didn't have to. It had started.

"Mr. Smith said they had stopped fifty out of fifty-three attacks. He as much as said we were heroes," I said as we lumbered back toward downtown Philly.

Nevertheless, the mood was sour as we walked to the train station. Nell and Spencer were heading south to Baltimore and Washington, DC. I was heading north, back into New Jersey. We said goodbye on the platform. Nell leaned in and gave me a kiss and whispered in my ear, "You better call me. You still owe me a date."

Spencer gave me a hug. "I'm not kissing you or whispering in your ear, buddy, but keep in touch," he said with a weak smile. We had saved each other's lives, and that was not a bond that could be broken.

My train came first, but I didn't want to get on. Despite the short time we had known each other, I wanted to spend more time with each of them. Saying goodbye was painful.

The ride back to New Jersey was wretched. Clouds were rolling in, and the sky was gray. A light mist started to fall as the train entered the congestion areas. I spent the first half of the trip looking for an update on what was happening in Mumbai. There wasn't any meaningful information. Frustrated, I wanted to scream into the phone. Not knowing what else to do, I started returning text messages and e-mails. Most I simply deleted.

I texted both of my kids, and neither responded. Just as well; I'd never be able to mask my feelings. After an hour, I felt utterly and completely depressed. Being with Spencer and Nell, I never had time to grieve for Alex. I didn't know him well, but I had never witnessed another person being killed. The horrors of the last several days surged into my consciousness, and flashbacks of all the physical and emotional outrages dragged me into a place as dark as the ocean's bottom. I was past all that now, but I faced a world where the prion was loose, wreaking havoc on those we had hoped to spare.

As the train started to slow down into the station, my phone rang with an unlisted number. What could Mr. Smith possibly want now, I thought as I answered. I could not believe my ears when the familiar voice of my old buddy David said, "Hello, John," in a deep voice dripping with rage.

I couldn't think of anything to say. This was surreal. "Is it true David? Are you somehow mixed up in all this?"

"You don't understand," he continued. "No one ever understands. This is something I have always had the responsibility to do. And you have ruined everything. I know you told them about me. And because of you, they have taken Adrienne. That is something that will have consequences. Everything you care about will be ripped from your life if it is the last thing I do."

The line went dead as I stared at my phone. Did that just happen? I let my head fall to my chest in despair and watched my tears stain the front of my shirt as the train jolted to a stop.

Chapter 20

IN THE ENSUING WEEK, THE world seemed to be falling apart. People began dying in Mumbai and then in Toronto and in Sydney—several hundred at first, and then a thousand and then ten thousand—rapidly overwhelming the hospitals in those cities. A week later, over a million people in each city were sick or dying, in a particularly cruel and grotesque way. The world watched in horror as health professionals proved helpless to save a soul. The prion was traced to the water sources in those cities, but no treatment worked, and there was no end in sight. No one survived, and stories circulated about mercy killings, to bring a quick end for those afflicted.

I tried to focus on my work, but nothing was the same. I went through my routines like a robot. I was constantly terrified that something would happen to my kids, my friends, my coworkers. David's threat hovered like a toxic plume. Then there was Mr. Smith, forbidding us to tell anyone about it, even though everyone around me was talking about nothing other than the mysterious illness. Somehow, I knew Mr. Smith would be watching. I was in hell.

"Word can't get out or it will jeopardize the greater good," he justified.

Always the greater good—what about *my* good? According to Mr. Smith, the fact that we had saved the fate of at least fifty more cities, registered in the win column. It certainly didn't feel like a win.

I wished I could curl up with Nell and forget. She was the only one I could confide in. Spencer was not reachable. I assumed he was recovering or busy tracking down leads. Nell and I had exchanged a few calls and texts, but she was in shock too. "Nothing seems real," she shared with me. "I feel like I'm encased behind glass, and nothing can reach me."

"Nothing but Mr. Smith," I said ruefully. "I long for a way to be free of that man and his looming presence."

The following Sunday morning, I was sitting on my deck and sipping my coffee, tossing the ball for Tallie. It was a peaceful moment that came as close to what I used to call *normal* as anything had. It occurred to me that maybe I needed to rebuild *normal*, consciously stacking up moments like this as a bulwark against the nightmare I was enduring.

My phone buzzed, and the caller ID registered an unlisted number. I went numb. Afraid to answer and afraid to not, I picked it up and just listened. My mug crashed onto the deck when I heard the voice of David through the receiver. Evidently, *normal* would remain a fragile state.

"Hello, John," he sneered.

"David, what's going on? You must know I did not give you up. I did not even know you were involved until the very end. You were my friend. Please don't do anything to my family."

"What about my family?" he snapped back. "My life has been turned upside down because of you. Worse, you've interfered with a crucial turning point in evolution. I could have saved the world. History would have celebrated me as a savior, but because of you, I will be judged as a murdering psychopath."

"David, I don't understand--"

"You of all people understand. You know me."

"The man I know would not murder innocent people."

"Wrong. You know that first and foremost, I am a scientist. You remember Koch's Postulates? The organism must be in every case where there is disease. The organism must be isolated from the host and grown in culture. And finally the organism must be reinjected and again cause the disease."

"What's that got to do with anything?"

"The same argument can be used for human overpopulation. It's so simple, I don't know how a guy as smart as you can't see it. Every city, in every country in the world is a disease center. People are the organism and nature is the host. Everywhere that people are introduced, the host is dying. Humans are the problem at the root of all evil."

"Since when did you become interested in overpopulation?" I asked.

"Remember the prion we tested from the Sarowitz Ranch?"

"Of course."

"I had never seen a prion that aggressive, that lethal. *All* of the samples were positive, and it came to me: if the crossover from cow to human could be perfected, we'd have the perfect paradigm for solving overpopulation."

He sounded deranged. Could I really have been working alongside a madman? I thought back to that night we tested the samples, all those years ago. David had been excited, but I assumed he was excited about the science we were performing. This leap to saving the world totally mystified me.

"That variation of the prion was different," he said, with an enthusiasm that made my stomach churn. "Nature had done most of the work, but it still needed a little tweaking."

"*You* took the samples that disappeared?"

"Not all, but enough of them before the government swooped in. And I found a sponsor with incredible lab resources, a man of genius and vision, and we formed a partnership to isolate and grow the protein, to perfect a paradigm for re-establishing balance in nature. Our prion was nearly perfect. The only flaw was how quickly the particle became deactivated in nature. One peptide bond, only one carboxyl group that wasn't strong enough, stood between a structure that lasted a week and one that would last a year. A few more months and I know I would have created the perfect structure—till you called, asking about BSE. I knew immediately they were on to me. I knew I had to disappear.

"But when I reached home, Adrienne was already being taken away in handcuffs. She knows nothing about what I've been doing. She's innocent, John. That's why I'm calling. That's the only reason you and your family are still alive. You have to make them believe she's not involved. I can't stand to see her locked up." There was a long silence, and I heard him snuffling, as though crying. Finally, he said, "Her life is all in front of her. I am asking you to do that for me. We are friends, and you can do that for me."

My heart sank even lower at the thought of yet another victim of this whole mess. But what could I do? "David," I said, "do you hear yourself? You're intent on killing billions of people, but Adrienne must be saved? You and Adrienne and Bakshii and God knows what other lunatics will be the ones to carry on?" I could hear the rage in my voice, and he certainly could too, but I was on a tear. "And you want *my* help, after what I've just been through—what *you* put me through? Do you have any idea--" I paused, as it seemed the line had disconnected.

"You will need leverage" David reluctantly continued.

"What do you mean leverage?" I asked, afraid to hear the answer.

"In order to set Adrienne free," David continued with obvious reluctance. It was clear he was struggling with what he was about to tell me. "I am not the only one working on the prion. In fact, a long way back, they even offered me a job."

"What are you talking about?"

"Your beloved government, the people *you* are working for. That's who I'm talking about. They have been working in parallel, doing the same work I have been doing. Not as well, I might add, but they are getting close. Think about it, John, what does the government do better than just about anything else? They design new and more terrible ways to kill people, always seeking the ultimate weapon. Think what a particle like this could do to those who the leaders deem a threat. Why do you think they are keeping a lid on all of this? They want me, they want what I have developed. That is your leverage. Now go and set Adrienne free."

The line went dead. I could barely believe any of this. I had thought returning home would be the end of the nightmare, yet David and his madmen were still working to end humanity, and if he was to be believed, our government was doing the same. How could this be? David, of all people. I had been friends with him. How had my friend become a mass murderer? And if I understood things correctly, he was going to continue.

I needed to do something. I needed to take control of my life again. Two separate people had threatened my family, and that was not something I could live with. Not anymore. I was tired of being debilitated with fear, waiting for something terrible to happen. Even though Mr. Smith was one of the ones who had done the threatening, he was the only one who had the resources I needed. I decided to do the only thing I could do. I got into my car and started the drive to New York City. I didn't know what would happen when I got there, but I needed to try.

I crossed under the Hudson and steered the car to Tribeca, parking the car right in front of the unusual windowless building, I started to realize how ill-conceived this plan actually was.

Walking up the stairs to the large, opaque doors, I expected to at least get into the lobby to be able to plead my case to someone, but the doors didn't budge. I tried pounding on them and only succeeded in hurting my hand. I walked slowly down the stairs and around the entire building. This was a fortress with no conceivable way in. I suspected it was the design.

What a waste of time. Defeated, I walked back to my car and sat down. I didn't have a plan B. I turned the key and listened to the engine turn over, ready for the long trip home. I was about to drive away, ready to accept defeat. As I put my car into drive, my phone rang with an unlisted number.

The annoyed voice of Mr. Smith rang out over my Bluetooth. "You should not be here. What do you want?" Big brother is always watching.

"We need to talk, and we need to talk right now," I said with an authority that surprised even me. A long silence ensued, but I sensed he was still there.

"Fine. But be careful what you wish for," came the voice back, and then the phone went dead.

As I got out of my car, the door at the top of the stairs silently swung open. I took a deep breath, not sure I was up for what would happen next. I thought about my kids as I walked up the stairs.

No one was in the lobby. I walked down the long hall to where I remember the elevators were. The door silently opened, and I stepped inside. To my surprise, the elevator moved down rather than up. The ride took much longer than it should have, considering I started on the ground floor.

When the doors opened, the hallway in front was dark and cold. I walked out and the elevator door closed behind me. I approached a faint light at the end of the hall, which smelled musty, with an underlying foul stench I could not place. The walk was unsettling, and I suspected that was the intension.

I entered a vast dimly lit room with rough black walls and floor which absorbed the light, blurring the contrast between open space and the cell I had willingly walked into. The darkness seemed to go on forever. A door closed behind me with a click. I couldn't even tell if I was alone or if someone was in the room with me. There was only the indistinct light coming from somewhere high above me and the deafening silence. I pulled out my phone. Of course, I couldn't get a signal, but I turned on the flashlight, which only provided a slight improvement in my surroundings, as if the light were being consumed by the darkness of this strange place.

I was alone. "Hello" I called out into the space, and only the echoes of my voice met me.

From all around me came the voice of Mr. Smith. "You wanted to talk Dr. Osler, so talk."

This was turning out to be a very bad idea. "I want this to end," I started. "I want to be out of this forever, and I want my family protected." I was met with silence. Taking a deep breath, I continued. "I have been contacted by David Fowler."

"I know," growled Mr. Smith. "I have heard your conversations. There is nothing I don't know about what is going on. You should know that by now. Moreover, whatever it is that you think you know, you have no idea what is truly going on. You are in no position to make any demands. You could simply disappear, and no one would ever know what happened to you."

I shuddered. I was way out of my element and now I was in trouble, a lot of trouble. "I recorded the conversation I had with David, and a copy will be sent to a *New York Times* reporter if I don't intercept it by tonight." Desperately I lied.

"I like you John," came the voice of Mr. Smith. "Don't lie to me or the room you are in will be your forever home."

This was going poorly. I had badly misjudged the situation and I knew it; Mr. Smith knew it. What could I offer that Mr. Smith needed? How could I get out of this terrible mess?

"You can't find David, can you?" This was met by silence, but I knew I was right. "As you know, he has called me, and he will call me again."

"Go on."

"We are going to trade," I continued. "I want my normal life back and a guarantee that my children will be protected. I also need Adrienne to go free."

The silence was deafening. Time passed with no response. "Hello!" I cried out to the darkness. There was nothing.

After what seemed like an eternity came a response, "This only works if David turns himself in. Do that, and you will get what you want." The door opened with a click, and I was free.

Chapter 21

Another week went by, sadly, slowly, without further word from David—and no indication there ever would be. I sat awake nights, wondering *what if.* I texted Nell every night and called twice. I confided everything I knew to her. Even if Mr. Smith was listening, I didn't care. We had good conversations, but somehow the relationship felt distant. Had it just been the shared experience that brought us together? Had I imagined that there was something more? Never had I felt so alone. Her absence, and the absence of answers, made me heartsick.

I had, nevertheless, continued my pursuit of *normal,* whatever my mood. I spent as many mornings and evenings as I could on my deck, with Tallie for company, drinking coffee and watching sunsets. One particular night, Tallie was chasing leaves and invisible monsters in the backyard. I had a scotch in my hand and twirled the glass, sipping absentmindedly, observing the colors in the sky change from yellow to red as the sun sank below the horizon, trying to resist a dull, deadened feeling within me.

"Wow, you really get terrific sunsets here!"

From the corner of the yard came the voice I was longing to hear. Nell opened the gate and let herself in. Tallie almost knocked her down, rushing to greet her. "She's great! What's her name?"

"Tallie," I answered, "and don't let her fool you, she can stand guard duty with the best of them." Tallie licked Nell's face with her tail wagging so hard it shook her entire body with every twist. I got up to greet Nell halfway across the deck. She grabbed me and pulled me close, and without a word, gave me a passionate kiss that seemed to last forever.

"Why is it every time I kiss you, you taste like scotch?" she asked.

"Sorry," I said, pulling up a chair.

"Don't be sorry, just share," answered Nell with a warm smile.

The world abruptly seemed to have value again. We talked for hours. Nell was having all the same emotions and problems I was. We had both been invited to a memorial service for Alex, to be held over the weekend. They were naming a wing of the hospital after him. I was sure Mr. Smith must have somehow been involved with that one.

"I guess we did some good. But it doesn't feel like it," she confessed.

The moon appeared. I watched the subtle changes in the night sky and waited, sensing she had more to say.

"I'm also torn about something else," Nell said.

"What?" I asked, pouring us each our third glass.

"Mr. Smith," she said without explanation. It hung in the air for a minute, and I waited for her to continue. "I can't decide if he's a hero or a criminal. He bribed and threatened both of us. He lied and put us in harm's way, and Alex was killed as a direct result of what he did. He must have known your friend was involved, or at least suspected it. That's too large a coincidence to overlook. He spies on everyone from his secret tower in New York. His assistant seems suspiciously involved on the side of the bad guys, and yet, *Mr. Smith* is supposed to be the good guy? And now, we're struggling to deal with the aftermath of all we went through, but we can't even tell anyone. We don't even know what is happening with all of this—and we don't even know if our government is also developing this prion as a weapon."

"Life isn't always like a movie," I reasoned. "There isn't always a good guy or bad guy."

"Except for us," interjected Nell. "We were the good guys or, more appropriately, good people, right?"

"Well, yes, of course, we were the good people," I said with a small laugh. "But within Mr. Smith's world, he saved fifty cities, millions of people and perhaps more from a terrible fate."

"I guess I just can't see the world the same way he does," admitted Nell. "I could never sacrifice someone to save someone else. It's not how I'm wired. Human life is human life, and none are expendable, even for the greater good."

"That's why Mr. Smith does what he does, and we do what we do," I responded. "I guess the world needs both kinds of people. The question is: can we co-exist?"

We fell silent, and my thoughts stumbled down a road of a future with Mr. Smith looming. And then I tried imaging a future with him absent, vanquished. What would come of my recent, inept attempt to bring that about? A week had a gone by; a very uneventful week.

Nell abruptly shifted my focus back to the present. "John, I want to be with you."

"I want to be with you too, Nell," I managed to fumble, feeling off balance yet alive inside for the first time since Philadelphia. I glanced toward my upstairs bedroom.

"No, not like that," she continued. "Well, actually, exactly like that, but right now I'm talking about life, not sex. I want to spend serious time with you. I haven't felt this way about anyone, ever, and that makes me feel scared and vulnerable."

I reached for her and opened my mouth to reply.

"Wait, don't say anything; there's more," she continued, clasping my hand and taking a deep breath. "Every time I've been with a man in a physical way, the relationship ended soon after. I'm so warped that I've come to associate physical intimacy as a prelude to the breakup. I'm scared because I don't want that to happen." A single tear rolled down the side of her face. "Truthfully, I'm terrified."

"You have to trust me, Nell," I said with a soft voice and brushed away the tear. "Besides, you're stronger than you know."

She looked at me, puzzled.

"That glass wall surrounding you? You broke through it. You're here. And now you're helping me to move past all that's been holding me down. Since I returned home, I've been feeling like I still wear that leaky diving suit, and it's been dragging me lower and lower—until this moment."

I leaned over and kissed her, and then pulled her up from her chair and led her inside. Tallie followed excitedly, and I closed and latched the door.

It was three in the morning when the phone rang. I woke from a dead sleep. Nell didn't move. I quietly walked out of the bedroom and answered.

"Is Adrienne free?" came David's voice from the phone.

"The only way that's going to happen is if you turn yourself in," I answered. "Your freedom for hers. That was the only deal I was able to make."

"What about my life for her freedom?" asked David, and the phone went dead.

Chapter 22

NELL AND I SPENT THE next day together, and for the first time in a decade, I felt whole again. We met Spencer in the city to attend Alex's ceremony, and I was astounded to see the Montgomerys there. Ella ran up and gave Nell a big hug. Carolyn walked over cautiously, leading Timmy by the hand. When Timmy saw Nell, he gave her a bear hug I thought might break her in half. He and Ella each grabbed a hand and pulled Nell over to some chairs, where they chatted and giggled. I felt glad to see the child in each of them had survived the ordeal.

Carolyn extended her hand to Spencer. "It's good to see you," she said softly. "After we were led away, we were questioned for days. It was awful. They separated the three of us, and we didn't know if it was day or night. Everything became so blurred. Five days ago, they let us walk out. No explanation, no apology—not even any transportation! We just walked away. I can't tell you the rage I felt inside, until I passed by a newsstand. I had no idea. Millions dead, and we helped those monsters make it happen—not purposefully or maliciously, but we had a hand in this. I will spend the rest of my life trying to make it up, but I don't even know how or who to make it up to."

Carolyn had been staring at Spencer, hoping for answers, but none came. She was still awkwardly holding his hand, almost begging for an answer, but he offered none. He had been holding her gaze but now looked down.

"You can make it up by raising Ella," I suggested, breaking the silence.

"What do you mean?" responded Carolyn with a confused glance. "I'm already doing that."

"How many ten-year-olds have already seen the world?" I asked.

Carolyn shrugged.

"Ella is a very special girl. She leads tours, and people listen to her. I have seen people's faces light up, just hearing her talk. She has knowledge well beyond her years. It puts her in a unique position to lead change. People like Ella don't come around very often. I think she's destined for greatness, and you can guide her. She has the power to make the world a better place, and that is not a gift to be squandered. That's how you make it up, and make it better."

Carolyn turned to me with tears in her eyes and smiled. "I don't know if I will ever forgive myself for the role my family played in this tragedy. I have never felt like a single person could change the world. It's too immense for anyone to have a meaningful impact. That was true until we survived the ordeal on Genovesa. The seven of us did make a difference that day, and perhaps mitigated a larger tragedy. Perhaps a girl as unique as Ella can make the world a better place or at least spend her lifetime trying. Thank you, John. For everything." She walked slowly back toward Timmy and Ella with her head high.

It was nearly midnight that night when the phone rang. Nell was lying next to me and didn't move as I quietly walked out of the room to answer. The number was unlisted, but I knew from the whisper on the other side, it was David.

"I am not sorry for what I have done, but Adrienne needs to live the rest of her life. This is the only way to make that happen.

This is not the end. Please let them know that. Raj is not the only one with this vision, or the means to see this through."

"David," I hissed into the phone. There was no response. A grainy video appeared on the screen. From the appearance of the image, it was being projected from a camera on David's chest. I pressed record on my phone to capture the video. He walked down a cobblestone street to an ultramodern house that seemed European. The walls of the house were mostly glass, with large balconies on the second and third floors. He was met by several security guards who knew his name as he walked through wide, ornate doors, through a large foyer and into a darker hall. He proceeded down a steep staircase to a large basement, a modified wine cellar. I counted ten people assembled in the basement. All of the faces displayed combinations of fury and dread. In the front of the room was Raj Bakshii.

There was a debate on the floor about which direction to go. "This was supposed to be a coordinated attack," said the man in the corner with a long gray, almost white, beard. "The particle was supposed to be supremely contagious and be released worldwide. Killing people to save the world is a noble cause. We would have been seen as saviors. Killing in three random cities just makes us mass murders and does nothing significant to further our cause. I fear that we will lose support over this failure."

His words were met by nods of agreement.

"Why was the prion released upon the world before it was perfected?" asked a man wearing a business suit—the youngest in the room. "We made so much progress over the last two years. The particle was becoming more dangerous. It was fatal, worked rapidly, and was becoming more contagious and stable with each modification. Six more months, and we would have nailed it. Disciples could have walked into any city square throughout the world, and one cough would have been enough to start the cleanse. We had no lack of volunteers who would have gladly distributed this. Now all is lost."

Again, his words were met with agreement throughout the group. All eyes were now turned toward Raj.

He scanned the group, looking for sympathy, but there was none. He let out a heavy sigh. "Brothers, this was my cause. I brought all of you into my vision, my dream, for saving the planet. We have planned and sacrificed for years. You have to trust me when I say this was the only way. We were being pursued, and our pursuers were close. We did not have six months to perfect the particle. I had to make an independent decision, and the decision was sound."

Still, no sympathetic glances. He continued, "We were betrayed by time. I too had a vision of the cleanse being spread by virtuous disciples willing to give up their own lives for the global good. Even though the majority of our glorious particles were discovered, as we speak, my factories are working to produce more of the noble protein. We will perfect its awesome power; of that you can be sure. Consider the cities we were able to cleanse, and let those be but a presage of things to come. Our vision will be fulfilled. The world will be cleansed, and those who remain will inherit a far more beautiful world."

He was starting to get nods of approval from the powerful men in the room. "All we need is time, for we have the mightiest of swords, and we have a vision. Our vision will not be denied by the ignorant. By the producers of filth. By the--"

Raj never got a chance to finish his speech. A bright flash and a loud explosion assaulted my senses as I stared at the screen, and then nothing. I stared at the dead screen in disbelief.

The prion outbreaks subsided as quickly as they arose. Millions died, but there were no lingering threats, and the cities where the devastation occurred were healing and rebuilding. Spencer told me Ponytail had disappeared from the face of the earth. What that meant, I didn't know, but I didn't want to know.

Spencer had taken a teaching job at West Point. His primary assignment was to teach cadets self-defense. He credited the job with saving his career. Spencer and Sarah had become friends and regular sparing partners.

He took a special interest in Sarah. According to him, it was only because Sarah was the best in the class. According to Sarah, it was because I was too old and slow to punch properly, and Spencer was convinced I would need someone to protect me some day. I watched a few demonstrations and would hate to be on the receiving end of one of Sarah's punches now.

Nell and I spent as much time together as we could. While we both had busy careers, we managed to steal at least a weekend a month together. On one of those beautiful fall weekends, with the leaves changing and the air crisp, we were wrapped in blankets, sitting on the deck of a bed-and-breakfast in Vermont. Everything was perfect. The proprietors had left a *New York Times* in front of our door. In this age of technology, I couldn't remember the last time I read from an actual newspaper. Nell was working on the crossword puzzle, and I had just finished an article on a new species of frog that was discovered in the Amazon. I turned to the last page and was about to drop the paper and head in to get ready for breakfast when a small article in the lower left corner caught my eye: "Hundreds of Macaques dying in a suburb of Kuala Lumpur of an unusual neurological disease." Before I could read the article, my phone rang with an unlisted number.

I looked at Nell, who smiled warmly at me as I dropped the paper and hit ignore on my phone. I returned the smile, took a deep breath of the crisp mountain air, and got up. "Let's head in for breakfast and enjoy the day."

About the Author

Dr. Garrett Davis is a board-certified veterinary surgeon, having obtained his bachelor's degree from Bowdoin College, DVM from Cornell University, and surgical training at the University of Pennsylvania. He has been practicing surgery for over twenty years, authored multiple journal articles, spoken internationally at veterinary  conferences, and currently is the director of the residency training program at the Red Bank Veterinary Hospital.

He spends his free time cooking, writing, and traveling the world on adventures with his family. He lives in New Jersey with his wife, two children, and multiple pets. *The Prion Paradigm* is his first novel.